Abou

Nick Thripp has an English degree from Cambridge University and an MA in Creative Writing from Kingston University, London.

Also by the author:

The Code

Tomorrow is Another Life

Nick Thripp

Matador
9 Priory Business Park,
Wistow Road, Kibworth Beauchamp,
Leicestershire. LE8 0RX
Tel: 0116 279 2299
Email: books@troubador.co.uk
Web: www.troubador.co.uk/matador
Twitter: @matadorbooks

ISBN 978 1800462 731

British Library Cataloguing in Publication Data.
A catalogue record for this book is available from the British Library.

Printed and bound in the UK by 4edge limited
Typeset in 12pt Minion Pro by Troubador Publishing Ltd, Leicester, UK

Matador is an imprint of Troubador Publishing Ltd

For my nephew, James,
for his constant support
and encouragement
of my writing.

Chapter 1

Leon, head in hands, rocked slowly back and forward on an IKEA chair in his white melamine kitchen. The photographs surrounding him had been turned towards the wall or laid face down. A pile of linguine with chicken and green pepper sauce lay untouched in front of him. Periodically, his rhythmic rocking motion was wracked by a seismic shudder as a memory scudded across his brain.

Ode to Joy rang out causing him to start. He really must change that ringtone. His adoptive mother's picture flashed up on the screen. He loved her dearly, but not now, oh God, not now.

'Hello Marianne.' They had always insisted he call them by their forenames. 'How's things? ...I'm fine... no, really I am... actually I've got a plate of pasta in front of me right now...no, out of a packet...yes, I know...yes, sugar and salt... work? Terrible.'

He wrinkled his nose and pushed his plate aside.

He'd already told Marianne they could be in for big redundancies, now she was fretting about it too.

'Another job?……I don't know, wherever I can find one… isn't much call for refrigeration design engineers round here……Clive? No, I've not heard from him. His things are still in the hall. Said he'd pick them up. Probably when I'm at work…I will…love you too.'

He carried his plate to the sink. He'd rather not have been reminded of the latest of many fixed-cost reduction exercises at work. Although he'd survived the last two, he had a bad feeling about this one. His premonition hadn't changed after that afternoon's interrogation by Alan, one of the consultants, from which he had emerged trembling, beads of sweat dew-dropping his brow and dark damp patches staining the armpits of his shirt.

He slid the congealed mass into the recycling bin and put the kettle on. A half-empty packet of cigarettes lay on the sideboard. Until last week he hadn't smoked for over four years. Giving up had been a torture made endurable only by Clive's anti-smoking vehemence. Taking them up again had been easy. The first had tasted disgusting and made his head spin. After that…he reached out. His body had assumed control. His hands opened the packet, pulled out a long white stem and lit it. He inhaled. Taste still slightly unpleasant. He drew in another lungful. Ah, so calming, so reassuring.

Slumping onto his grey fabric two-seater sofa,

his thoughts were back at the St George's Club in Antigua, on whose sparkling silver sands he had met Clive, skinny and white, pontificating about the dangers of skin cancer to an uninterested and bronzed group of sun worshippers. Typical Clive. Always opinionated. Never wrong, at least in his own eyes. What a bastard! Turning the TV on, he flicked through the channels hoping for something funny, or at least mildly interesting. Nothing but cooking programmes. He groaned. To him ready-made meals were a lifeline and the microwave a fifth limb. He switched the set off. Sighing, he picked up *Martin Chuzzlewit*, a present from Clive. 'You need to develop your mind,' he'd been told as the neatly wrapped gift was pushed across the kitchen table one evening. No doubt developing his mind was what Clive was doing at this very moment with that muscular Australian swimming coach he'd met at the health club. Sod fucking Clive. He threw the book on the floor. He hated Dickens. And he hated Clive. *Ode to Joy* blared out again and his heart missed a beat. Could it?...no, it was his mother again.

*

'Well matey, at least *you* know you're safe, you lucky bastard.' Sam prodded Leon's shoulder gently. 'Getting rid of you would ruin their diversity statistics.' Fiddling with a loosely knotted bright red tie, Sam

3

surveyed the rapidly filling auditorium. 'Loads of Pakistanis, some Filipinos, a few Chinese. No genuine blacks, er, I mean, Afro-Caribbeans, apart from you. You know man, this consultation process is a farce. We know what they're going to do. They know what they're going to do. They're going to chop forty per cent, like they said they would.'

'Right-sizing. What the hell is that? More consultant-speak,' Leon said, and Sam nodded.

Tiny Withers, the bald, six-foot-eight CEO, stalked in, flanked by two sleek and glossy consultants, like seals in their shiny grey suits. He was followed by the rotund figure of Sheila Barnett, the HR Director, more walrus than seal and weighed down by a bulging briefcase.

'So that's where all the pies went,' Sam said, and a few people laughed. Leon, uncomfortable at hearing her ridiculed for her appearance, looked away.

'Tiny's wearing that tie again,' Sam added in a hushed whisper. 'Never lets you forget he went to Harrow.'

Withers cleared his throat as the last few stragglers shuffled into the auditorium and pushed along the crowded rows looking for empty seats.

'Ladies and Gentlemen, good morning. You'll remember the business case I outlined in January.'

A low murmur grew, spread across the hall, and subsided.

'Let me run through a summary of it again, just

in case anyone is in any doubt.' A succession of charts flicked rapidly across the screen: competitor advances, reductions in revenues, increases in raw material prices, vanishing profits and then, miraculously, after a reduction by forty percent in fixed costs, ker-ching! A promised land of market share growth and fattening profits.

'Crap,' whispered Sam. 'The Chinese are skinning us because their products are better and cheaper. Redundancies will make fuck-all difference.'

'Any questions?' Withers glared at the audience. His thick black eyebrows, like two fat caterpillars squaring up to each other, quivered menacingly in the harsh lights directed at the podium. He cleared his throat, preparing to continue.

Leon put his hand up. 'Excuse me, Dr Withers.'

Withers stared into the crowded auditorium, trying to locate the owner of the voice. 'Yes?'

'What makes you think cutting costs will make us competitive? The Chinese cost base will always be much lower than ours. Wouldn't it be better to invest more in new technology, grab the top end of the market and generate higher margins?'

Withers' expression was incredulous. 'You can't just magic new technologies out of thin air. They need substantial investment and time. If we don't cut costs now, we won't be in business long enough to develop any. Any more questions?'

The room remained silent.

'Let's talk about the future then,' Withers said, outlining in a monotone revised vision and mission statements, which sounded like Japanese technical instructions translated badly into English. He flashed up the new strategy chart. Apart from no mention of Business Development, previously a core activity, and little of Technology, it was indistinguishable from its predecessor. Leon's stomach cramped. He was in Business Development.

'Let's talk about the reductions.' Withers wiped his glistening forehead with a silk handkerchief. 'We've decided—'

Sheila Barnett's cough stopped him, and he shot her a malevolent look.

'What I meant to say is that we propose to make some significant changes, which will be consulted fully with employees and their elected representatives.' He drew breath and cleared his throat. 'I don't believe in trimming. If I snip a bit off a bush, what happens? It grows even more vigorously than before.'

'Obviously what he did to his eyebrows.' Sam sniggered, fingering the knot of his tie.

'We will therefore disengage from some areas completely,' Withers continued. 'Let's start with Technology.' He ran through swingeing reductions in which whole technologies were abandoned and entire departments removed. Several people in Technology hung their heads. A few stormed out, slamming the door behind them. Withers, his eyes fixed on his prompt cards, waited for the commotion to die down.

Leon raised his hand. 'Excuse me, Dr Withers.'

Withers' look was one of disbelief. 'You again? What is it?'

'If Technology is cut, how will we ever get a technical edge over our competitors?'

'You'll get plenty of opportunities to ask questions like that during the consultation phase.' Withers looked at his watch. 'As time is limited, I suggest we get on now. The second major change will be the cessation of centralised Business Development activities. Again, returns have been well below plan and show no sign of improving.' He revealed a bar chart showing the previous five years' worth of costs towering over corresponding profits like skyscrapers over bungalows. 'We propose to transfer all BD activities to Marketing, which will undertake them within current resource levels.'

Leon's brain froze. The rest of Withers' presentation faded into background noise. Not only had his job gone, his department had disappeared. Accepting that promotion into Business Development from Marketing, which had seemed such a good idea at the time, looked like a career-terminating decision now. When he tuned in again, Sheila Barnett was speaking. Fragments penetrated his consciousness: 'redeployment where possible... re-training... outplacement,' all the usual organisational consolations for the terminally unwanted, thrown like so many sun-bleached bones to an enclosure full of starving dogs.

'What a shitload.' Sam put his arm round Leon's shoulders. 'So sorry mate.'

Leon was too numb to respond. No partner and no job. The taunts hurled at him at school came back to him. 'You Coconut, you're not wanted here,' they'd shouted, sometimes leaving an actual coconut on his desk to taunt him. The black kids had resented him because he'd been brought up by whites, while the rest, psyched up by mob hysteria, joined in because that was safer than taking the risk of being picked on themselves. He thought he'd put that all behind him when his family moved out of the inner city. Yet all his efforts to educate himself, carve out a profession and sustain a loving relationship had come to nothing. A thirty-year-old failure, not wanted by anyone, he had become Coconut again.

★

Leon was returning from buying more cigarettes when Frank sidled up to him.

'Hi Leon. Everything OK? Heard about the redundancies at your place.'

'Fine, thanks,' Leon said, determined to avoid a conversation.

'Haven't seen Clive around lately.'

'He's away.' One of the advantages of having black skin was that few noticed when you blushed.

'He's always away. Another business trip?' Frank nudged him. 'Better keep an eye on that one.'

Chapter 2

'Fuck them all.' Leon made the pile of final demands and threatening letters into paper darts. With only enough money for one, or perhaps two of them, he would launch the darts out of the ground-floor window and pay the one that went furthest. He hoped it wouldn't be that unpleasant letter from the agents threatening eviction. In any case, what he had in the bank would hardly make a dent on the rental arrears. Marianne had offered to help, trying to press money on him and encouraging him to move in with her. He'd declined for several reasons, but mainly because she was living in a one bedroom flat on a meagre wage herself.

He averted his eyes and chose a paper dart at random before launching it out of the window. In a way that reminded him of his career, it surged upwards briefly, then flopped to the ground, barely clearing the window box.

He leant out and peered at it. The logo of the letting agents stared up at him.

'Yeh, result.' He punched the air.

Bzzzzzzzzzz.

A burly figure loomed through the frosted glass of the front door, the shadow of his hand on the bell. Though Leon had never seen a bailiff before, in his imagination they were all that shape and size. He froze.

Bzzzzzzzzzzzzzzzzzzzzzzzzzzzzzzzzz

Another slimmer, shorter person joined the first one, who turned as if to speak to him. Leon strained his ears. He didn't recognise the gruff voice. The other sounded like Frank's. With the help of his GCHQ-standard surveillance techniques, Frank would know he was still inside.

'OK, I'm coming,' he shouted. Opening the door slowly, he revealed Frank, hopping from one foot to the other, and an Afro-Caribbean man dressed in an immaculate charcoal grey suit, white shirt and what looked like an Old Harrovian tie. He was carrying a briefcase. Leon examined the stranger closely. He didn't have the swagger of the Nigerians he'd known, nor did he look like any Somali he'd encountered. He did have a v-shaped scar which stretched the length of his left cheek.

'He said he's got to see you,' Frank announced. 'Matter of the highest importance.'

'I'm Mr Bankole. You got my letters?'

Leon stared blankly at him before vaguely remembering a couple of official looking letters from some African country which he'd torn up thinking them yet another Nigerian scam. 'Er, no, I don't think so.'

'That's strange. Then we must talk. Alone.' He directed a withering glare at Frank who, at first, looked affronted, then, with a flick of his head, flounced off.

'You bailiffs are more polite than I expected,' Leon said.

'Bailiffs?' Bankole's brow furrowed. 'I'm here from Mutabe on a mission of the utmost urgency. You are needed there. Now.'

Mutabe! His birthplace, where his natural parents had disappeared, presumed dead; the country out of which he'd been smuggled into the UK by Peter and Marianne.

'Please, can we go inside?' Bankole said. 'I'm not comfortable discussing this in the open. We could be under electronic surveillance.'

Leon hesitated, not sure whether it would be wiser to close the door in the stranger's face, but good manners prevailed. 'All right, if you promise you're not a bailiff.'

'I promise,' Bankole said, extending his hand. 'You can call me Mr B.'

Leon proffered his own, which the other gripped tightly. He showed his visitor into his sitting room, where, without being invited, Mr B placed himself in the armchair, took a cigarette out of a slim silver case and lit it.

Leon stared at Mr B's behaviour, deciding on the spot not to offer his arrogant guest any refreshment. 'Do make yourself at home, why don't you?'

Mr B leant forward. 'It's taken us a long time to find you, Leon. Your kidnappers covered their tracks well.'

Leon frowned. 'Kidnappers?'

'The Cartwrights.'

'My adoptive parents?'

'They spirited you away after your parents died and before we could come to your aid.'

'What the hell are you talking about?'

Mr B delved into his briefcase and produced a sheaf of documents, which he waved in Leon's face. 'This is the official Government report corroborating what I say.'

Leon grasped his wrist and pulled the papers towards him. 'I can't make out a word of it. What's it written in?'

'Mutabese of course.' Mr B took the papers back and pointed to several places where Leon's adoptive parents' names appeared. 'You can see that the Cartwrights feature prominently. I'll translate what it says about them if you like.'

Leon shook his head. He needed time to think.

Mr B placed the documents back in his briefcase. 'Now do you believe me?'

'But they rescued me. I've seen the newspaper cuttings. I was in a house which was blown up. My birth parents' bodies were never found.'

'Never believe the pap that lazy journalists regurgitate. You were abducted by British agents.'

'They were aid workers. When he went back years later, Peter was killed by rebels for trying to alleviate the poverty there.'

Leon's mind replayed that dreadful internet video he'd forced himself to watch. It had caused Marianne and him so much grief. The indelible images of Peter blindfolded, on his knees, hands tied behind his back and a pistol aimed at his temple. His so-called confession, recited in the stumbling monotone of one who, after unbearable pain and sleep deprivation, is indifferent whether he lives or dies. Then a shot like the crack of a whip and a six-inch spurt of blood from his head, followed by the dull thump of his lifeless body toppling onto the ground. Finally, a close-up of a placard blaming Britain for its role in supporting the ruling regime, held up by his masked but beaming executioner.

Mr B's lips curled into a sneer. 'Peter Cartwright was an MI6 agent.'

'I don't believe you.'

'At their bidding, he committed despicable crimes against the Mutabese people.'

'But he was so gentle and caring.'

Mr B emitted a harsh laugh and, stubbing out his

cigarette, stood up to face Leon. 'He was a trained assassin. Including your birth parents and your sister, we've identified a dozen or more victims.'

Leon covered his ears. 'No, I can't listen to this.'

Mr B wrenched Leon's hands from his head, gripping them tightly in his own massive fists. 'You have no choice. The Foreign Office knew how valuable you were and got the Cartwrights to seize you. Your parents and your sister paid the price.'

'It's ridiculous. Everything you say is nonsense. I want you to leave now.'

Mr B shook Leon, who struggled to free himself. 'Listen to me. Do you have a scar on your left thigh, a little above the knee?'

Leon stopped wriggling. He did have such a scar.

Mr B's expression softened. 'A careless nanny took her eye off you and you fell off the table, cutting yourself badly. It's in your medical records, which I have here too. Do you want to see them?'

'No, this is all some trick.'

'On the contrary. Everything is documented.'

Mr B released his grip and Leon's hands fell to his sides,while hot tears pricked his eyes. Unaccountably, the sense of confusion, interlaced with anger and sorrow, brought back his bewildering first day at school when nothing seemed real and he yearned to be back in his cosy bedroom at home.

'You've got the wrong person!' he cried, trying to put the evidence of his scar out of his mind.

Mr B placed a comforting hand on Leon's arm and spoke in a soothing voice. 'Listen, Leon, do you know who you are?'

Leon swallowed hard. 'Yes, of course. I'm Leon Cartwright.'

'No, who you really are.' Mr B paused as though for dramatic effect. 'You are the grandson and only remaining male blood relative of Chief Onagaku.'

Leon shook his head, as though to clear it. 'Chief on a what?'

Impatience battled with restraint for primacy on Mr B's face. 'Chief Onagaku, the founder of our nation, leader of the Mutabese people and first President of the Democratic Republic.'

Leon's eyes narrowed. 'So, my mother was Onawhatsit's daughter?'

Mr B shook his head. 'No, your father was Onagaku's son.'

'But I was told my family name was Nwagbara not Onagaku,' Leon said, secretly proud to have torpedoed this canard so easily.

Mr B gave an exasperated sigh. 'So many questions. Your parents adopted a false identity after your grandfather was murdered.'

Leon rubbed his hands, distractedly. He was beginning to feel faint. 'I can't take all this in. It's so far-fetched.'

Mr B nodded. 'I understand why it's come as a shock, but we have incontrovertible evidence. We've been tailing you for some time and have collected DNA samples. The match confirms it.'

Leon, realising he was clutching the door frame, released it and straightened up. 'Tailing me?......
DNA? ... bizarre...though I'm not sure I believe anything you say. So what if I am this chief's grandson?'

'Mutabe has been suffering under the dictator Oblanga's rule for many years. The people are primed and ready to rise up. All they need is a figurehead to unite them. That person is you. You are very important – critical – I might say, to their future happiness.'

Leon scratched his head. Was this one last cruel trick on Clive's part to pay him back for that terrible last evening when, as Clive was in graphic mid-confession about the swimming coach, Leon had caught him full in the face with a chicken tikka masala?

'Go and pack your bag,' Mr B said. 'Our plane leaves at nine-thirty tonight. We have two hours to get to the airport.'

'I'm not coming. This is all some monstrous scam.'

Mr B's eyes roved around the room, finally coming to rest on a magazine lying face down on the coffee table. Its back cover was emblazoned with an advert entitled, 'Find your Family,' sponsored by a DNA tracing company.

'Don't you want to try to track down your other sister?'

'My other sister?' Leon wiped his forehead. 'What other sister? I only had one.'

'As far as we know, only one was killed in the blast. The other may well have survived. She may not have been with you and your parents at the time.'

The sound of an aeroplane passing overhead shattered the peace and afforded Leon a few moments for reflection. He'd been so lonely as a child; he'd always been desperate for siblings and had even urged Marianne to have children, so he'd have someone to play with.

'How old would she be?'

Mr B's eyes slid away to the left before returning to fix him with a stare. 'Oh, about five or six years older than you.'

'You're sure she exists?'

Mr B nodded. 'Sure. Though we have no idea what became of her. But, given a bit of effort on your part, it wouldn't be beyond you to track her down.'

'Why didn't you mention her before?' Leon asked.

Mr B sighed in a long-suffering way. 'Because it didn't seem relevant, it slipped my mind.'

Leon peered at Mr B's expression. He couldn't read it. He had no idea whether he was lying but, even though he harboured doubts, the image of a sister floated tantalisingly in front of him. What had become of her? Had she family of her own? Was he an uncle now? He took a deep breath and silently urged himself not to get carried away.

'Even if I believed you about my grandfather and this sister, I couldn't go with you. I can't leave my mother without saying goodbye. And what about the flat…?'

'It's not your flat and she's not your mother. Pack your bag.'

'She's treated me like a son, better than most mothers treat their sons.'

Bankole's laugh was hollow. 'Because of her, you, a chief of the Mutabese, have been brought up by whites, with no understanding of your own people, of your own culture. Brown on the outside, white inside. It's an abomination.'

'I've got to go and see my mother,' Leon insisted.

Mr B drew himself up to his full height as though to demonstrate what a backbone did for a man. 'If you really must. We can still make the flight. I'll see you back here in one hour's time. Make sure you're ready to leave.'

Despite Mr B's exhortation, Leon dawdled on his way to Marianne's flat, his mind struggling to weigh the likelihood of his parents abducting him against that of Mr B lying. And yet, even if Mr B were trying to trick him, what did he have to lose by taking up his offer? His life had been boring, humdrum, for a long time. Now it was downright depressing. A change of scene, adventure, living instead of existing; they held their attractions.

Chapter 3

A large yew sideboard, a scuffed oak table, some battered dining chairs and other assorted clutter took up most of the space in the two-room flat, leaving only four feet between the television and the stained armchair on which Leon perched.

Marianne, her eyes brimming with tears, leaned against the doorframe, her hands trembling. 'Why do you keep asking me? You were a baby buried in a pile of wreckage. We thought everyone was dead. Then we heard you cry. Peter and I scrabbled away, lifting rubble till our hands bled. No one helped, though, goodness knows, enough of them were standing there gawking.' She dabbed at her nose with a wrinkled hankie. 'Finally, we got to you. A beam had collapsed above your cot and held the worst of it off. It's what we've always told you.'

'How come I was the only survivor? How could a baby live through a bomb blast?'

'I don't know, Leon. I can only say what happened. Why do you believe this Bankole instead of me? How did he track you down anyway?' She reached out a pale hand, the fingers thickened by arthritis, and placed it on Leon's arm. 'I'd steer clear of him. He's probably a confidence trickster, after your money or identity.'

'I don't have any money, Marianne, and he's trying to give me a new identity, not steal mine.'

Leon looked into his mother's grey eyes. She held his gaze. He'd never known her tell a lie.

'It is strange he's turned up here though,' he said. 'I'll ask him.'

'You should. Expose him for the fraudster he is. Otherwise you'll risk everything, maybe even your life, and for what? Some nonsense story told you by someone about whom you know nothing.'

'At least it would be different, exciting, maybe even satisfying if I'm helping downtrodden people shake off a despot. And what have I got to lose here? I've slogged my guts out for years, putting up with all sorts of nonsense from assorted pricks and what have I ended up with? Nothing. Even if I die doing it, going to Mutabe would be an adventure.'

Marianne folded her hankie and wiped her eyes. 'Please don't go.'

The image of his older sister coalesced in Leon's mind and then evaporated. 'I'd like to trace my sister.'

Marianne looked at him sadly. 'Do you mean the

little girl who was with you in the house? I'm afraid she died in the blast.'

'No, the other one.'

Marianne's face screwed into a puzzled frown. 'What other one?'

'The older one. I had two sisters, according to Bankole.'

Marianne looked doubtful. 'I don't think you did.'

His missing sister's phantasm danced into his mind again. At every appearance she became more substantial, more real. 'Well, I'm determined to find out,' he said. 'Even if I don't go with Bankole, I'll definitely make the trip sometime. By the way, what was my parents' surname again?'

Marianne exhaled. 'It was Nwagbara, as we've always told you. Why do you ask?

'It wasn't Onagaku?'

'The local police told us it was Nwagbara. That's also the name reported in the newspaper.'

Leon stroked his chin. 'So, you had no idea my birth parents were using false identities?'

Marianne's eyes, normally a cool grey, flashed. 'No, of course not.' She steadied herself. 'If they were, that is, though I suspect it's another fabrication on the part of your mysterious friend.'

Leon didn't know what to believe. Was Bankole making things up or was Marianne withholding facts? 'I'd better go now,' he said after a pause. 'Things to do.'

'All right, dear,' Marianne said, and Leon felt a pang of sorrow at the look of resignation – almost defeat – on her face.

As he negotiated the small gap between the sideboard and dining table, the urn containing Peter's ashes teetered before succumbing to gravity and falling into a hand Leon had stretched out at the last moment.

'Phew!' Leon wiped his brow with his other hand. 'That was close.'

'Do be careful,' Marianne said, and Leon wasn't sure whether she was referring to his safe exit from the apartment or his possible trip to Mutabe. Depositing the urn on a shelf by the front door, he turned to face her and extended his arms. 'If I do decide to go with Bankole, I'll let you know straight away.'

They kissed and hugged.

Leon opened the door to the apartment. Through the landing window he could see a bulky African in a light grey trench coat at the entrance to an alley way, lighting a cigarette.

'See you soon then. Bye,' he said to Marianne as he headed for the stairs. The rear entrance to the block was not obvious from the front of the building. With luck he'd be able to shake his tail off. That would give Mr Pushy something to think about.

★

23

His flat looked different, more spacious, more airy. It took Leon a few seconds to realise that not only had Clive's things gone, so had all the moveable IKEA furniture, the TV, the CD player and the mock polar bear rug. And in less than an hour. Without exception, they had been bought on credit by Leon. All that was left was a note on the kitchen work surface.

Hi Leon,

You never did appreciate the finer things in life. They'll be better off with Mike and me. I'm sure you'll soon fill the house with old tat without too much difficulty. Perhaps Marianne can give you some of her junk.

Best we don't keep in touch. I didn't realise till I met Mike just what an emotional drain you are and how toxic our relationship was.

Thanks for the good times,
Clive

Bzzzzzzzzzzzzzzzzzzzzz

Leon saw Bankole's shape and opened his front door.

'Are you ready?' Bankole pushed past him and into the sitting room.

'I haven't said I'm going.'

Bankole turned, towering over Leon. 'Of course you are. It's in your eyes. I've awoken something in you, something that's been dormant since you were a baby. You can hear your destiny calling you. It's so loud, I can hear it myself.'

'That's my tummy gurgling. In any case, you've got to answer some questions first.'

Bankole grabbed him by the collar. 'There's no time for questions. Not now. You can ask them on the plane. Get your bag.'

'First I need to know about my grandfather, my family.'

Mr B tightened his grip. 'Later!' he snarled. Then in a more conciliatory tone he added, 'I promise, you'll find out everything you need to know,' and relaxed his hold.

Leon shook himself free. He surveyed the empty flat, his gaze alighting on Clive's note, on the pile of paper aeroplanes, on the picture in the hall of him and Clive arm in arm in dinner jackets. He peered past Bankole through the still-open front door. Some purposeful men dressed in black had jumped out of a van and were heading in his direction. So that's what bailiffs looked like.

'All right. I'll be two minutes. Oh, and we'll have to go via my mother's. I promised her. You stall these guys. They can't enter unless you invite them in. Bit like vampires. Tell them it's your flat and you've never

25

heard of me. I'll slip out the back and meet you in Queen's Road. It's the next street along.'

★

Bankole stopped drumming his fingers on the window of the black BMW 7, leant forward and spoke to the chauffeur, before swinging open the nearside rear door for Leon to hurl himself aboard. The car roared off with Leon still closing it behind him.

Nervously Leon patted his pockets to make sure he hadn't forgotten anything. Money, mobile, passport. All there. Idly he pulled the passport out, flicking through its pages. 'Shit! It expired a month ago. I can't go.'

'Pull in!' Bankole shouted at the driver. Without looking at Leon, he produced a phone, pressed a few keys and started gabbling in a foreign language. Sliding the mobile into a trouser pocket, he said, 'I'll take care of it. Give me that.' He plucked Leon's passport from his hands and stuffed it into his briefcase. 'It'll take two hours. I'll pick you up then.'

The car swung into a U-turn, and Leon was deposited back on Queen's Road. He glanced over his shoulder. No sign of the bailiffs. He opened the maisonette's back door and, looking all around, shuffled in. No sooner had he put the light on than the doorbell rang.

'Oh no, not them again!' He peered at the caller's silhouette through the frosted pane of glass. 'Oh, it's him.' He strode towards the door, pulling it open.

'Leon, what's going on?' Frank said. 'These bailiffs were here. Waved something at me but I didn't have my glasses. They wanted to know if that car was yours.' He nodded at a neighbour's Vauxhall Astra parked outside the front wall. 'Said they'd take it if it was.'

Leon laughed. 'I hope you said yes, Frank. Would have served that homophobic old bastard right.'

'Are you in trouble, Leon?'

'It's Clive's warped sense of humour. Set me up as a joke.'

Frank chuckled. 'You're not wrong there. I've seen what he's got up to in the past. Is he coming home soon?'

'Actually, I'm flying out to meet him for a week or two. Leaving in a few hours.'

'Somewhere nice?'

'Mutabe.'

Prompted by Frank's quizzical expression, Leon added, 'West Africa. Fashionable holiday destination.'

'Ah, yes,' Frank said in a way which confirmed he'd never heard of the place.

★

Shortly afterwards, Leon found himself standing outside Marianne's apartment block again, pressing the bell. He looked over his shoulder. Two solidly built black men were loitering on the street corner, apparently immersed in their smartphones. Mr B must still have him under surveillance.

Marianne took a while to answer. When she did, she embraced him clumsily, transmitting the tension locked in her body. Even her voice sounded strained.

'Leon, what are you doing here?'

Out of the gloomy recesses of the flat loomed a thin man with a hook nose, dressed in a pale grey suit.

'This is Charles,' she said.

Charles stepped forward into the light, extending his hand for Leon to shake. Then he picked up his briefcase and edged towards the open front door.

'I'll be in touch, Marianne,' he said with a slight incline of his head, pulling the door shut behind him.

'Who's Charles?' Leon asked.

'Oh, just a friend.'

'Didn't look much of a friend. Didn't even say good-bye.'

'More of an acquaintance really.'

An anxious expression gripped Marianne's face. 'You haven't come to tell me you're going?'

'Yes.'

Marianne wrung her hands. 'When?'

'Pretty well straight away.' Leon saw Marianne draw breath. He didn't want her to speak. 'I've made up my mind,' he added quickly.

Marianne folded him in a tight embrace. 'Oh, my

boy, my darling boy. I've been dreading this moment. Do be careful. And you know, don't you, that whatever happens, I'll always love you.'

Nodding, he turned towards the front door.

'Hold on a moment.' Marianne scurried into her bedroom, returning with something in her closed fist. 'I want you to have this.' She opened her hand to reveal a silver elephant charm attached to a thin chain.

'Is that yours? I've never seen it before.'

'It was in the sheet you were wrapped in when we found you. Take it with you for good luck.'

Marianne fastened the charm around his neck and kissed him.

★

When Leon got back, the black saloon was already waiting outside the maisonette. Bankole lowered the window at Leon's approach. 'You took your time. Get your stuff.'

Leon rushed into the maisonette, grabbed his bag and ran back to the car.

'Here you are,' Mr B said as they started moving. He pushed a British Passport towards Leon, who took it gingerly, riffling its pages.

'Is it genuine?' Leon tried to mask the anxiety in his voice.

Mr B laughed. 'You don't think I'd risk everything by giving you false documentation?'

'No, I suppose not.'

The car made its way slowly through mounting traffic. Leon looked at his watch. 'We're going to miss it.'

Bankole withdrew his head from a copy of the *Financial Times* and yawned. 'Relax, young man.'

'It leaves in forty minutes, and we haven't even reached the airport, there's security to go through—'

'They'll wait for us.'

Bankole immersed himself once more in the newspaper while Leon fidgeted in his seat.

'Why should they?'

'Because they will.'

Finally, they arrived. Bankole strolled to the check-in desk while Leon bobbed up and down beside him. A solidly built woman, her cheeks scored with tribal markings, flashed them the perfunctory smile of someone whose shift is ending, ran through the standard questions and pushed their boarding passes towards them.

'As soon as you've cleared security, go straight to the gate. It's fully boarded and ready to leave.' She didn't bother to look up. 'Have a good journey.'

Leon grasped his boarding card and snatched up his bag, anxious to join the long queues snaking their way up to the security screening area. Bankole carefully placed his passport in the inside pocket of his jacket. 'There's plenty of time.'

'We'll hold the plane up,' Leon said, darting ahead and then stopping.

Bankole ambled up to him. 'Air Mutabese planes are always late.'

Mr B shepherded Leon through the fast track security lane. After a stately walk through the teeming corridors of the airport terminal, they arrived at the flight's departure desk and were waved through. At the cabin, they handed their boarding cards to the attendant.

'Your seat is down here, third on the right, Mr Bankole,' she said, pointing to the business class cabin. Leon shuffled up close behind, ready to follow.

'And you're down there, fourth on the left, sir,' she added, indicating the economy cabin.

'But, I thought—'

Bankole cut him short. 'I always travel business class.' He turned his back and made for his seat, pulling his suitcase behind him and leaving Leon with his mouth agape.

'Please take your seat, sir.' The attendant put her hand on Leon's forearm and nudged him in the other direction.

The seat was easy to find; it was the only empty one in a packed cabin. A woman nursing a bawling infant stepped into the aisle to let him sit down, a complicated exercise which involved gathering up the child, its squidgy toys and a blanket that smelled of urine. He settled eventually into his seat and the woman back into hers. Prompted either by malevolence or flatulence, the child stared pop-eyed at him. He looked more

31

than two years old, but couldn't be, as at that age he would have had his own seat. The aircraft accelerated for take-off, the child's screams matching the roaring thrust of the engines in volume, and his already chunky fists flailing and often catching Leon's arm. Hoping for moral support, or at least some sympathy, Leon looked at the large man on the other side of him who, with his eyes closed, his head lolling back and his mouth open, emitted a single, long drawn out grunt like that of an amorous pig in heat, a clear precursor to a night's heavy snoring.

★

The baby finally fell asleep half-sprawled across Leon's lap. Its mother, having gulped down two large gin and tonics, joined Leon's other neighbour in a stereophonic snoring symphony. It was a relief when the crew finally emerged in the morning, turned on the cabin's lights and trundled a trolley down each aisle.

Breakfast consisted of a large blob of what smelled and looked like builder's putty, three electric pink biscuits and a piece of fatty meat soaking in its own grease.

Leon pushed the plastic tray to one side, as he had done with the uneatable dinner they'd served earlier, and his stomach emitted a deep, volcanic rumble. Marianne's worried frown kept materialising and then disappearing in his mind. Who was Charles?

He'd displayed a coolness and detachment more befitting a rent collector than a friend.

'Everything all right?' Mr B's voice startled Leon. From his relaxed manner, it appeared he'd eaten and slept well. His gaze alighted on Leon's untouched meal and his tone was more accusatory than concerned. 'You haven't eaten your food. You're not ill?'

Leon pulled a face. 'I would be if I ate it. Anyway, I thought we were going to talk on the flight. I've got lots of questions.'

'All in good time. There'll be plenty of opportunity when we arrive. I only popped back to see how you were. Better return to my seat.'

By now Leon's neighbours were tucking into their meals.

'How are things in Mutabe, sir?' Leon addressed the question to his male neighbour, who was wiping a streak of brown grease off his chin with a paper tissue.

'Terrible. I only use Mutabe City for flight transfer.'

'Me too.' The woman on the other side ceased slurping to join in. 'My parents say it nice country before troubles. In past, people holiday there from all over.'

'When was that?' Leon wished he'd spent more time researching the land of his birth. When he was young, he'd shown a lively interest and had even drawn a Mutabese flag in crayons on his bedroom wall. But when they'd killed Peter he painted over the flag and tried to forget the country.

'Thirty, thirty-five years ago,' the man replied. 'Hard to remember. Seem like forever.'

'Didn't Oblanga bring stability?' Leon said, relying on a *Wikipedia* entry he'd glanced at on his phone on the way to the airport.

The man laughed. 'So he claim. Not stopped bombs going off though.'

'Who's responsible for them?'

The man stared at Leon. 'Who isn't? Communist rebels, fascist rebels, Muslim fanatics, gangsters, police, army, probably even old Oblanga himself.'

Leon scrutinised his neighbour. 'Why Oblanga?'

'Where you been? In cave or top of mountain? Power. If everyone scared, he get away with murder.'

'They say he kill millions,' the woman added. 'I not like changing planes there. Have to this time. So happy when we take off again.'

The man looked out of the window. 'Crossing coast now. Port Villis below.'

'What's that like?' Leon asked.

'Main town in Tribal Lands. Shithole. As Americans say, cowboy country. They say they semi-autonomous. I say they semi-civilised.'

The fasten seat belts sign came on and Leon strained to catch a glimpse of Mutabe through the small window beyond his corpulent neighbour. The aeroplane turned in a wide arc prior to landing. The airport was served by two heavily congested grey roads and surrounded by small shacks interspersed with lush, dark green vegetation and linked by pale yellow tracks dotted with ant-like people.

Leon's stomach churned with fear, excitement and anger. Even if everything goes wrong from now on, at least I've made it to my birthplace, he thought, as the aircraft landed and taxied down the bumpy runway. No one can take that away from me. And if this Mr B turns out to be a phoney, I'll go to the British Embassy and get them to repatriate me. It won't be a problem.

★

Mr B was waiting for Leon in front of passport control. 'You'll need a visa,' he said, extending a handful of what looked like Monopoly money denominated in thousands.

Leo was amazed. 'How much does that cost?'

'Five thousand shillings. The rest is for the official.'

Leon smoothed the back of his head with the palm of his hand to calm himself. His irritation at his treatment by Mr B, simmering since he left the maisonette, was bubbling up into anger. Yet he must remain cool, at least as far as outward appearances were concerned.

'I refuse to bribe anyone.'

Bankole patted Leon's arm. 'Facilitating payment. Not a bribe.'

'Whatever you dress it up as, it's against my principles.'

'Then you'll have a brief but unpleasant stay at the airport until you're deported, probably on this aeroplane. I hope you've worked out what you'll say to those bailiffs.'

The sweat was running in small rivulets down Leon's back and he silently cursed the air-conditioning for its inefficiency.

'But I can negotiate, right? I'll get one without paying *all* this money?'

'Possibly. Meanwhile, Immigration will carry out a full body search and then hold you in an internment room for a couple of weeks. No air-con, no bed, no shower, several room-mates, not very pleasant.'

Leon looked down at the wad. 'How much is this worth?'

'Today, fifty dollars. Tomorrow, who knows? Perhaps forty, perhaps thirty.'

Leon put the money in his pocket and joined the long, stationary line of Economy Class passengers. 'How do people live with inflation like that?'

Mr B pulled out his wallet to reveal a wad of hundred dollar bills. 'By using these. Unless you're poor, of course, in which case…' He didn't bother to finish the sentence before turning his back and heading for the short and rapidly moving Priority Passengers' queue.

★

Leon felt soiled yet relieved when he emerged with his visa still wet in his passport. The immigration officer had wanted more, forcing Leon to bargain hard. He'd eventually thrown in ten pounds to clinch the deal. At one point, he'd thought he might also have to sacrifice his watch, which the official had been eyeing. He wondered how badly the shilling had fallen in value in the few days since Mr B had been away.

A chauffeur in a pale grey suit and peaked cap, who Mr B introduced as Adwin, met them and saluted. He took Mr B's bag and led them through the swarms of people struggling with suitcases, large plastic bags and battered wooden boxes, to an automatic door. When it creaked open, they found themselves in a dense and noisy crowd outside the terminal building. A wall of heat smacked Leon's face and the reek of pungent body odour robbed him of breath. They picked their way through tangled masses jostling in haphazard fashion for transfer buses and, fanning themselves with their hands, worked their way towards a small carpark only twenty metres away marked, 'Reserved for VIPs.' By now Leon's shirt was clinging to his back like a second skin. With a click of the chauffeur's keys the lights of a silver Bentley Continental flashed and its boot opened with the faintest of whirrs. Leon threw his bag in. Adwin lifted Mr B's calf-skin case and laid it down with all the care one would a newborn baby.

As he slid in beside Mr B, Leon said, 'You must

answer my questions before we go any further, starting with my Mutabese family.'

Mr B inclined his head towards Adwin, shaking it almost imperceptibly.

'Later. We'll meet for dinner. Meanwhile I'll drop you at your hotel.'

Chapter 4

The Hotel Britannica was a conservationist's dream and a guest's nightmare. Built in the late nineteenth century of imported greyish yellow London brick, it had resisted all attempts at modernisation, thus preserving the charms and discomfort of a building completely unsuited to its environment. As a security measure, its large sash windows opened only a little, while its bricks soaked up the sun's rays so that, by mid-morning, its rooms were like kilns. Meanwhile the plumbing and drainage system coughed and spluttered like a smoker on his deathbed.

As the bellboy put his shoulder to the door and gave a hearty shove to let Leon in, small pieces of plaster tumbled from the crumbling ceiling and lodged in his tight black curls.

Leon stepped over the threshold and onto floorboards that sloped away from him. The spacious room was furnished with a brass bed, a threadbare grey tartan wingback armchair, an IKEA-style bedside table bearing a kettle, teapot and two cups, an orange plastic chair and a large oak wardrobe with two drawers. Its windows, their frames almost entirely denuded of paint, looked out onto the street. A cracked washbasin, elaborate Victorian cornices, and a ceiling rose, at the centre of which an electric fan rotated with the speed of a tai chi grandmaster, made up the room's fittings.

Sensing Leon's plummeting mood at the news that the shared bathroom was at the end of the corridor and despairing of a tip, the bellboy left, slamming the door behind him.

Longing for water and a snack, all Leon found in the wardrobe was a trouser press, vintage 1970. Minibars evidently had yet to make an appearance in Mutabe City.

A sudden movement caught his eye. A speckled brown gecko had darted out of a minute aperture and scaled the wall in pursuit of a purple fly, which was taking a rest from hurling itself, along with several similarly coloured fellows, against the dusty window panes. A treasure trove of brilliantly marked dead moths lay on the windowsill beside a withered black and gold hornet, its spiky legs pointing stiffly upwards.

Leon, his ankles still swollen from the flight, stepped out of his shoes and shed his socks. The creaking wooden boards beneath his feet were warm.

Slipping out of his sweat-drenched shirt he was about to take off his lightweight suit trousers when he spotted something black and furry scuttling across to the far corner of the room. Terrified, he edged towards it, craning his neck to get a better view. Whatever it was had disappeared behind the wardrobe.

It's probably more scared of me, he thought, failing to convince himself. He mopped the sweat trickling down his face with his shirt. It was no good; no sooner had he done so than he was wet again. Everything seemed damp except his mouth and throat, which were sandpaper dry. Had there been a phone, he would have called reception to ask whether the water was potable. As there wasn't, he risked it and, bending over, cupped his hands under the tap and lifted them to his mouth. Despite the faintly sulphurous taste, he slaked his thirst before running some water into the basin to have a wash, only noticing then its brown colour. Perhaps drinking it hadn't been a good idea.

Mr B had promised to pick him up at 7pm. It was now 4pm. He considered exploring the nearby streets, thought better of it and, instead, stretched out on his bed, his leaden eyelids drooping. He was woken from his stupor by a sharp rap on the door.

'Who is it?' he called out.

'Room service,' a female voice replied.

Heaving himself up, he stumbled to the door, which, using considerable force, he prised open. He was greeted by the sight of a woman of about forty-five with a too-friendly smile, wearing grey overalls and flip-flops.

'Yes?' he said, inclining his head.

'Room service.' She breezed past him, slamming the door behind her and stopping by the bed.

'I didn't order anything,' he said, adding, under his breath, 'What the hell's going on?'

'You not have to,' she replied, unzipping her overalls and stepping, naked, out of them. She was well-built, with pendulous breasts, a luxuriant pubic bush and muscular legs. 'Uncle already pay. You enjoy.' She waved her hand towards the bed. 'Come on. Bet you real animal.'

'I don't have an uncle. You must be in the wrong room,' Leon said, hovering by the door.

The woman advanced towards him. 'Course you do, sweetie. Man with big scar. He send me. Now come here. No point lonely.'

'I'm not lonely. I'm absolutely fine. Never been better. Kind of you to call, but I think you should go now. Please.'

He was conscious of the pleading tone in his voice. Perhaps he should try to be more assertive.

The woman shook her head. 'What wrong? Make you relax.' She took another couple of steps, reaching out towards him.

'I'm engaged,' he blurted out.

'I married,' the woman replied. 'Your wife to be, she never know. I…' her face puckered with the effort of trying to remember a word. 'Discreet,' she added moments later with a triumphant smile.

'Look, I don't have any condoms. Nothing personal, it's just we don't know each other.'

The woman smiled. 'No problem.' She padded over to where her overalls lay on the floor, stooped down and pulled a packet out of the pocket. 'Here!' She flung it and it fell at Leon's feet.

'All right, if you must know, I'm waiting for the results of an AIDS test. I can't risk infecting you.'

'L'il rubber friend protect me, mister. Come on.'

Leon shook his head.

'You not gay boy?'

Leon was silent.

'You gay, yes?'

Leon looked out of the window. Through the dusty panes mountainous black clouds were congregating.

'You tell me, sweetie. No tell anyone, promise.'

Leon nodded.

Her eyes opened wide and she drew a deep breath.

'Be careful, sweetie. Abomination, Bishop Mbutu say.' She walked slowly over to her overalls and stepped into them, pulling them up with a flourish. 'Not my business.'

'No, it isn't,' Leon mumbled, resenting her inquisitiveness, and realising he was now at her mercy.

She gave his upper arm a gentle shove. 'You no tell uncle no pokey-pokey, I no tell him you gay. I keep

43

uncle money. Deal?' Her tone was brisk and business-like.

Leon nodded again. 'By the way,' he said. 'What's your name?'

She laughed. 'Usually men not ask. Primrose. You?'

Leon hesitated. Perhaps he would be less vulnerable if he didn't tell her. Then again, there was something about her he instinctively liked. 'Leon.'

'Nice name. I call you Mr Lion.'

Failing to close the door quietly, she slammed it behind her. With his heart still pounding, trying to rest would be pointless. He needed a drink, and something a lot stronger than tap water.

After the chugging brass shower had intermittently squirted lukewarm water over him, Leon put on clean clothes and headed for the Hippo bar, named after the pygmy hippopotamus's head mounted there. The room was half-full of what looked like businessmen and hookers. Perching on a stool, he ordered a beer from an aged barman, whose yellowing white jacket matched his teeth.

Embarrassed by the intimate scenes unfolding around him, and with nothing else to do, he read the label on the bottle, noticing it was more than two years past its sell-by date.

'This beer's old,' he said, pointing at the label.

The barman, his forehead knotted, stared first at him, then at the date and shrugged.

'Get me another bottle, will you?' Leon said.

When the barman had been through all the bottles in stock and not found any more recent, Leon screwed up his face and his courage and swigged his beer.

'What the hell.' He wiped his mouth with the back of his hand.

'Hello Mr Lion.' A few feet away, Primrose stood arm in arm with a fat man wearing a shiny blue suit. She flashed him a smile and winked as she and her companion secluded themselves in the corner.

What was he doing here? This was a mistake. He could have got another job, confronted Clive, got his stuff back, and found somewhere to live. Instead he was oozing perspiration in a crumbling hotel-cum-brothel and drinking out-of-date beer. A bellhop approached and handed him a message:

Delayed. Cancel dinner. Pick you up 09.00 tomorrow. Mr B.

Leon knocked back another couple of beers and was holding his next chilled bottle up to his moist face when a hand was placed on his thigh. Its owner was a broad-shouldered young woman in a low-cut scarlet dress which revealed an ample cleavage glistening with sweat.

'We go to your room,' she purred.

'I'm waiting for someone.'

'You waiting long time. I watching. You get message. She stand you up.'

'No, I'm busy.' Leon wondered whether he would ever succeed in shaking these prostitutes off.

'You leave Mr Lion. He my friend. Right Mr Lion?' Primrose, arms akimbo and looking ready to hit her, had squared up to the other woman, who turned away with a loud harrumph.

'Thanks Primrose.' Leon wiped his brow with a handkerchief.

'It nothing, Mr Lion. What friends for.'

'Speaking of which, where's your friend? The man you were with.'

'Gone home to wife.'

Leon felt the urge to confide. 'I was meant to be meeting Mr B tonight, but he cancelled.'

'Not surprised, Mr Lion. Two bomb explosions tonight. One by FMF, other PRF.'

'That's terrible. Many hurt?'

'No, lucky this time. No injuries.'

'Who are these people and why are they doing these things?'

'They rebels, Mr Lion. It what rebels do. One lot is Fundamentalist Muslims, the other Communists. They compete with each other.'

'What's the Government doing to stop them?'

Primrose shrugged. 'Not much. They say one part of Government sponsors FMF, another part PRF.'

'How could any Government have anything to do with extreme factions which want to bring it down and replace it with their own regimes?'

'Everything for sale in Mutabe. Just depend on the price.'

This all sounded crazy. Leon sank his drink and wiped his mouth on the back of his hand. Not normally much of a drinker, after only a few beers he was becoming sentimental. Primrose was the closest thing to a friend for several thousand miles. He gazed at her fondly, the embarrassment of their encounter in his room receding rapidly.

'If you're free, can I buy you a drink?'

Primrose shook her head and laughed. 'Been on back all day. Go home now. Family. You enjoy evening.' She patted Leon on the arm and left the bar, swinging her hips.

In the near empty hotel restaurant, with its smell of decomposing mushrooms and its waiters dressed as relics from an imperial past, Leon struggled with a glutinous stew of leathery goat followed by a local fruit that was more pips than flesh. Although he was now aching to get out of the hotel for a while, torrential rain accompanied by thunder and lightning dissuaded him. He was in bed by half past nine, certain he would sleep deeply.

He woke up at midnight in acute discomfort and, curling himself up round the pedestal in one of the two toilets on that floor, periodically retched up the contents of his stomach. Shortly after, diarrhoea set in.

★

When Adwin hopped out of Mr B's limousine in the hotel forecourt and marched into the lobby to summon him, Leon, shivering and with a blanket draped around his shoulders, sent him away saying he was ill and would contact Mr B when he was better. Adwin, after some minutes shuffling back and forth between the foyer and the car, gave him a number where he could leave a message.

Chapter 5

The English edition of *The Mutabe Times* was delivered to Leon's room both days he lay in bed, facing the wall and refusing all but a jug of water. When he finally dragged himself to his feet on the third morning, he picked up the latest edition and collapsed, exhausted, into an armchair to peruse it. The newspaper was one long paean of praise to Oblanga, ingenious in its insertion of his name into every article, whatever its content. Even the national football team's recent 1-0 victory over regional rivals, Ghana, was attributed to his wisdom, foresight and encouragement. Leon was about to throw it out when he noticed an article tucked away on page 7, headlined *Social Cleansing Continues*. His eyes scanned the report, which announced the execution of *four hardened deviants convicted of unnatural acts*, going on to claim each had *undergone extensive curative treatment at the Government's expense but had relapsed into abominable and diabolical sexual practices.* Bishop Mbutu was reported as saying that Mutabe would be all the better *for the elimination of insidious elements who had spurned the help generously offered by President Oblanga and his chief Medical Officer and were intent on corrupting Mutabese society from within.*

Leon had been queasy when he had picked the newspaper up. Now, feeling deeply sick, he took to his bed again, unable to move. As he drifted between wakefulness and sleep, he kept wondering why gays were so hated in Mutabe.

★

Leon had lost half a stone by the time he got over that bout. On the fourth morning he emerged from the hotel into the blinding glare, his legs wobbling and his hands shaking. With Adwin's help, he eased himself onto the car seat beside Mr B.

'I've never known a man take three days to recover from sex with a hooker. It must have been a hell of a session,' Mr B said.

The car set off along the rutted road at little more than walking pace, splashing through the large puddles left by several days' rain.

'Where are we going?' Leon asked.

'To meet some friends.'

'Who?'

Mr B inclined his head in Adwin's direction and put a finger to his lips.

They arrived at a 1960s brutalist, concrete building, surrounded by a high metal fence topped with razor wire. Two white-helmeted, khaki-clad soldiers stood rigidly to attention by sentry boxes on either side of the gate. A couple of scruffily dressed policemen with cigarettes hanging from their lips inspected the documents of a driver while several vehicles queued patiently behind him.

Adwin, approaching at speed, hooted twice, put his headlights onto full beam and drove in through the exit lane, causing one of the policemen to jump out of the way, screaming abuse. Mr B, leaning out of his window, silenced him with a couple of words. Then Mr B, with Leon trailing apprehensively behind, stepped out of the car by the main entrance.

'Bullet proof,' Mr B boasted, touching the thick glass, and swaggered through into the building.

Two guards with machine-guns stood in the lobby. Another, a pistol bulging in his leather holster, cowboy style, sat behind a desk. Mr B flashed a card, they saluted, and Leon and he took the lift to the fourth floor. As soon as the doors opened an icy blast hit them which froze the sweat under Leon's shirt and sent shivers rippling up and down his body.

Mr B pointed towards a door on the far side of an open-plan office full of people at their workstations, or scurrying silently between them carrying files.

'Wait for us in there, and don't come out before we arrive.'

At the centre of the large conference room stood an oval wooden table surrounded by ten chairs. In front of eight of them was a printed name card showing the title 'Mr' and a letter. The ninth bore the words *Bishop Mbutu* written in neat red felt-tip pen. At the far end of the table was an overhead projector and a screen, both of a type Leon remembered from his early days at work. A flip chart on a stand had been parked in one corner, and along a wall there were a couple of low cupboards which Leon found contained spare flip charts, marker pens and a sign which read: *Highways Committee in session. Do not disturb.*

Leon pulled out a chair and waited. After twenty minutes, he put his head round the door. The outer office was deserted. 'Hello, anyone there?' he called. There was no answer. 'Hello!' he bellowed, punching his palm with his fist.

Several individual office doors faced onto the communal area. He knocked on each in turn and, on receiving no answer, poked his head round. All were empty. He decided to try another floor and took the lift to the fifth. Then the sixth. Finally, having established that the whole building was unoccupied, he went back to the ground floor where the desk was unmanned. A security camera, set high in the ceiling, made a buzzing sound as it swivelled around to track his movements. He tried the main doors. They were locked and despite strenuous efforts, he couldn't find a release mechanism to open them. Where was everyone? Why had he been brought here? Was this an ingenious test, or had an emergency occurred and, in their haste, they had forgotten him when they abandoned the building? He tried the doors again. The glass looked thick and strong. He went to the reception desk only to find its drawers locked. And all the time the camera followed his every move. He felt like hurling himself against the glass, crying, curling up into a little ball on the floor. Instead, deliberately affecting a nonchalant manner, he drew a deep breath, seated himself at the desk, put his feet up in front of him, and stared back at the camera, challenging it to blink before he did.

He must have been there for more than an hour when a panel in the wall opposite opened and two security men toting machine-guns strolled in. One of them pointed his weapon at Leon, and then jerked it away to indicate he should move. Leon drew himself up slowly. Although trembling, he wasn't going to hurry for these goons.

The other guard unlocked the drawer and took out a remote control. The main doors swung open and, in an instant, a silent stream of people entered, some taking the lift, others climbing the stairs.

'Can you tell me where Mr Bankole is?' Leon asked the guard, who shook his head.

'Mr Bankole.' Leon shouted the words, but the guards merely stared at him. He took the lift to the fourth floor and stood in the middle of the once-again teeming open-plan office.

'Anyone seen Mr Bankole?' he yelled. No one paid any attention. He opened the conference room door and jumped back in surprise. It was full of men in suits seated around the table, one of them wearing a cleric's collar.

Mr B's look of censure mirrored that of the men around him. 'Ah Leon. At last. We wondered where you'd got to. You've kept some very important people waiting.'

'You wondered where *I'd* got to. Where the hell were *you*? I've been left here for hours, on my own.'

Mr B's face remained impassive. 'You're being most discourteous. You owe our friends an apology. We were having a brief pre-meeting.'

'You owe *me* an apology,' Leon yelled back. 'You abandoned me. That's not very courteous.'

'I think we'd better get on with the business in hand.' From his place name it was Mr C.

Leon's stomach knotted. 'No, let's sort this out now. You've brought me to Mutabe and then done nothing but mess me about. I've had enough. I'm going home on the next available flight.'

The room fell silent, all eyes turning to Mr B.

'Out of the question,' Mr B said after a short pause.

Leon stepped forward and slammed his fist on the table. 'You try and stop me.'

'Precisely what I will do. You're here on an A4B visa. That means you must obtain official clearance before you can depart. All immigration staff will be advised that it's denied.'

'You can't do that!' Leon shouted.

Mr B stared at him. 'Yes, I can.'

'I'll go to the British Embassy. They'll repatriate me.'

'I doubt they would be particularly impressed that you travelled here on forged documents.'

Leon experienced a sudden sinking sensation. 'You promised me the passport was genuine!'

Mr B gazed at him. 'You're misremembering. In any case, the fact is, you are here illegally, so no one in your embassy is going to intervene.'

'Especially as we have film evidence of you bribing an Immigrations Officer,' Mr C added. 'That's a charge carrying a minimum fifteen-year gaol sentence.'

'He wasn't even much good at it,' Mr E said. 'Should have got in for a tenth of what he paid.'

Leon stuttered and stammered, but no coherent words came, and he lapsed into silence, staring nervously at those around the table as he tried desperately to think how he could escape.

Mr B took a deep breath. 'Well, I think that's settled. Now, as Mr C said, let's get on with the matter in hand.'

Having silently worked through all his options and drawn a blank, Leon said, in a wavering voice, 'You mean I'm a prisoner in Mutabe?'

'You are our honoured guest,' Mr B replied in a solicitous tone, which then hardened. 'If you continue to offend us, you may well, of course, find your status diminished. That's rather up to you. I suggest you sit down and listen.'

All eyes were now on Leon. He curbed his impulse to make a break for the door. What would be the point? He was in their power. He slumped into the empty chair, his head in his hands.

'Let me summarise,' Mr B said, looking at Leon. 'We have with us the grandson and only remaining blood relative of Chief Onagaku, leader of the Mutabese people and first President of the Democratic Republic.'

A ripple of spontaneous applause broke out. Mr B raised his hands to silence it.

'We are now in a good position to throw off Oblanga's yoke. As soon as the people hear that the young Onagaku has returned they'll rise up and, using the armaments we've secreted around the country, overthrow the old despot.'

'About time too,' Leon said, brightening a little. Perhaps all the indignities he was suffering would prove worthwhile. 'Then let the people decide what happens.'

Nine pairs of eyes focused on him. The man to Mr B's left spoke. 'Of course not. That's what got us into this mess. Oblanga couldn't resist pandering to the Americans by pretending to listen to the rabble.'

Leon, disappointed by his cynicism, suspected he already knew the answer to the question he had to ask. 'So, who's going to replace Oblanga?'

Mr B stiffened. 'Why, we are, of course.'

Leon scanned their smug, self-satisfied faces. 'What gives you the right to run the country?'

Bishop Mbutu, small and pock-marked, stood up and declaimed, 'It is God's will!' and sat down again.

Mr E spoke. 'Between us, we have considerable experience of domestic and international affairs, of the exchequer and all the service ministries. There's no group better qualified to govern.'

'How do you know?'

'Because we have access to data on all citizens, at least those who matter. No one else has any relevant experience. We are, after all, the existing Government.'

Leon's head was swimming. 'If you're the Government, why do you want to carry out a coup? Aren't you rebelling against yourselves?'

Mr B intervened. 'You ask too many questions. Leave the politics to us. All you must do is learn the scripts we give you and stick to them whenever you're interviewed. We'll do the rest.'

The sound of thunder prompted Leon to look out of the window. Outside, hard pellets of rain were being hurled down from the mountainous clouds.

'What if I say no?'

'We can always find someone else,' Mr B said, as a fork of lightning lit the grey sky.

'Even though I'm the only surviving male blood relative of Chief Onagaku?'

Mr B smiled. 'Perhaps there are others we haven't found yet. Now, would you like to hear a little about yourself?' Without waiting for an answer, Mr B advanced to the overhead projector and placed a transparency of a bombed-out building on it.

'This is where you were kidnapped by the Cartwrights. We think they placed the bomb here.' His thick finger jabbed at the far side of the site. 'Their intention must have been to blow that wing of the building in. Unfortunately, they used too much explosive and the whole thing collapsed.'

'They saved me. They dug me out of the rubble,' Leon said quietly.

'We believe they removed you and then blew it up. Then they scrabbled around to make your rescue look authentic. A cold, calculating act.'

'No,' Leon exclaimed. 'They're kind, caring people; they aren't kidnappers.'

Mr B flashed up a transparency bearing a photograph of his adoptive parents.

'The man on the left, Peter Cartwright, born Peter Moynihan in Brighton 18th April 1953, known British MI6 agent, working in the guise of an aid worker. His wife, Marianne, born Riga, Latvia, 3rd June 1956, naturalised 1976, ostensibly employed by the British Government in various low-level roles all strangely carrying high level security clearance, until she resigned to join her husband as an aid worker here. They left Mutabe in 1988. Cartwright returned several times on operational missions, was captured and executed by PRF rebels in 2000. Marianne now lives in a small apartment in Feston-on-Sea.' A fuzzy picture of Marianne's block of flats, which looked as though it had been taken from a speeding vehicle, appeared on the screen.

'No, you're wrong,' Leon, slack-jawed, muttered. Though shaken by what he'd heard, he couldn't think of anyone less likely to be a secret agent than Marianne. Her forgetfulness had been a family joke. As for Peter, he was the least practical person ever. His attempts at DIY were positively dangerous, like the time he had put up a shelf in Leon's bedroom which collapsed in the middle of the night, showering Leon with magazines and notebooks. It was lucky it had been mounted at the foot of the bed, not at its head. Weren't secret agents meant to be ruthless killers too? When Leon's goldfish had developed a large grey growth, and Leon wanted Peter to put it out of its misery, he was too squeamish. Eventually Marianne, with a determined grimace, despatched it with a hammer.

Another picture followed. Leon gasped. It was the man who had been at his mother's flat.

'Charles Forrest, Head of B214, MI6. The

Cartwrights' superior,' Mr B said. 'Now, Leon, is it all starting to fall into place?'

Only partially suppressing the doubt gripping him, Leon shook his head. Yet the aloof and evasive Charles could easily have been a spy, in which case, what was he doing at Marianne's apartment? Agents, of course, were skilled at dissimulating, at passing as ordinary citizens, but Marianne? So much of what he'd been told didn't make sense. He needed to know more.

'Why would anyone kidnap a baby? And if they did, why didn't they try to make use of me?'

'The British Government was supporting Oblanga. You were their insurance policy. If they fell out with him, which they're doing right now, they had Onagaku's grandson, and they could use you to destabilise him.'

So, if Bankole hadn't turned up when he did, Leon wondered, would MI6 have approached him and asked him to return to Mutabe to oust Oblanga? He doubted it, but in any case it would be better to go along with what he was being told, for the time being at least. The phantasm of his missing older sister insinuated itself in his mind.

'What happened to my sister?'

Mr B waved his hand. 'Killed in the blast.'

Leon shook his head. 'No, the other one. The older one.'

Mr B looked puzzled, then his puckered expression reconfigured itself as a perfect blank. 'Oh her. I've no idea.'

Leon's anger grew but, breathing deeply, he made a strenuous effort to calm himself. He needed their help to track her down. 'I mean, wouldn't it be useful to have two of Onagaku's grandchildren supporting you?'

Mr B's face betrayed no emotion. 'She's only a woman and, in any case, it would be impossible to find her. Even if she is alive.'

'Impossible? But you said—'

'Let's cut the chit chat,' said an enormous man with cauliflower ears who had introduced himself as Mr D. 'We're wasting time. Tell him what to do.'

Mr B cleared his throat. 'You're going to declare publicly who you are, denounce Oblanga and demand his resignation. We'll provide DNA evidence to support you. The people don't like Oblanga and will be pleased to see him go.'

Leon struggled to get his mind round these instructions. He'd made sales presentations and addressed technical conferences, but denouncing a president? And he still hadn't been given the opportunity to find out more about his family.

'I'm not doing anything until you tell me what happened to my grandfather.'

The room fell quiet.

'OK. He lost the presidential election to Oblanga and was subsequently assassinated by Communists who wanted to radicalise the Tribal Lands,' Mr B said.

'But what was he like?' Leon insisted.

'He was a dreamer who lost everyone's support with his ridiculous ideas,' Mr D chipped in.

'Then how come his name is so important to you?'

Mr D eyed Leon balefully. 'He lost the support of everyone who matters. The masses, who don't, fell for his bullshit. Many still think him some sort of tribal saint.'

Leon wanted to probe further but could detect fidgeting around the table. There was, however, one more question he had to ask. 'My natural parents. Why were they murdered?'

'Probably incompetence on the part of your adoptive parents,' Mr B said, 'but we can't be sure. With that name there was always the risk they'd become someone's puppets, so perhaps Britain did decide to neutralise them just in case.'

A knot form in Leon's throat and tears welled up in his eyes. How could they talk so cynically of innocent humans being murdered as a contingency? He looked around the table, trying to control his emotions. Nine pairs of eyes were fixed on him.

Mr B walked round the table and placed his hand on Leon's shoulder. 'What we've said may have come as a shock, but you wanted to know, and there's no easy way to tell the truth.'

Leon took out a handkerchief and blew his nose. He would give anything to spirit himself out of this ghastly country.

'Let's get on with it,' Mr D said brusquely. 'I have an appointment in ten minutes.'

Mr B removed his hand abruptly. 'Yes, we'd better.' He cast an impatient glance at Leon's downcast face. 'Well, Leon, this is the plan. We'll create a social media storm. That will get all those leftie students buzzing. Then we'll make sure there's full coverage in all mainstream media of your demand that Oblanga quits and your call for a mass demonstration outside the Presidential Palace. We reckon a hundred thousand will turn up. You'll address them using our scripts. Once he realises the strength of public opinion, Oblanga is bound to go into exile.'

Leon sat up straight and stared Mr B in the eye. Not only did morality and justice not cohabit in Mutabe, it was as though they'd divorced and were completely estranged.

'And you'll let him swan off to Switzerland to be reunited with his plundered millions, will you? No plans to bring him to trial?'

Mr B's posture stiffened. 'Of course not. Why would we do that?'

'Because he's a mass murderer?'

Leon's question was greeted by a sudden inhalation around the table. Mr B stared at him. His tone was harsh.

'Where did you hear such drivel?'

'On the aeroplane. People don't even like changing flights here.'

Mr B's upper lip curled. 'Oblanga made lots of mistakes, that's why he must go, but that stuff about killing people is nonsense.'

Mbutu stood up again. 'Turn the other cheek!' he exclaimed and sat down.

'Amen, Bishop!' Mr D thundered.

Mr B towered over Leon, scrutinising him as an eagle might a rabbit. He stretched out his left arm, opened his palm and clicked his fingers. Mr E scuttled over and placed a bundle of papers in his hand. Mr B threw them down in front of Leon.

'Homework. Your public appearance is on Saturday. That gives you three days to learn these.' He turned to his colleagues. 'I think that concludes today's business.' He looked at Leon. 'I'll drop you back at your hotel.'

'I haven't agreed yet,' Leon said.

'You'll do it whether you want to or not,' Mr C replied. 'We know enough for you not to have a choice.'

Leon froze. Did that mean they'd dug into his past, maybe spoken to Clive even and discovered he was gay? If so, they could out him at any time and he would be as good as dead. He wiped his brow. He was over-reacting. If they had any evidence, they wouldn't be associating with him. He tried to control his breathing and picked the papers up. He had three days to find a way to wriggle out of this nightmare.

Mr C turned to Mr B. 'When he's finished this

little job for us, we need to send him down to the Tribal Lands. They're getting restive again.'

'I heard they're building up their militias,' Mr E added. 'We don't want them to get any ideas about breaking away from Mutabe.'

'His family name, used wisely, could help settled them down,' Mr D said.

'What exactly are the Tribal Lands?' Leon asked.

'It's a semi-autonomous region down by the coast. It's where your grandfather came from,' Mr B said.

Mr D wiped his forehead with a handkerchief. 'While he's there, maybe he could find out what the deal is between Mrs Daniels and the Tribal Chiefs. She seems to have a monopoly in trading their diamonds.'

'I think the answer to that question could lie closer to home,' Mr B said, staring at Mr E, who kept his eyes firmly on the papers in front of him.

Mr D snorted. 'No response from our friend, despite all the reports of his being seen at Morowa Daniels' house.'

'She's just a friend,' Mr E said and the room erupted in laughter.

'That's what they all say,' Mr D said. 'On that note, I suggest we ajourn the meeting. Please keep us updated on any developments, Mr B.'

While walking back to the car, it struck Leon that Mr B's tie looked familiar. 'That isn't an Old Harrovian tie?'

'Yes,' Mr B replied.

'I suppose all your colleagues went to Harrow too.'

Mr B sighed. 'Thankfully not all of them, though most went to your famous British public schools and top universities.' He paused thoughtfully. 'Except Bishop Mbutu, of course. God only knows where he was educated, if at all.'

'So, you're all bilingual?'

'Certainly not. I speak five languages: English, Mutabese and three dialects.'

'And if I were to take on the suicidal task you're intent on setting me, how would I get by? I only speak English.'

'When the British arbitrarily drew some lines on the map to create the country, they took no account of the tribes. Even now, fifty plus years after independence, only sixty percent speak Mutabese, forty their own dialects, and the young, the wealthy and the old generally understand English.'

'So, I'd only be able to communicate with juveniles, plutocrats and geriatrics?'

They had reached the car. Mr B put his finger to his lips and nodded in the direction of the driver, who opened the door for them.

'Thanks, Adwin,' Leon said, pleased to have remembered his name. Adwin, for his part, looked nonplussed at being recognised.

Mr B leaned forward when they were in the car. 'Get Akello to contact me,' he said hoarsely. 'I've got a job for him.'

Adwin nodded. Shortly after, the car came to a halt in a traffic jam. Dense black smoke was curling up into the sky in the distance. Adwin opened his window and an acrid burning smell filled the car. He closed it immediately.

Mr B pulled out a phone. After a brief conversation in Mutabese, he turned to Leon. 'PRF again. Seventeen killed or wounded.'

Adwin sighed. 'Those Communists are doing a lot of damage. People are scared now.'

Mr B tucked his phone back into his trouser pocket. 'It's all in hand.'

Adwin turned the car round and they took another route, driving in silence until they pulled into the hotel forecourt. Mr B placed his hand heavily on Leon's arm.

'Don't leave the hotel. You can take all your meals there, and I'll arrange for that woman to call on you every evening. If there's anything else you need, I'll be on this number.' He handed Leon a scrap of paper. 'And remember. You'll be under constant surveillance.'

Leon got out without saying a word.

'I'll be there at 15.00 on Friday for the dress rehearsal,' Mr B shouted after him.

Chapter 6

Leon slammed the door behind him. As the limousine pulled quietly away, he surveyed the crowded forecourt. There must be at least a dozen possible candidates for the role of minder, and it was probably the least likely one who was keeping tabs on him. He shuffled up to his room, his limbs aching with fatigue. On opening the door, he reeled back. His mattress was upended, his clothes strewn everywhere and his suitcase in the middle of the floor with its sides slashed. The lining of his jacket had been ripped and the heels of his shoes torn off. His sponge bag had been turned inside out and its contents deposited under the basin. Whoever had searched his room had been thorough.

With his heart pounding, he ran down to the phone booth in the lobby and dialled the number Mr B had given him, only to get the unobtainable tone. With fingers now trembling so much he could barely control the telephone's keys, he repeated the process. Still unobtainable. He scrutinised the piece of paper. Perhaps his rebellious fingers had slipped. He tried again. Perhaps the number had been written down incorrectly. He double checked and tried once more but without success. Typical of this bloody country, he thought. Bankole's phone must be out of order. Nothing worked here. Cursing loudly, he crumpled the piece of paper into a ball, flung it onto the floor, smashed the receiver back onto its cradle and then retrieved the scrunched-up ball of paper. Stuffing it into his pocket, he rushed back to his room, where he stood, paralysed.

'Big mess.' Primrose joined him, hands on hips, shaking her head. 'Done you over good, Mr Lion. I tidy up.' She gave him a kindly smile that made him want to burst into tears.

Leon shut the door and watched her as she stooped to gather his clothes, draping them over the crook of her arm, while a large bluebottle alternated between dive-bombing the room and hurling itself noisily against the window.

'Why are you even here?' he asked, wondering whether her broad face was as innocent as it appeared.

'I paid, so I here.' She handed him the pile of clothes and nudged his stomach. 'What you like? Blowjob? Rub and tug?'

Leon brushed the fly away and nodded at the teapot. 'You could make us a cup of tea. And you can tell me how you know Mr Bankole.'

Primrose emitted a wheezy laugh as she filled the kettle. 'All the girls know uncle. We go his parties, entertain friends; money good, men clean.'

'What's his actual job?'

Primrose rolled her eyes. 'He Mr Fixit. Fix everything and everybody.' Reaching in her handbag, she produced a small fly swatter with which she deftly squashed the bluebottle, which was resting on the sugar bowl.

Leon considered her answer. The man who had brought him here was still a mystery. 'What about his personal life? Is he married? Does he have children? What sort of house does he live in? What does he like to do when he's not working?'

Primrose's gaze slid, fixing on one of the many stains on the ceiling and she paused for a few moments before replying. 'No one really know him. They say wife long dead from fever. Son had brain cancer.' Primrose's eyes met Leon's and held them. 'Clever boy. Take long time. Uncle not same. Before, many people think he follow Oblanga as leader. Now just ficky-ficky all time and do things no one want to. He the President's balls. Without him Oblanga impotent.'

'He told you to come here now?'

'I no speak to uncle. Man give me orders. Uncle pay.'

Leon gave up. But perhaps Primrose could tell him about his own background.

'Did you know my family?' he asked.

'No. Meet grandfather at big rally. I little girl. Give us all sweets. Nice man.'

'Why did they kill him?'

'They say he communist. Destroy country. Give rich men's farms to the workers. Rich no like. Lost election. Oblanga president. Maybe Oblanga think grandfather a threat. Life cheap here.'

'Do you think Oblanga killed him?'

'Maybe, maybe not. Never know. Say Americans involved. They think he communist too.'

Leon sighed. In his experience, 'never know' were the operative words in Mutabe.

Primrose chucked two teabags into the pot, which she filled with boiling water. 'You very thoughtful, Mr Lion. What worry you?'

'Primrose,' Leon began tentatively. 'If you were looking for a missing person, where would you start?'

'We all missing in Mutabe. Missing everything: food, power, clean water, proper houses—'

Leon interrupted. 'I think I may have an older sister here who's still alive, but I don't know how to track her down.'

Primrose's face became serious. 'What her name?'

'I don't know.'

Primrose looked at him incredulously. 'There millions in Mutabe. How you know her, even if you find her?'

'I'm hoping she has one of these.' Leon removed the elephant charm from his neck and held it out in his palm. Primrose stared at it for a moment or two.

'Very pretty, Mr Lion, but you look at necks of all Mutabe women? Take long time. And what if it lost or stolen?' Her large brown eyes stared up at him. 'Sorry. I see you upset.'

Leon brushed his eyes with the back of his hand and took the cup of tea she proffered. He felt stupid. They drank in silence, then Primrose sat back in the armchair with her eyes shut. Within seconds her lower jaw dropped open and her heavy rhythmic breathing became a light snore. Leon raised himself quietly to his feet so as not to disturb her and paced the room. None of this made sense. It was as though he'd fallen through a trapdoor into an alternative universe, where all norms are reversed, where you can't get through immigration without a bribe which instantly makes you a criminal and where the Government is instigating a rebellion against itself.

Half an hour later Primrose sat up, looked at her watch, and said, 'That it, I go now.' She sprang out of the chair. 'You be careful, sweetie. Bad men here. Hurt you big-time. Specially gay boy.'

When she'd gone, Leon read through the papers he'd been given. Radio and TV interviews had been scripted, both questions and answers. At the back was a speech which opened:

I am Leon Onagaku, heir to the last Chief of Mutabe. I come to claim my tribal rights and free my people from the yoke of oppression.

Leon sighed. He wasn't really expected to spout this nonsense, was he? He looked again. The speech was five pages long. It would take an eternity to learn it.

He managed to get through to Mr B later that evening to report the break-in. Mr B dismissed it as the work of petty criminals, brushing aside Leon's rejoinder that they had searched everything.

'It's the one profession in this country where people get a thorough training,' Mr B said. 'They start at the age of five or six as lookouts, move on to street crime as young adolescents and become armed gang members in their late teens.'

Chapter 7

For the next three days Leon sat hunched over his papers or rehearsed in front of the mirror. Food was provided by room service and every afternoon Primrose would appear, tidy his room and make him a cup of tea, staying for precisely half an hour. On Friday evening, there was a rap on the door.

'At last, my wicked uncle,' Leon said, opening it. Mr D filled the frame. Behind him stood two ebony-skinned heavies wearing pinstriped suits and dark glasses. Without a word or a nod, Mr D lumbered in, his flunkies in train, and squeezed himself into the armchair. Nodding at one of the men, he said, 'Shut the door.' He turned to Leon. 'Give Donald here your papers. He's going to test you.'

'Where's Mr Bankole?'

'You'll be dealing with me from now on. Get on with it.'

Donald removed his dark glasses to reveal penetrating blue eyes, something Leon had never seen in an African before. He read the first question in a lazy drawl.

'You went to Oxford too?' Leon asked.

Donald cast a disparaging glance at Mr D, who was extracting a slim cigarette from a gold case and reaching in his pocket for his lighter. 'Had my mother and the rest of my family to support. No silver spear for me.'

'Enough chit chat,' Mr D barked.

Donald directed a malignant look at Mr D, then resumed asking questions for Leon to recite the answers.

'More energy, more heart, more passion,' Mr D said, looking up from an extended scrutiny of his cuticles. 'I've heard more animated train announcements.'

Donald and Leon ran through it again. Acting had never been Leon's strong suit so all he could think of doing was to increase the volume and wave his arms around.

'Better,' said Mr D. 'At least you know the words. Now the speech.'

Leon took a deep breath, fixed his eyes on the far wall and launched into it.

'Terrible,' Mr D said when he'd finished. 'Get Mhlambo to give him a lesson.' He heaved himself out of the chair and dusted his suit down. Turning to Leon as he was about to leave, he said, 'The social media storm starts tonight. We'll pick you up at twelve tomorrow. The demonstration starts at one.'

Donald stayed with him, making a brief call on his mobile before immersing himself in video games which pinged occasionally.

'Tell me a bit about yourself, Donald,' Leon asked. 'Were you born in Mutabe City?'

Donald didn't look up.

'How many in your family?'

Donald shot Leon a venomous glance. 'I'm trying to concentrate.'

Leon lay on his bed, his hands over his eyes, lamenting his stupidity in agreeing to accompany Mr B. He looked at his watch. Back home, he could be in the pub now, or watching television, or relaxing on his old sofa. Instead he was in this lousy vermin-infested room with a few lizards, spiders and the personality-free Donald for company. He also had the prospect of making a fool of himself in front of upwards of a hundred thousand people tomorrow to look forward to. He'd been an idiot getting himself into this situation.

Half an hour later, a fat man, sweating profusely and breathing heavily, waddled through the door, his stomach protruding over his belt and his shirt tail hanging out. He and Donald spoke rapidly and increasingly loudly in Mutabese for several minutes. Then Donald said something to the man which brought his invective to an abrupt halt. The man nodded and turned to Leon.

'I have to turn you into an actor overnight, so let's get started. I'm Mhlambo. Stand up.'

Leon dragged himself to his feet with a weary sigh. Mhlambo looked him up and down with thinly disguised contempt.

'Oh dear,' he said softly. 'This may take some time.'

Donald sat down, playing games on his smartphone, while Mhlambo showed Leon how to breathe, when to pause, where to look, what to do with his hands, what stance to adopt, and many other things. Despite his brusque manner he was clearly a professional and his advice was good. When, at last, they paused, it was nine o'clock. After a ten-minute break they carried on, Mhlambo fortifying himself periodically with deep draughts from a hipflask. At eleven Donald stopped the lesson. He and Mhlambo left, and Leon, his stomach rumbling, crumpled onto his bed, too tired even to stagger downstairs and order some food.

A soft tapping on his door made Leon start. He opened it cautiously to reveal a swarthy man with a small moustache wearing an oatmeal coloured linen suit and holding a notebook.

'I'm Jeff Gbeho from the *Record*, Mutabe's only truly independent newspaper. I'd like to interview you about tomorrow's demonstration.'

Leon rubbed his eyes. 'Do you know how late it is?'

The reporter smiled in a conciliatory manner. 'Sorry if I disturbed you, but this is important.'

Leon stared at his bed. Even if this stranger were a reporter, which seemed unlikely, he was far too tired to speak to him. 'Sorry. I'm not doing interviews. I'll talk to you afterwards.'

He pushed the door closed, staggered to his bed and toppled onto it.

Another knock. This time louder. Then an insistent voice.

'Chief Onagaku, please open up. The *Record* can help you. I only need five minutes.'

Leon scrambled off the bed and stood against the closed door. 'Go away! I told you. I'm not doing interviews. Tomorrow. I'll talk to you then.'

An exaggerated sigh came from the corridor. 'Have it your own way.'

Leon listened carefully, certain he could hear feet padding away into the distance. He waited for a few moments, eyelids drooping, then tottered to his bed, threw back the sheet and fell into it. He was fast asleep within five minutes.

He was roused by a frantic knocking on his door. Oh no! Not that bloody reporter again, he thought, holding a pillow over his head.

'Open door, now!' Even though it was muffled, he recognised the voice. Dragging himself to his feet, he released the catch and pulled the door open. Primrose burst in.

'Demonstration tomorrow, Facebook. Your picture. You no go. Police kill you. Trap. Client tell me.'

Leon stared blankly. He tried to speak but no words came. His mind was in turmoil once again. Was she telling the truth? Judging by her stricken expression, she genuinely feared for his life. Either that, or it was some big act. If so, what had she to gain? At last, he collected his thoughts. 'How do you know your client isn't working for Oblanga?'

'He not, Mr Lion, I swear. He not know I know you. Men fall asleep after sex or talk big, want you to think they know everything. He talk big. He in trouble if leak traced back to him.'

'And you'd be in trouble if anyone found out you passed it on to me. Why did you take the risk?'

Primrose started to cry. 'I like you. Too many die already.'

Leon put his hand on her heaving shoulder. 'Sweet of you to warn me, Primrose, but I'll be fine. Mr Bankole promised they'd look after me.'

Primrose's eyes looked ready to burst from her skull. 'Mr Bankole gone, sweetie. No one can find.'

'Perhaps he wanted a little private time.'

'He go nowhere without bodyguard.'

'Are you sure?'

Primrose nodded. Leon scrutinised her tear-stained face, trying to decide whether to believe her.

'What do you think's happening?'

Primrose dabbed at her eyes. 'I not know. You want, I help you disappear.'

Disappear. What he'd wanted to do for so long, but now the opportunity was offered, he was paralysed by doubts. What if Mr B was dead and Primrose was working for others who wanted him out of the way?

'I need time to think. So much going on and I don't understand any of it.'

'Mutabe, sweetie. Mutabe.'

There was a loud knock on the door. In seconds Primrose pulled Leon towards her and, with one practised hand undid his belt, unzipped his fly and let his trousers drop round his ankles while the other whipped off her blouse to reveal a lacy black bra. She wrenched open the door just as Leon was pulling up his trousers.

Donald stood leaning against the door post, a half-smoked cigarette hanging from his lower lip. When he saw their state of disarray, a sleazy smile spread across his face.

'Sorry to disturb you.'

'I should think so.' Leon did up his belt and stared at Donald.

'We've received some intelligence that Oblanga's agents may try to subvert you before tomorrow. If anyone, and I mean anyone, contacts you, let me know.' Donald pressed a card with a telephone number scrawled on it into Leon's hand. 'I'll leave you two to get on with it.' He smirked and started to pull the door closed behind him, then had second thoughts and pushed it open a fraction. 'We'll pick you up at eleven tomorrow. Wait for me in the lobby.'

'I thought you said twelve,' Leon said, as the door shut. 'Ah well, eleven then.' He turned and stared at Primrose. 'You tried to stop me from going. You're not working for Oblanga, are you?'

Primrose met his eyes without flinching and emitted a deep, frame-shaking belly laugh. 'Me sweetie? You joking. You go, you have more holes in you than my roof.'

'Strange though, isn't it?' Leon rubbed his chin. 'Your turning up here at crucial moments.'

The smile disappeared from Primrose's broad face. 'I tell you sweetie. I work for uncle.' She emitted a deep sigh. 'If not have Mr Fixit behind me, I find own customers. Not so clean.' She looked at her watch. 'Cup of tea? Five minutes I go.'

'No, but I'd die for a cigarette.' Having reawakened the nicotine monster, Leon had tried to curb it again, repeating to himself that it was only a matter of will power; he'd given up before and could do so again. Now it was proving too strong.

'Like man with firing squad?' She rummaged in a small purse and produced a pack of ten, offering him one and smoking another herself. He drew deeply on it, his body relaxing as the drug hit his system.

'That's better.' He stretched out on the bed, then sat

bolt upright. 'Hold on. You said there's five minutes left. That means you're still billing your time. Who are you charging?'

Primrose, lounging in the armchair, shrugged. 'Someone take over; someone always take over. Uncle Mr Fixit number four in ten years. Now be five.' She got up. 'You come, or stay be killed?'

Leon gazed at her open, smiling face. No one looked so sincere, so honest. She must be lying.

'I'll go through with it,' he said at last, stubbing out his cigarette in his saucer.

'Primrose sad. You easy customer, sorry lose you. Good luck, sweetie.'

Primrose's sadness appeared genuine. She must have had a hard life and her concern for him, despite all the problems she must face daily, touched him.

'How did you get into this game? It can't be much fun.'

Primrose shook her head. 'Work at factory owned by Chinese till it close. Husband no good, drinking, gambling and all that. Then big man come, say husband owe money and break his leg all bent and he no work now. Big man always come, ask money. I got no money, so he tell me get this job and he take most. No choice. But then Police Chief become client, and he like me. I tell him, he arrest big man, throw him in jail. Then I meet first Mr Fixit and find rich clients so can feed five children, two at college. One may be doctor one day. No can pay college fees with job in factory.'

'What about your husband?' Leon asked.

'Drunk, useless. Not care. No do ficky-ficky with him.'

'That's a terrible story, Primrose,' Leon said. 'You deserve better. This place needs to be turned upside down. Perhaps if Oblanga goes— '

'Others as bad. Seem better now, but after six months, a year, all the same.'

'Isn't there anyone who wants to change things for the better?'

Primrose shook her head. 'Meet no one like that, and I meet many people.'

She opened the door, pausing before exiting. 'Good-bye, Mr Lion. You good man. Sorry no see you again.'

Chapter 8

Leon lay awake most of the night, as thoughts of his own survival entwined with others about his missing sister, Primrose's grim life, and the exploitation of the Mutabese people by a corrupt leadership. If his actions tomorrow contributed to the overthrow of a ruthless despot, whatever the risk, he would see them through. For achingly long hours, he listened to the sluggish groaning of the ceiling fan and the whine of frustrated mosquitoes constantly testing the net draped over his bed. It was only a matter of time before an ingenious – or lucky – malaria carrier found its way through one of its several holes. He curbed an urge to get out of bed and set about the predacious insects with a towel. If Primrose was right about his own life expectancy, mosquitoes were low on the list of things he need worry about now.

The next morning a young bellhop, balancing a tray loaded with eggs, bacon and toast, together with a steaming silver coffee pot and matching milk jug, knocked on the door.

'What's this?' Leon had only ordered a bowl of cereal. The boy looked at him blankly.

'Your breakfast, sah.'

'You must have confused the order with someone else's.'

The bellhop shook his head. 'You only person have breakfast in bed, sah. I collect order from door myself.'

Leon took the tray and rummaged for a tip. 'The condemned man,' he said softly. It was the sort of joke Clive would have played, except Clive was several thousand miles away. Who else would have? It must be Primrose, but how could she afford it? Touched by the generous gesture, he was overcome by tenderness towards her which soon gave way to hunger. The smell of bacon and eggs was making him salivate, so after a few moments' deliberation, he sat down and munched his way through them, wiping his plate clean with a slice of buttered toast. He looked at the clock. Eight thirty. Two and a half hours to go. He took his scripts from a drawer and stood in front of the mirror, rehearsing in his deepest voice.

His worries about his own survival had receded with every delicious mouthful of his breakfast. He convinced himself he needn't worry. He wasn't Coconut; he was someone important. He was Chief Onagaku's heir and overlord of the Tribal Lands.

They, whoever they were, needed him and would protect him. He promised himself he'd buy Primrose a drink in the hotel bar that evening to thank her for her generosity. He could see her in his mind's eye now, laughing about her baseless fears and complimenting him on his oratorical skills.

★

The darkened glass in the windows of the blue Toyota that pulled up promptly at eleven in the hotel forecourt rendered its occupants invisible. Leon peered out from the lobby door and waited for five minutes. No one emerged. No other cars arrived. 'It must be,' he said to himself and walked slowly towards it, trying hard to make out who was inside.

As he drew alongside, one of the back doors opened and a voice rasped, 'Get in, Leon.' He surveyed the man on the back seat. He didn't recognise him, nor the unfamiliar men in the front.

'Excuse me, is this the car that's been sent to pick me up?'

'Yes, get in.'

'Where's Donald?' Leon asked, backing away.

'Donald sent us,' the man replied. 'Get in.'

Leon looked around. He glanced at his watch again. Still no other cars had arrived. This *must* be the one. He slid onto the back seat and closed the door, only to hear the lock click.

'How long will it take to get there?' he asked.

The three men stared ahead in silence.

'To the demonstration,' Leon persisted.

'Change of plan. You're going for a holiday in the countryside,' the man in the front passenger seat replied. His nose was bent, as though it had been broken and had never healed properly.

'The countryside?' Leon said. 'What's going on? Who are you?'

The three men remained impassive. As the traffic on the road – vehicular, animal and human – thinned, the car built up speed. What would be his chances of escaping if he had to, Leon thought, his bowels uncomfortably liquid. He looked around nervously at the car's other solid and muscular occupants and concluded they wouldn't be high.

'Is the demonstration cancelled?' he asked, trying to keep his voice level.

No reply.

'Look, what's going on? Where's Donald?'

Still no reply. They drove on. They had reached the outskirts of the city and were in the depths of shanty town, the shacks stacked back to back.

The car swung suddenly onto an unmade road, along which it continued for several miles, lurching up and down like a poorly maintained fairground ride as it struggled over cavernous potholes and jagged ruts. The road narrowed to a lane and eventually to a dirt track, at the end of which was a tall fence, topped by barbed wire. They ground to a halt and Broken Nose got out and swung the gate open to reveal a single-storey brick building with what looked like a steel front door and steel shutters over its windows. The car eased into the compound and stopped. Its rear door was flung open and Leon, propelled by a sharp push in the small of the back, found himself ankle deep in a puddle.

The Neanderthal-like man who had sat beside Leon seized his shoulder and impelled him in the direction of the front door. The car, with its remaining two occupants, completed a U-turn and headed back up the track, while the Neanderthal punched numbers into a security code pad fixed to the steel doorframe.

'Where are we?' Leon demanded. His companion pushed the door open. The shaft of light revealed only a sliver of the interior, leaving the rest in darkness. They entered and the Neanderthal fumbled on the wall. Click. The room was filled with lights so bright that Leon shielded his eyes with his hand and squinted to pick out a rough wooden table, three chairs, three single beds and a washbasin. One corner housed a kitchenette comprising a sink, and a cooker and a fridge both attached to butane cylinders. As his eyes adjusted to the glare it struck him that the room resembled the set from a low budget crime movie. Even though the main door was still ajar, the heat was intense; it was like walking fully dressed into a sauna, and sweat soon glued Leon's clothes to his body. He glanced at his swarthy companion who was gazing around as though looking for something. He was so muscular, so determined, Leon's chances of overpowering him were nil. But who was he? And what did he want?

The Neanderthal opened a cupboard and, with an exasperated sigh, produced a small table fan, which he plugged in, its feeble whirring barely shifting the treacly air. Then he went to the corner and, with a flourish, removed a cloth to reveal a sleek television set, which he zapped on with a remote control from the drawer in the table. The hysterical voice of a commentator, shouting in a language Leon couldn't understand, flooded the room. The pictures showed panicking people running in all directions as a phalanx of helmeted police wearing full riot gear sprayed them with bullets. Bodies, some still writhing, lay thick on the ground, as dark viscous rivers snaked their way from the thoroughfare to a gutter.

Leon stumbled backwards, his hands covering his eyes.

'That's your demonstration,' the Neanderthal said, and switched the TV over to a channel showing football. 'Ah, Mutabe playing Sierra Leone,' he added. 'Should be good game.'

Leon, oblivious to the chants and cheers now filling the room, slumped onto one of the chairs, sickened by the horrific carnage. 'Why? Why would they kill people like that?' His voice cracked and his eyes filled with tears. 'So brutal, so vicious.'

The Neanderthal stared at the screen, alternately groaning and cheering softly, while Leon huddled on the chair in shocked silence, the violent scenes replaying in his mind. He couldn't make sense of any of it.

'Was Donald killed today?' he finally asked in a small voice.

'Donald probably organised it,' the Neanderthal said in a neutral tone. He took his shirt off and hung it carefully on a hook on the back of the door.

'But why?'

'To get rebels to show themselves so he could eliminate them.'

'I could have been killed.'

'Maybe. Maybe they have use for you and save you before it all go off.' The Neanderthal sat down, kicked his shoes off and swung his feet onto the table. A sweaty odour permeated the stale air. A big toe peeped through a hole in his sock.

'Who are you guys? Leon asked.

'We look after you. All you need to know.'

'Do you work for Donald?'

The man snorted.

'Well, who do you work for then?'

'If you not ask questions, you likely live longer.'

They both turned their heads at the sound of a car screaming to a halt outside. Within seconds, the

Neanderthal was up and bounding towards the door. Before he could slam it shut, it swung open, there was a burst of gunfire and he crumpled to the floor. A tall thin man wearing a black hood with slits for eyes stepped over his body and waved his gun at Leon.

'Come with me.'

Although his tone was harsh, there was something familiar about his accent which, in his fear and confusion, Leon couldn't place. Leon glanced down. Rivulets of blood from the gaping wounds in his erstwhile captor's body were flowing into a small pool. Putting his hand over his mouth to stop himself from retching, he tried to stand up, but his rubbery legs gave way and he collapsed back onto the bed.

'Now!' the masked man shouted, firing a round into the ceiling and causing a cascade of plaster dust. Leon crawled off the bed and onto the floor, taking a long route round the cadaver and its growing pool of blood. The gunman grabbed him by the collar and yanked him to his feet, and then, with a mighty push, propelled him through the door so that he fell sprawling into the mud outside. Another hooded figure sat in a Toyota pickup, its rear door open and its engine running. Confronted by an automatic gun, Leon allowed the gunman to steer him into the front passenger seat. When he was inside, the door slammed shut and the hooded man jumped in behind. As they sped off, a pad was clamped over his nose and mouth. He tried to push it away before realising the hard metal object being placed against his head was the barrel of a pistol.

'I'd relax – that is, if you want your brains to stay inside your skull.'

Leon dropped his hands to his lap, and seconds later, he passed out.

Chapter 9

He came to slowly, remaining still while collecting his scrambled thoughts. His brain was mush, his mouth was dry, and his eyes burned. He had no idea where he was or who he was with. Only slowly did it dawn on him he was still in the pickup, and had been unconscious, though he didn't know for how long. Through the window he could see that the lush tropical vegetation had given way to patchy semi-desert scrub clinging to the sandy soil. His captors were still in situ. Though his heart was thumping, Leon determined not to show how frightened he was.

'How long was I out?' He rubbed his throbbing head in what he hoped passed for a casual manner. The emptiness of his stomach suggested it had been some time.

No response.

'Where are we?' His right arm was sore and he

ran his hand over it. Had they injected him with something and, if so, what?

'What did you do to me when I was unconscious?'

No reply.

He refused to acquiesce to the silent treatment.

'Where are we going?'

The two hooded figures remained mute.

'Who are you?' By now Leon was so used to people refusing to say who they were, he was taken aback when, in a clipped English voice, the driver replied, 'We're the FMF.'

'What's that?' Leon asked, realising he might be pushing his luck.

'The Fundamental Muslim Front,' the driver replied, swinging the pickup into a sharp swerve to avoid a pothole. 'We will expel or eradicate all non-believers and deliver our country to the true faith.'

Even in Leon's muzzy-headed condition, something didn't make sense. It was to do with that voice. Its modulated tones conjured up cricket pitches and warm beer rather than the arid sand that surrounded them. It might incur their wrath to ask yet another question, but after a few moments' reflection, he decided to take the risk.

'You don't sound as though you come from around here,' he said tentatively. 'You sound English.'

The driver nodded. 'I'm from Cheltenham, actually. I've been here four years.'

'Was your family from Mutabe originally?'

'I wish,' the driver said. 'They've always lived in Cheltenham. Generations of them.'

Leon turned round to the other gunman, who was holding a pistol aimed directly at him.

'Are you Mutabese?'

The man didn't reply. After a few moments' silence, the driver said, 'No, he's Damian. He's from Tunbridge Wells.'

'I'm Aazim, you idiot,' Leon's other captor snapped.

'Sorry Aazim,' the driver said sheepishly.

For the first time Leon noticed that both his hooded captors had white hands.

'What the hell are you two doing here?'

'We're on our gap year,' the driver replied.

'But you said you've been here four years—'

The other hooded figure broke in. 'You're telling him too much, Jace – er Nabhan.'

Leon was horrified. 'You mean you're both British students, and yet you go around killing people in cold blood?'

'You should be grateful,' Nabhan said. 'We rescued you from the PRF. They're hard-line Marxists. Having the grandson of old what's-his-face, the last remaining sprig of local royalty, wasn't exactly going to advance their cause, was it? They probably planned to discredit and then execute you.'

Leon wasn't sure this so-called rescue had made his predicament any better. Not only were his captors hardened psychopathic killers, they were smug and cocky English upper-class twats who could murder him at any time for any reason or no reason at all.

'What are you lot going to do with me?' he asked, trying to mask his growing panic.

'We're going to give you the opportunity to convert to the true faith, so you can join us,' Nabhan said.

'And if I don't?'

The two exchanged glances.

'Put it this way. You won't need your ticket home,' Nabhan said, swerving late to avoid a goat.

Arriving at a makeshift checkpoint, a posse of masked gunmen waved them down, spoke to Nabhan in hushed tones and examined some papers he was carrying. Then they peered into the vehicle and finally waved it on.

A further twenty minutes' silent drive followed, during which they encountered no one. Leon spent his time thinking through how he could escape and came up with nothing. His captors were heavily armed. They must be miles from Mutabe City and the terrain was increasingly inhospitable. As there was nothing he could do about his situation, Leon reasoned, he must remain vigilant until the opportunity to escape presented itself.

'Where is everyone?' he asked. 'Even for a semi-desert, it's deserted.'

'This is the part of the country under our control,' Nabhan said. 'Some fled when we took over. Others we've had to expel. Only true believers have been allowed to remain.'

'Doesn't look like there are many of those,' Leon said. 'If you lot do take over, it could get pretty lonely.'

'It's no joking matter,' Nabhan replied. 'When we do take over, with the help of our true-faith international friends, we'll begin a thorough programme of re-education.'

The pickup slowed as they approached the gates of a large wooden stockade around which milled twenty or so hooded figures, like so many black ants, machine-guns slung casually over their shoulders. Then it screeched to a halt, kicking up a mini sandstorm. Leon was shepherded into a compound containing several huts made from mud bricks, and guided, with none too gentle shoves, towards the biggest.

Coming in from the glare, it took his eyes a minute to adjust to the darkness inside. As they were doing so, a voice with a thick Mutabese accent said, 'Good day, Mr Onagaku,' and he found himself in front of a seated figure in white flowing robes, topped by a small round gold hat perched on his head like a walnut on a sherry trifle.

'Who are you?' Leon said, stifling his inclination to swear. His emotions were vacillating between fear and anger. Something about that ridiculous headgear was now pushing them towards the choleric.

With apparent equanimity, the man replied, 'Zaynabou.'

'I suppose, like everyone else here, you see some use for me in whatever plans you are hatching and want me to mouth some nonsense in support of you.'

Zaynabou cast his eyes down for a second, as though in sorrow. When he spoke, his voice had a hard and determined edge. 'There's nothing nonsensical in my beliefs. I hold to the true way. It is those who disagree who spout nonsense and will suffer for it.' He took a deep breath and his tone softened. 'In any case, welcome to your new home. I will be your guide and mentor, although, of course, I will not give you religious instruction myself. We will leave that to our Imam.'

Leon exploded. 'I have no intention of taking religious instruction from anyone.'

Zaynabou brought his hands together in front of him so that his fingers were touching and shook his head slowly.

'That would be regrettable. If you cooperate with us, we can assure you of a future spent in a state built on the solid foundation of the true faith, where the words of the Prophet, blessed be his name, will be implemented rigorously, and order and stability will prevail. If you do not…'

Zaynabou lapsed into silence. He sat so still he appeared to be in a trance, breathing loudly and rhythmically and with his eyes tight shut. Leon moved his weight from one foot to the other and back again. Everyone wanted to play mind games with him, no doubt to intimidate him into doing their bidding. Well, he wasn't going to put up with it. Coconut would have. Chief Onagaku definitely wouldn't.

'You, overthrow the state? Judging from the drive here, you've about as many supporters as my local football team, and they've just been relegated to League Two.'

Zaynabou opened his eyes, exhaled slowly and motioned for Leon to sit down. Leon glanced at the proffered chair and instead paced to the other side of the room, where he stood with his arms folded.

'It would be unwise to allow yourself to be deceived by appearances, Mr Onagaku,' Zaynabou said. 'We have friends at the heart of Government and many people in important positions. We have ten thousand armed men, and we have promises of support from powerful interests outside. Within six months we will have taken over the country.'

'Then why do you need me?'

Zaynabou pursed his lips. 'You are a dispensable nice-to-have. If you don't join us, I will let your two young countrymen take you into the desert for a little fun. They do so miss foxhunting.'

'You haven't answered my question,' Leon insisted. 'You've gone to a lot of trouble to bring me here. Why? You must have something in mind.'

Zaynabou frowned, as though puzzled by the question and then rocked his chair back onto its rear legs.

'Because of your grandfather, of course. He still counts for a lot, and it is an established fact he renounced Christianity for the true religion towards the end of his life, which is why the British arranged for him to be killed. With a history like that, and a similar conversion on your part, you would make an admirable figurehead.'

Leon dumped himself into the other chair. 'My grandfather was a Muslim?'

Zaynabou nodded. 'Even then we had plans to lead this country to the true faith and shake off Britain's imperial yoke. Unfortunately, our noble intentions were discovered and when Chief Onagaku was targeted and killed in a street battle, the British managed to suppress all information about his conversion for fear he become a martyr.' He leaned forward abruptly and grasped Leon's hands. 'Well, what do you want to do, die like a dog or honour your grandfather's memory and create a legend of your own?'

Leon pulled his hands away and stood up. 'And die anyway?'

'Maybe, maybe not. That's a chance you'd have to take. But if you did die, the payoff would be a fast track to heaven as a martyr.'

'I don't believe in heaven.'

'That's another chance you'd have to take. But the choice is pretty stark anyway, isn't it? A sandy anonymous grave here now or the chance of living and becoming famous. The life of ease accompanied by forty compliant virgins if you're killed fighting for our cause is really by way of being a bonus.'

Leon rocked back on his heels. The wonderland he found himself in grew more surreal with every encounter. First the Government had wanted him to lead a rebellion against itself, then the Communists had, for reasons known only to themselves, saved him from death and now the FMF wanted him, an avowed atheist, to become their figurehead. None of it made sense.

'I have to think about it. You're asking me to lead your revolution when I'm not even a Muslim. Why should your followers accept me?'

'You wouldn't be leading it exactly. But if you need time to consider, I'll give you twenty-four hours. You must remember, however, the alternative.' Zaynabou clapped his hands. 'Perhaps a period of quiet reflection will help you arrive at the right conclusion.' An armed guard entered. Zaynabou pointed at the door. 'Take our friend to the honeymoon suite.'

Leon was pushed out into the heat, his eyes seared by the glare. He shook his head and a cascade of sweat spun off, spotting the ground around him. He tried to swallow but his mouth was too dry. They walked around the main hut. Hidden behind it was a low corrugated-iron shack. The guard produced a key and undid the padlock holding the makeshift doors together, stood back and waved his hand for

Leon to enter. As Leon stooped to go in, a wall of heat slammed against his face and a faecal smell gripped his throat. He tried to back out only to feel the guard's boot propelling him forward. He sprawled into the hut and the doors shut behind him, leaving him in darkness. The padlock clicked.

'Shit, shit, shit,' he intoned quietly, mopping his brow with his sleeve. Then he heard a noise, like that of a large animal, and detected the rank odour of someone else's sweat commingling with the other smells assailing him. He was not alone.

'Who's there?' he shouted, his voice rising to a falsetto.

A large, sweaty hand on his thigh made him start. He'd read about what happened in prisons, and that was in England. It must be ten, a hundred times worse here. 'Get off me!' he yelled, trying to pull himself away. The hand gripped his ankle. By the force it was exerting, he wasn't going to succeed.

'Sssssh, speak softly. Even then we may be overheard.' The voice was familiar.

'Who are you?' Leon whispered.

'Bankole,' the hoarse voice whispered back.

Leon recoiled in shock, his hand to his mouth. 'No!'

'Fraid so,' Mr B said, and his voice sounded almost wistful.

Leon's mind raced through the implications. If his erstwhile principal protector was being held captive here, what chance did he stand of being rescued? None. The TV footage of the bloodshed at the rally replayed in his mind along with the suggestion that Donald had organised it. And Donald, he knew, now worked for Mr D, so how likely were they to launch an attempt to free him? His prospects were even bleaker than his surroundings.

'It's Leon,' he said at last, feeling stupid he hadn't said something as soon as he realised it was Mr B.

'I know,' Mr B replied with gruff contempt.

'Why are you here?'

'I was sent to open discussions with these people and they threw me into this stinking hole. And you?'

'Kidnapped from the Marxists who seized me just before the demo.' Leon unbuttoned his shirt, slipped it off and started to fan himself ineffectually with it.

'Is there any water? I'm desperate.'

'None left. What happened at the demonstration?'

Leon whimpered softly. He'd never been so thirsty and didn't know how he'd survive the night.

'Well?' Mr B insisted.

Leon gathered his strength, sucked in his cheeks in a vain attempt to salivate, and gave as good an account as he could of the scenes he'd witnessed on television, and the allegation that Donald had arranged the massacre.

'Hmmmm,' Mr B murmured and lapsed into silence.

'Was Donald working for you?'

Mr B hesitated. 'Yes. At least I thought he was.'

'Not for Mr D?'

'Certainly not. Why?'

'Because he came to the hotel with Mr D. Could he have betrayed you?'

'It's possible. I turned up to the meeting place and my bodyguard didn't. Only Donald was aware of my movements.'

'Could Mr D be in on it?'

Mr B sighed. 'Unlikely. We were at Harrow together.' He paused. 'Donald, on the other hand, could well be working for a foreign power, or even freelancing. Whatever brought it about, now I'm in the hands of these jokers, who are quite capable of killing me through sheer incompetence.'

'What does the FMF want from you?'

Mr B hesitated. 'Not sure. Maybe use me as a bargaining counter, or perhaps upload my execution onto the internet to show how powerful they are.'

Leon collapsed onto the wooden floor. If he didn't get a drink soon, he'd pass out. As his thoughts wandered, muddled dreams coalesced in his mind and then evaporated so that he wasn't sure whether he was awake or asleep. Time passed, though he didn't know how quickly. He must have fallen into a deeper sleep eventually because he was awakened by the sound of the door opening and a breezy home counties' voice saying, 'Morning Leon. Come with me please.' Blinded by the brilliance of the morning sun as he crawled out of his improvised cell, gradually Leon was able to make out the tall, pink-cheeked face of a blond English boy.

'Sleep well?' the lad asked.

'Water,' Leon croaked. 'Please.'

'We'll get some on the way.' The boy stuck a Kalashnikov into Leon's ribs. 'Let's get going, shall we?'

When Leon was steered into his presence, Zaynabou calmly laid down a half-eaten slice of mango and wiped the juice that was smearing his face with the back of his hand. To Leon the mango, which glowed in the gloomy room, looked like the heaven he didn't believe in. The young Englishman was now loafing at the back of the hut, cleaning his gun. From outside came the noise of soldiers being drilled.

'Good morning, Mr Onagaku.' Zaynabou waved a casual hand in the broad direction of a wooden chair. 'Please take a seat.'

'I need water,' Leon gasped, falling onto the chair and clinging to it to avoid sliding to the floor.

'All in good time.' Zaynabou swept the remnants of the mango off his table and into a bin beside him. 'Have you an answer for me?' He sat back, a half-smile pinned to his face.

'Water first,' Leon said.

Zaynabou shook his head. 'Answer first. Why would we waste good water on someone we're going to kill?'

Leon recognised Zaynabou's logic was both unanswerable and a good indication of how close to death the wrong response would leave him. In his lucid moments during the night he'd decided he'd have to play along, whatever that entailed, to buy time. He just hoped too much wouldn't be asked of him before he could escape.

'All right. I've thought about it. What would I have to do?'

Zaynabou smiled. 'Easy. Say a sentence called the Testimony of Faith.'

'One sentence? Is that all? I thought I'd have to study for months. What is it?'

'A common mistake,' Zaynabou said. 'It's a few Arabic words to the effect that there is no true god but Allah, and Muhammad, blessed be his name, is the Prophet of God.'

'If that's all, and you tell me the Arabic, I'll say it.'

'Well there are a few other things, but they all flow from that.' Zaynabou's eyes narrowed. 'Of course, you must understand and mean what you say, but the Imam can help you with that.'

'Could I have some water now?'

'Certainly, my friend.' Zaynabou clapped his hands and a boy who had been squatting unseen in the shadows hurried out, returning a few minutes later with a thin metal tray on which balanced a mango, a cluster of fresh dates and a large glass of water.

Leon seized the glass and drained it in two noisy gulps. He then set about the food, not looking up till the plate, apart from mango skin and several stones, was empty. When he raised his eyes, he saw Zaynabou staring at him, a quizzical look on his face.

'You have a good appetite for food, my friend. I hope it is matched by your appetite for the struggle of the true believers against their oppressors.' Zaynabou turned to the young Englishman. 'Take our friend to his new quarters. I'll arrange for the Imam to visit tomorrow to start his instruction and, once they've had a discussion together, we'll start his military training.'

Leon started. 'Military training?'

Zaynabou laughed. 'Now that you have become one of us, you will, of course, take part in our operations. We'll give you small tasks to start with, planting a bomb in one of those schools where the infidel corrupt young women with seditious nonsense, that sort of thing, and build up to more demanding missions, like the assassination of government officials.'

Leon's knees buckled. He tried to speak, but no words would come. Zaynabou waved a dismissive hand and looked down at some papers. There was a push in his back and he found himself outside in the blinding light, in front of a squad of barefoot teenage boys in brown fatigues, who were standing to attention.

'Squad, take aim,' a voice shouted in received-pronunciation English. The boys raised their rifles and pointed them at Leon.

'Squad, ready.'

A wave of nausea surged through Leon. So this was how it was going to end. Everything that had just taken place was a hoax, a massive wind-up. They'd meant to kill him all along. Well, there was no escape, so he might as well exit with dignity. Despite the cramping of his stomach, he forced himself to stand erect and stare down the barrels of the dozen or so guns.

'Nice posture.' It was a voice he recognised as the other Englishman's. 'OK guys, put your weapons down.' As the youths complied, Leon found his hand being shaken warmly.

'Hi, I'm Nabhan and this, if you remember, is Aazim. Glad you decided to join us. I'd have hated killing you.'

'Me too,' Aazim added. 'We had to have this firing squad ready in case you gave the wrong answer. I hope you didn't mind our little joke. You reacted really well.'

Leon shook his head, though at that moment he would have liked nothing more than to decapitate them both.

'Let's go and have a brew,' Aazim said. 'You don't mind goat's milk, do you? It's got a bit of a tang, but you get used to it.'

They walked slowly in the broiling sun until they got to a low, two-man tent.

'Home, at least for now,' Nabhan said, squeezing through the aperture and emerging with a small stove, a kettle and three cups.

'I'll go and get some water and some milk.' Aazim disappeared carrying a large plastic container and a jug.

'What brings you here?' Leon asked. 'You said you were on a gap year.'

'Yah!' Nabhan shook his head and, with the hot dry wind behind him, it haloed his long fair hair. 'We were on our way to Sumatra to work in an orphanage when we met these guys from Birmingham. It was their idea.'

'Are they still here?' Leon asked.

'Hell no. They blew themselves up a couple of months ago. Good guys, even if they were Villa fans.'

Aazim, his face red and glistening with perspiration, appeared lugging the plastic container, his thin body bending under its weight.

'Aren't you afraid of dying?' Leon asked.

'We're not part of the suicide team,' Nabhan said. 'They gave us a special exemption on condition that when we finally get to uni, we recruit people to the cause.'

'You're not going back to the UK?'

'Sure.' Nabhan flicked a fly off his leg and it lay on its back on the ground buzzing, its wings a blur. 'All part of the masterplan.'

'First thing we must do is film you.' Aazim produced a smartphone. He read from a crumpled scrap of paper that he pulled out of his trouser pocket. 'Now say, "I am the grandson of Chief Onagaku and heir to his title. I have converted to Islam, the true path to heaven, and am committed to the overthrow of Oblanga's corrupt and degenerate regime, the expulsion of his western allies and the introduction of sharia law. I am determined to bring down decadent western civilisation by whatever means are necessary. I will fight wherever I am called upon by my faith to do so. I am willing to die in the cause of the true prophet, blessed be his name."'

He handed the piece of paper to Leon, held up his smartphone camera and nodded at him to start. Leon, his mind floating some feet above his body, mumbled his way through the words, stumbling a few times over the near illegible writing. When he finished, Aazim clapped him on the back.

'Well done. That'll be on the internet tonight. Wouldn't surprise me if it went viral.'

The implications struck home. A lot of people would be shocked, especially Clive who had always accused him of being staid and set in his ways. As a cure for a broken heart, becoming a leader of a fundamentalist sect bent on destroying western civilisation was even more dramatic than joining the French Foreign Legion. And what would Marianne make of it? And his ex-work colleagues? He imagined journalists and cameramen door-stepping them and asking when and where he'd been radicalised. His old teachers would be interviewed, as would all those school bullies who'd thought him such a wuss, such a Coconut. Well, they'd have to think again. There might even be questions in Parliament—

His thoughts were interrupted by Zaynabou's runner, who padded up to them in his bare feet and whispered something to Aazim who, excusing himself, left without finishing his tea. When Aazim returned five minutes later, his face was drained.

'It's your first job, Leon. Zaynabou wants it done now. If you've finished, we'll set off.'

Leon's eyes searched Aazim's face for a clue. 'What is it?'

'A bit more than I expected for a first assignment. No probs, though. We'll talk you through it and film you. You wait here. We'll get things ready. Come on, Nabhan.'

Chapter 10

Left on his own, Leon sipped the remainder of his tea. It was disgusting; the milk tasted of goat and had curdled. This assignment, whatever it was, sounded worrying. He had to get out of this place, but without knowing where he was, he didn't stand a chance. Then he thought of Mr B. He was a local. If he could extricate him from the cell and nick a vehicle, perhaps Mr B could guide him back to Mutabe City. Until then he had to play along. He was wondering what the job could be when he heard Aazim summoning him. As he trudged round the corner of the building he was surprised to see Mr B, his shoulder poking out of a torn t-shirt, his tree-trunk legs protruding from his boxer shorts, sitting in the front passenger seat of a gleaming open jeep, his hands apparently secured behind his back. Nabhan was sitting in the driver's seat, a pistol in his hand. Aazim, mid-way between Leon and the jeep, waved his gun in the air and shouted, 'Hurry up Leon, hop in!' Then he strode back and jumped into the seat behind Mr B. As Leon advanced towards them, Mr B turned his head. Leon nodded and Mr B gave him a baleful stare. Leon eased himself into the back seat behind Nabhan.

'Where are we going?' It was very convenient Mr B would be with them. It saved Leon the bother of having to get him out of his cell. All they had to do now was give the two young Englishmen the slip and they could make a bid for freedom.

'Reconnaissance,' Aazim replied.

'Into the desert.' Nabhan added.

Leon eyed the implement lying behind him. 'What's the shovel for?'

'You never know when you might need to dig yourself out of a sand-dune.' Aazim's tone was curt.

'Sand-dunes are a bit like snowdrifts,' Nabhan said. 'They move around in the wind.'

Mr B stared ahead. Aazim played with a satellite phone. Nabhan whistled tunelessly as he negotiated the undulating terrain and Leon marvelled at the miles of sand which surrounded them on all sides. They drove for at least an hour before Nabhan turned the jeep in behind a sizeable dune.

'Everybody out,' Aazim ordered. Nabhan leapt down and grabbed the shovel from the back in the time it took Leon to get out of the vehicle. Mr B didn't move.

'Get down,' Aazim shouted, walking quickly round to Mr B and pointing his pistol in his face.

'You're going to kill me anyway. Why should I put myself to any trouble? Do it here, if you must.'

'They're not going to kill you,' Leon said, though his entrails were telling him a different story.

Mr B looked at Leon. 'You fool. You absolute bloody idiot.'

'We'll shoot you where you are if you don't move.' Aazim's voice was now a croak.

'Makes no difference to me,' Mr B said. 'You'll make your nice new jeep dirty if you do.'

Aazim grabbed Mr B's arm and tried to drag him from his seat, but his slim frame was no match for Mr B's bulk.

'Help me, Jace,' Aazim panted, and Nabhan threw himself back into the driver's seat and pushed as Aazim pulled.

'And you,' Aazim yelled at Leon, who stood rooted to the ground. Before Leon could move, the combined efforts of the two student assassins finally dislodged Mr B, who slid out of his seat and sat, propped up, against the vehicle. For a couple of minutes, they tried hauling him to his feet, but to no avail.

'I know,' Nabhan said as he hopped into the jeep. He started its motor and drove ten feet away. Mr B, deprived of his support, slumped to the ground.

Aazim, his eyes ablaze, thrust the pistol into Leon's hand. 'Now, shoot him.'

Leon stared back at him, then at the pistol, then at the recumbent figure on the ground. Finally, he looked at Nabhan, who had the other pistol trained on him.

'Hold on,' Nabhan said, lowering his gun. 'We haven't made the film.'

'Oh shit!' Aazim bounded to the back of the jeep and produced a banner in Arabic, which he stuck in the sand. Then he handed a black t-shirt with some Arabic writing on it to Leon. 'Put this on. Now!'

Leon's eyes glazed over. This couldn't be happening. Yet it was. As soon as he'd taken his own shirt off and replaced it with the t-shirt, a piece of paper was pushed into his hand and Aazim said something in his ear that echoed through his head.

'Read these words, and then shoot him.'

'He hasn't dug his own grave yet,' Nabhan said.

Aazim looked at Mr B's inert body. 'He's not likely to, is he?'

Nabhan took his mobile out of his pocket and pointed the lens at Mr B.

'Leon can bury him after he's shot him. He's done bugger all else so far. Now, Leon. Walk up to him, read the words out loud, hold the pistol to his head and squeeze the trigger gently. If you don't, you're dead meat.'

Leon looked at the weapon trained on him, at Mr B, who still lay sprawled on the ground, and at the two young Englishmen. He had to do something to prevent the murder; he couldn't kill someone in cold blood.

'Come on guys. This is another of your jokes, isn't it?'

Their faces remained impassive.

'You can't be serious. You can't kill people like this.'

Nabhan nodded. 'Sure we can, when they're enemies of the true religion and have committed atrocities against our brothers and sisters.'

'What about justice? Due process? Giving him—'

'This is justice,' Aazim snarled. 'The type he deserves. Now do as we say, or you'll join him.'

Leon stared at the four cold eyes drilling into him. Aazim did something and his gun clicked. It must be ready to fire now. There was no way out. The nightmare had enveloped him again. Leon walked numbly towards Mr B and stood over him. Softly, he read out the words he'd been handed. When he finished, Aazim said, 'OK, now raise the pistol, point it at him and shoot.'

Leon lifted his arm millimetre by millimetre, wishing himself a million miles away. He suddenly had a strong need to evacuate his bowels. 'Guys, I need to go to the toilet. Urgent like.'

'Just shoot the bastard,' Aazim screamed.

'I can't wait. I'll crap my pants.'

Nabhan lowered his phone. 'He's spoiled that take. We're going to have to refilm the whole thing anyway. What does it matter if it takes a little longer?'

Aazim sighed. 'All right, you've got two minutes.'

Leon found a shaded spot behind a neighbouring dune and squatted. He thought about running away. It was hopeless. They would catch him easily. While buckling himself up he heard a phone ring. When he returned to where Mr B still lay, he was surprised to find only Nabhan there.

'Where's Aazim?'

'His girlfriend phoned. He's talking to her now.'

Leon could hear a few words wafting on the light desert breeze. 'Yah, honey. I'm fine. Me 'n Jace are having a wicked time......'

'You'd better save time by digging his grave now,' Nabhan said, handing Leon the spade. Leon thrust the blade into the soft sand, lifted a spadeful and threw it over his shoulder. A gust caught it and blew it back in Nabhan's face.

'You fucking idiot—' Nabhan shouted, but was silenced by Mr B who, with an unsuspected nimbleness jumped to his feet and head-butted him. Mr B, now standing next to Nabhan's comatose body, turned his back on Leon, pushed his hands out towards him and hissed, 'Untie me, you idiot.'

Leon did as he was told. Mr B picked up the pistol and then sat down again, his hands behind him. Aazim sauntered back, the satellite phone in his palm.

'What the fuck's happened?' he demanded, looking at Nabhan's body lying in the sand.

'Heat stroke,' Leon said.

Aazim took a couple of steps towards Nabhan, then turned on Leon. 'If you're trying anything—' His threat was interrupted by a blow on the back of the head from the butt of the pistol Mr B was holding.

Leon gawped, transfixed by a combination of disbelief and amazement that his prayers had been answered.

'Now let's get out of here,' Mr B said, searching Nabhan's pockets for the jeep's keys. 'Out here with no vehicle, these two are as good as dead. No need to get our hands dirty.'

'We can't leave them to die,' Leon said. 'Can't we tie them up and drop them off somewhere?'

Mr B waved his pistol at Leon. 'Any more idiocy like that and I'll leave you here with them. They're killers. Now grab that sat phone and get in the jeep.'

Leon looked at the two unconscious figures. Nabhan was beginning to stir.

'Now,' Mr B shouted, revving the engine. Leon grabbed the phone, plucked his shirt from the ground and jumped onto the jeep as Mr B let out the clutch. The vehicle surged forward, a cloud of sand kicking up behind its spinning wheels. He clung on, pulling himself into the front seat where he tore off his t-shirt and put on his own shirt. Looking back, he saw Nabhan sit up, rub his head, catch sight of them and, a second later, raise a pistol and take aim.

'He's going to shoot,' Leon cried, as Mr B swerved the jeep.

As they sped away, putting a sand-dune between them and Nabhan, Leon sighed with relief. They'd escaped, and it was largely thanks to him. Perhaps subconsciously he'd meant to throw sand—

Mr B interrupted his train of thought. 'Why the hell didn't you get their gun instead of your shirt?'

Reality bit and Leon hung his head. He wasn't very good at this James Bond stuff. He hadn't even taken their mobile phones so, if Nabhan and Aazim did survive, they would have all those pictures of him declaring himself to be a Muslim and threatening to kill Mr B.

The satellite phone rang. Reflexively, Leon answered. A young woman's voice breathed seductively in his ear.

'I'm naked now, babes, just me and Mr Porker's photo –'

Deeply embarrassed, Leon hung up.

'Who was it?' Mr B demanded.

'Wrong number,' Leon replied, adding quickly to change the subject, 'We didn't take their smartphones.' He expected his admission to elicit another tirade.

'Doesn't matter. No signal for mobiles out here. We've got the sat phone.'

They drove in silence across swirling, searing sand for hours. Eventually Leon took the handkerchief away from his mouth.

'Do you know where we are?'

'Somewhere in the north,' Mr B replied. 'I'm navigating towards Mutabe City by the sun.'

The landscape started to change. Unbroken sand gave way to tufts of grass, straggly bushes and stunted trees until, finally, they arrived at a dirt track.

'Seem to be approaching civilisation,' Leon said.

'This is the North Super Highway,' Mr B replied.

Leon peered at Mr B's face, searching for a sarcastic smile, but his jaw remained set and his expression grim. A herd of goats clustered by the road, tended by a wizened man wearing a loincloth, who stared as they passed.

'We must be close to a village,' Leon said.

Mr B, still bent over the wheel, replied, 'Not necessarily. Goatherds often live in the wild, miles from anyone.'

As he spoke, the jeep started to slow down.

'Are we stopping to ask the way?' Leon asked.

Mr B turned to him, his eyes blazing with contempt. 'No, we're running out of fuel.'

The jeep's engine cut out, and they glided down a slope, coming to a halt where the track started to rise again.

'What do we do now?' Leon asked.

Swearing softly, Mr B searched the jeep, pushing Leon roughly aside to look under his seat.

'Damn! No spare fuel can. We'll have to walk.'

He picked up the pistol, the satellite phone and a two-litre plastic water container and set off. Leon hurried behind him.

'Where are we going?'

Mr B, staring ahead, said, 'South.'

'Can't we use the phone to summon help?'

'They're not secure.'

'Isn't voice traffic encrypted?'

Mr B's upper lip curled. 'That's what the makers would like you to think. Even our security services have managed to reverse-engineer their encryption algorithms. We'd be broadcasting our position to the people who betrayed me and to the Fundamentalists.'

They trudged on for two hours, periodically pausing for a sip of water. Now and then they encountered more goats nibbling at the desert scrub. The daylight was beginning to fade.

'We're coming to a village,' Mr B said.

Fifteen minutes' more trekking brought them to a row of huts made from what looked like brown mud and straw. As they approached, three naked little boys jumped out, stared and ran away giggling to hide.

Mr B shouted and a skinny old woman in a faded red dress emerged, her back bent and her hair white. She stood, hands on asymmetrical hips, waiting for them to approach. A couple of younger women in tattered yellow garments slipped out of the door and stood behind her, looking around anxiously.

Mr B spoke. The old woman engaged the two younger women in an animated discussion before waving her arms and gabbling at him through toothless gums.

Mr B turned to Leon. 'We're still in Fundamentalists' territory. They've taken the men. They may come by anytime. These women will put us up for the night, but we must pay. Got any money?'

Leon took off his shoe, lifted the insole, and held out a crinkled hundred shilling note, which had escaped confiscation by his captors. For the first time since they took flight, Mr B smiled at him, then uttered some words to the woman, who shook her head. It appeared they were negotiating.

Finally, after a lot more toing and froing, Mr B and the old woman clasped hands and were all smiles. The two young women half-smiled, their mouths revealing the gaps in their teeth, adjusted their ragged dresses and averted their eyes.

'They'll give us shelter, goat stew and water but we have to leave first thing tomorrow.' Then he nodded at one of the young women, who stood leaning against the doorway. 'She's yours. I'm having the other one.'

'I don't want her,' Leon said.

Mr B stared at him for a moment. 'Please yourself. We've paid for them, so I'll have both. If you change your mind, you'll have to make do with granny.'

'Won't the Fundamentalists find the jeep?' Leon asked. 'Then they'll be able to track us down.'

'The wind will cover our footprints and they'll have to guess where we went. It'll be dark soon and we'll leave at dawn, so we should get away all right. What happens tomorrow is a different matter.'

The old woman went indoors. She reappeared, struggling to carry an earthenware pot, which she finally succeeded in balancing on the bricks above the already laid fire. Soon the smell of goat stew had Leon salivating.

They ate in silence. Immediately after, Mr B took hold of the young women's hands and led them away to a neighbouring hut. The old woman pointed at another hut and Leon went in and settled himself down. It was still suffocatingly hot, so he stripped down to his underpants and lay on top of a pile of foul-smelling goats' skins, promptly falling asleep. He awoke shivering a couple of hours later, put his clothes on and pulled the skins tightly round him.

Chapter 11

Leon was roused by vigorous shaking from a dream in which Clive was cooking him a teddy bear stuffed with sage, onion and sausage meat for his Christmas lunch.

'Wake up,' Mr B's voice boomed. 'We have to leave before light.'

Leon rubbed his eyes, which seemed to have sunk deep into their sockets. Clive, what a waste of time he was, he thought. Why did I care?

They drank a cup of mud-flavoured water and set off into the dark, stumbling as they felt their way through the scrub to the track.

'Did you sleep—?' Leon's question was interrupted by three burst of gunfire coming from the direction from which they had set out.

'It's from the huts where we stayed,' Leon gasped.

Mr B clamped his hand over Leon's mouth. 'Ssh! I can hear something,' he whispered, dragging Leon off the path. They lay on their bellies, squeezed in behind a scraggy bush.

Headlights played along the track, then off it, then on it again. These were accompanied by the uneven growl of a diesel vehicle crawling slowly towards them in low gear. Leon flattened himself. Mr B held his pistol out, two-handed, ready to fire. The jeep was now parallel with them. Behind the swarthy driver, Nabhan, Aazim and a wiry local were sitting nursing Kalashnikovs. Leon held his breath as they rolled past. The moment their rear lights disappeared, Mr B grabbed Leon's arm and hauled him up.

'Let's get moving, and fast.'

For a man of his bulk, Mr B moved surprisingly quickly, half-loping, half-jogging, and Leon had difficulty keeping up. They stuck to the middle of the track, pausing to listen and look around every few steps. The darkness had given way to a grey dawn, and Leon's stomach was rumbling. An hour later the sun broke through and sweat, induced by both exertion and fear, poured off him. Crude mud shelters, dogs sunning themselves and malnourished chickens scratching around in the dirt all appeared in increasing numbers, and every so often someone could be seen setting about the dusty earth with a crude instrument or hacking at some of the scanty vegetation. In the distance, a translucent blue row of mountains glowed.

'Why is it so dry here?' Leon caught his breath sufficiently to ask. 'It was raining in Mutabe City.'

'Probably still is. Mutabe City is one of the wettest places in the country and this is the driest.' Mr B pointed at the distant peaks. 'It's in the rain shadow of the Panmuir Highlands.'

'You don't mean Mutabe City is the other side, do you?'

'Yes. We're going to cut across on a mountain path.'

Leon swallowed hard. As a little boy, his heart had always pounded when the fair came to his local green and Peter would offer to take him on the rides. Even glancing over the side of a nearby bridge down onto the railway lines had been enough to induce vertigo.

'Although it's very narrow,' Mr B continued, 'and there's a sheer drop on one side, it's in pretty good condition. Or at least it was when I was last there.'

'When was that?' Even to himself, Leon's voice sounded strangulated.

'Twenty years. I did my army training here.'

They plodded on without pausing to rest, the mountain range apparently as distant despite their efforts.

'We'll never make it,' Leon moaned.

'Well, I will,' Mr B replied, not breaking his stride. Seconds later, surprised at the rumble of another approaching engine, they flung themselves behind a sandy hillock. A lorry was progressing slowly along the track, its wheels clanking as they struck the many potholes. Mr B peeped out.

'It's only got a driver,' he whispered. 'Come on.'

As the lorry groaned slowly past Mr B grabbed at it and hauled himself aboard. He beckoned to Leon to join him. Although Leon, some yards further back, caught up, his arms were too weak to pull himself up. All he could do was hang on. They started to gather speed and Leon was sure he'd be hurled off onto the stony track to die a slow and lonely death. Just before his strength gave out, Mr B's powerful hands gripped his forearms and heaved him up. He pivoted on his stomach, tumbled into the back and came to a jarring halt against a pile of something unyielding covered by a tarpaulin.

While Leon rubbed his head, Mr B pulled the cover from the wooden crates and threw it down.

'We can hide under this if necessary.'

The track had, by now, broadened into a dirt road and the lorry bounced along at increasing speed. Leon lay on his back gazing at the cloudless sky while Mr B scanned the countryside.

'I wonder what's in those crates,' Mr B said. Within seconds he was prising one open. After pulling at it for a couple of minutes the wood gave and the lid flew off. They both peered inside.

'Oh my God,' Leon said, looking away. Mr B placed his hand on Leon's shoulder.

'Steady.'

Several skulls grinned at them. Behind these, tightly packed were other bones, pieces of pottery and wooden and stone ornaments.

'The Fundamentalists must be trying to get rid of the evidence,' Leon whispered.

Mr B shook his head. 'With miles and miles of sand, why didn't they bury their enemies' bodies out there where no one goes?'

Leon could see his point. You could dispose of that number of people in one large pit without too much difficulty.

Mr B was examining the find more closely. 'These aren't recent remains. They're too faded and chipped. But why would someone transport old bones? And why is the other stuff mixed in with them?'

'Perhaps, instead of burying them, someone recently dug them up, and wants to get them away from the desert,' Leon suggested.

Mr B's brows furrowed. 'The FMF certainly don't like scientists and would regard archaeologists in the same light. They've also been destroying some of our oldest historic sites. Perhaps someone is taking these bones and the other artefacts to a safer place.'

'Which means,' Leon said, pausing while the implications sank in, 'this lorry is not a safe place for us to be. The FMF may well be looking out for it.'

As Mr B replaced the lid, the lorry slowed. He knelt up and peeped over the driver's cab. 'Roadblock. Let's get out of here.'

They jumped off the back and rolled behind thick bushes by the side of the road. Fifty metres further on, the vehicle ground to a halt outside a cluster of cabins. Armed men, their heads and faces covered by black hoods with slits for their eyes and mouths, surrounded the driver's cab, while others climbed into the back and opened crates. A few minutes later, the driver was dragged screaming out of Leon's sight. A burst of gunfire rang out and the screaming stopped.

Leon lay on the ground, unable to move and barely able to think. One of the men parked the lorry behind a clump of trees. Another got a shovel and started to dig. The rest formed a circle in front of the nearest cabin, squatting on their haunches, chattering and laughing.

'Come on,' Mr B said, assuming a crouching position. 'Now's our chance.'

Leon tried to stand, but his arms and legs trembled so much that he slid back down. Just then a couple of the men stood up, looked down the track, picked up their guns and walked slowly towards where Leon and Mr B were hiding. Mr B flattened himself on the ground, his arms outstretched, his pistol directed at the advancing men. Leon, motionless, held his breath. A tickling sensation on his leg made him turn his head. Crawling across the back of his knee in the direction of his buttocks was a six-inch black scorpion, its tail curled.

By now the men were only twenty metres away.

'Mmmmm.' Leon's suppressed squeal drew Mr B's attention. He looked at his companion and then at the scorpion.

'Sssh!' he said in the softest of whispers and looked away.

By now the arachnid was advancing up Leon's left buttock and towards the small of his back. Leon wriggled, trying to dislodge it, but the scorpion continued its steady march up his rigid body.

The men, ten metres away now, surveyed their surroundings and then turned back. A whimper escaped Leon's pursed lips. The men stopped, their eyes roving all around. They spoke to each other, shrugged and walked back to their comrades.

'Scorpion,' was the only word Leon could squeeze out of his fear-dried mouth.

Mr B brushed the creature from Leon's shoulders. 'Only an Emperor. Virtually harmless. Come on, let's get going.'

Then they were up and jogging through the tangled scrub in a wide arc to avoid the roadblock. When they hit open ground beyond the bushes, Mr B sprinted, his burly figure receding rapidly into the distance as Leon trailed, panting, behind. Looking over his shoulder, Leon expected to see a line of men taking aim. Instead, all was calm and peaceful. After about a quarter of a mile of lung-bursting, sweat-drenching running they slowed and walked in the direction of the highest mountain.

'Need to keep moving quickly,' Mr B said, his breathing again normal.

Leon, still fighting for breath, remained silent as

the sun roasted the nape of his neck. Mild pinpricks of soreness on his feet grew into bud-like blisters, then blossomed into full-blown crimson sores; his tongue was sandpaper. Each step was like hoisting and lowering a twenty-kilo weight. Small black flies surrounded him like storm clouds around a mountain peak, lifting every time he raised an arm to dispel them and returning to clog his eyes and ears as soon as he lowered it again.

Mr B forged on, untroubled by the heat or the insects, his attention fixed on the craggy mountains ahead.

'We don't have to climb those?' Leon gasped.

'No. There are paths between them. We only need to climb for a couple of hundred metres then scramble across to the other side.'

After a few more hours, as the sky was darkening, a breath of air from the west afforded them some relief from the heat. They were in a rocky landscape of abandoned army vehicles: one badly damaged lorry but with its cab intact, another completely burnt out, the remains of a blistered jeep and a scorched tank with its blackened gun pointing at the sky.

They heard a high-pitched bleat, followed by the deeper more resonant answering call of a goat. Mr B, with the speed of a panther, leapt into the outcrop of rocks, emerging moments later with a black and white kid the size of a small cat in his hands. Its yellow eyes looked beseechingly at Leon as it cried in anguish for its mother, who bleated plaintively back.

'Supper,' Mr B said triumphantly, dashing the kid's head again a boulder until it lay limp and lifeless in his arms. The nanny goat staggered back onto the rocks, its bleating, at least in Leon's imagination, now suffused with both grief and outrage. Leon looked away, put his fingers in his ears and dry retched.

'We'll eat it raw,' Mr B said. Leon turned back and stared at his companion's bloodied hands. Somehow Mr B had wrenched the body apart and was drinking from the bleeding wound. He held it out towards Leon.

'Drink some now before it dries up. It's the only liquid we'll get.'

Leon averted his eyes, unable to blot out the image of the dead animal, its head lolling, its eyes staring, its limbs hanging limply. When he next looked, Mr B was gorging on the entrails which he'd ripped out.

'This would be better cooked,' Mr B said, a trickle of blood oozing down through the stubble on his chin. 'Eat.' He held out a bloody kidney.

Leon, now crouching, shook his head, knowing beyond any doubt that he'd spend the rest of his life as a vegetarian. There must be ways of surviving which did not involve the slaughter of young animals, if only he could bring them to mind. Had he persevered with being a boy scout, perhaps he would have picked something up about survival in the wild. Seconds passed. Mr B gnawed the raw flesh off the kid's bones. The nanny goat bleated in the background. A column of large red ants marched towards the pieces that had fallen to the ground. Leon patted his head with the palm of his hand, unsuccessfully urging inspiration to come to his aid. When it didn't, he reconciled himself to a night of hunger and thirst. He hadn't paid a lot of attention to religious studies at school, but hadn't Jesus spent forty nights in the desert, resisted temptation and emerged all the stronger? Perhaps the privation he was undergoing would have the same effect on him.

'It's getting dark. We'll spend the night here.' Mr B announced.

Leon shivered. 'Shouldn't we light a fire?'

Mr B looked at him with contempt. 'With what as fuel?'

Leon gazed around at the arid soil, feeling foolish.

'We can sleep in there.' Mr B nodded at the cabin of the lorry. 'It's going to be cold.'

Chapter 12

Had Leon listed the people he would least like to spend the night cuddling in the lorry's cab, Mr B, who reeked of blood and stale sweat, would have been at or near the top. But the freezing temperatures made him grateful for all the warmth Mr B's muscular frame generated. Even so, by midnight his teeth were chattering and by the early hours of the morning he was racked by seismic shivers. He drifted in and out of unsettling dreams: Clive chain smoking, Marianne complaining about her council tax bill, Donald and Mr B – dressed in sequined gowns — competing as a couple in *Strictly Come Dancing*. Afflicted by worsening bouts of dizziness, he became so sure he wouldn't survive the night that the first eager streaks of crimson light piercing the sky surprised him.

With his tongue fissured by an aching thirst that gripped his entire body, he at first dismissed as a hallucination the heavy dew that lay all along the lorry's chassis and collected in pools in the two large indentations in its bonnet. A second, more careful inspection had his heart thudding inside his chest with excitement. It was a miracle, like finding manna in the desert. Leon extricated himself unsteadily from Mr B's snoring embrace, staggered outside and ran his tongue gently along the pitted surfaces of the metal, trying to ignore the acrid flavour. The tank yielded an even greater bounty from a deep crater in its armour, though the burnt taste made his cheeks pucker.

With the sun now ablaze, the moisture was evaporating rapidly, so Leon woke Mr B and pointed to the diminishing reservoirs. Mr B smiled warmly at him, even with something approaching gratitude, and Leon felt a sense of achievement. Perhaps the privation had made him more observant, more self-sufficient.

A flock of birds passed overhead, heading towards the hills. At the sound of their wings, Mr B looked up. 'We'll follow them. First rule of desert survival: the wildlife will lead you to water. And now for breakfast.'

He pulled the kid's carcass from its hiding place under the lorry. It was seething and boiling with a thousand ants, scores of which ran up onto his hand, doubling over as they bit him. He shook the kid in vain. Hundreds more streamed up his arm and on to his body. With a shriek, he let the blood-stained remains drop and thrashed at the marauders attacking him. 'Let them have it,' he growled. 'We'll find something else.'

They set off, Mr B striding in front and still rubbing himself vigorously, Leon shuffling behind, his feet re-glued to his socks by his bleeding blisters. Hours passed and the heat increased. There was no sign of the birds or any other creatures. Weak from hunger, Leon stumbled to his knees and wasn't able to get up. With Mr B a speck in the distance, Leon slumped forward and lay flat out on the roasting sand, his head resting on his arms. He wondered when Mr B would notice he wasn't following. The sky was an impossible blue. In it a large bird, probably a vulture, circled. He closed his eyes, determined to block out his surroundings and replace them with thoughts of the most beautiful places he'd ever been.

He was roused by having one arm pulled and then the other, until he was suspended in mid-air. Mr B was hoisting him onto his shoulders, like a hunter with a trophy antelope, while muttering unintelligible words, none of which sounded complimentary. Soon he was being jolted up and down as his rescuer struggled to gain a firm foothold in the soft sand. They continued like this for an hour or more before Mr B dumped him roughly on the ground. They had come to the hills at the base of the mountain. Mr B grabbed a large, vaguely spade-shaped stone, stooped and started to scrabble, chucking earth behind him as the hole he worked at deepened. After an hour, during which he paused only occasionally to wipe the sweat from his brow, he dropped his makeshift tool and rocked back on his heels. Leon, intrigued, crawled up alongside him and peeped into the by now sizeable cavity. It was filling with water.

'Desert survival lesson,' Mr B said, in a kinder manner than Leon expected. 'Water can often be found at the base of mountains.'

They knelt, cupping the water in their hands, and only pausing occasionally to spit out some grains of sand. It tasted good, better than any wine or beer that Leon had ever sampled. They drank until the hole had run dry and their stomachs were bloated.

With a surge of energy, Leon jumped to his feet, ignoring the pain from his blisters. 'I'm ready to go on.'

Mr B smiled wryly. 'I had thought my next job might be burying you.'

'What happened to my friend?' Leon shielded his eyes and scanned the sky. The bird was still there, higher now and accompanied by two other vultures, all wheeling on the thermals generated by the rock face.

Mr B squinted at the circling scavengers. 'Word's got about. One slip and you're lunch.'

Leon followed Mr B's gaze as it moved over towards what was a near vertical climb. His heart sank. This was going to be even worse than those rope climbing sessions he'd endured at school.

★

The vultures continued to circle as they approached the rock face. Mr B scrambled up, hauling himself from boulder to boulder and grasping the few tufts of vegetation that had insinuated themselves into cracks and crevices. Leon, breathing hard, started tentatively, certain that as he lifted himself clear of the ground the sound of beating wings drew nearer. He neither dared look up in case the challenge ahead disheartened him nor down and risk vertigo. He'd never realised how hard climbing was; every finger ached, his shoulders were rigid and his legs wobbled from the strain of supporting his weight. They climbed for about an hour before the slope flattened out and they could walk, though by then he was finding it difficult to persuade his rebellious muscles to place one foot in front of the other. Mr B held out his arm for Leon to stop.

'There,' he said, pointing. Leon followed his gaze. On a rock face to their right, about twenty feet higher up, was a colony of squawking birds.

'So?'

'Our restaurant.' Mr B quickly scaled the rock face amidst a cloud of its screaming, dive-bombing inhabitants. Despite bleeding profusely from direct hits to his head and shoulders, he rose triumphantly on a ledge and plundered several nests. One courageous parent came too close and was seized by its neck, which Mr B broke with a single flick of his wrist before throwing the body down to within a yard of where Leon was standing.

'Delicious!' Mr B announced, his face smeared yellow with yolk. 'Come on up.'

Leon stood transfixed. He couldn't face climbing again, nor all that avian wrath. Mr B must have read his mind.

'Catch,' he shouted, lobbing an egg. To Leon's surprise he caught it, and though it broke in his hand and its contents slid over his palm and between his fingers, he succeeded in cramming most of them into his mouth. Another egg followed, and then another. Soon his shrunken stomach rebelled, and he called to Mr B, who was still fending valiant birds off, to stop. Mr B re-joined him, picked up the corpse, plucked its feathers and scattered them in the wind.

'Want some?'

'No thanks.' Though he'd compromised his vegetarianism by eating viable eggs, the idea of ripping into raw flesh with his teeth disgusted him.

'No wonder you're so weak,' Mr B said as he tore the bird's near-naked torso apart. 'When we get back to safety, I'm sending you to military camp to toughen you up.'

Leon looked at the darkening sky. 'Will we make it across today?'

'No, too dangerous in the dark,' Mr B replied. 'I know a cave where we can spend the night. We may have to throw a wild dog pack out when we arrive. I did last time I was there.'

★

Untroubled by wild beasts of any type, except for the occasional saucer-sized spider, they slept soundly. Awaking early, they breakfasted on more stolen eggs before setting out. Although the sun was already hot, they remained in the shade, shuffling for several hours along the narrow strip of rock which snaked between two precipitous peaks. When they emerged on the other side of the mountain range, they stood for a moment's rest on a ledge surveying the verdant farmland stretching out below. Mutabe City shimmered in the distance. Mr B was the first to spot the building close to the foot of the hills and the van parked beside its barn.

'Our limousine awaits.'

It took them another hour to reach it, skirting around the farm's perimeter before darting towards the ageing van while the labourers toiled in one of the fields. Within seconds, Mr B had hot-wired the ignition. Asthmatic coughs alternated with black exhaust fumes, until finally the engine settled into a steady rhythm. As they climbed aboard a shot rang out and a bullet smashed into the tree beside them. Mr B stamped his foot on the accelerator and they careered down the drive, the spinning wheels hurling thick clumps of mud behind them. Leon turned and looked through the rear window as the farmer threw down his rifle and ran towards the farmhouse.

'They're bound to call for help.'

Mr B didn't appear to care, and Leon wondered whether he could really be that cool, that fearless.

'No phones out here and it's miles to the next farm,' Mr B drawled, gunning the vehicle along a rough track. 'In any case, this isn't rebel territory, so if they summon anyone, it'll be the police and I can sort them out. It's our friends in the city we have to be on our guard against.'

They drove the rest of the way in silence, pausing only occasionally so Mr B could drink from the large water container in the back of the van.

Chapter 13

They rattled into the city as shops' shutters and houses' security grills were being slammed down and locked in readiness for the night.

'We'll stay in a cheap hotel and reconnoitre,' Mr B said. 'I know one nearby. Serves as a brothel too, so we'll be all right.'

You might be, Leon thought, dreading the prospect of having to fight off another prostitute's advances.

They squeezed along narrow streets, steering round piles of rubbish, cardboard boxes and the occasional corpse. Eventually, they pulled up at a door, its cracked wood bearing vestiges of flaking green paint. Mr B hopped out, knocked three times and called out in Mutabese. A female voice answered and a few moments later a large, crimson-lipped woman in flip flops emerged, securing the cord of her voluminous orange kimono.

She and Mr B conversed rapidly, making occasional glances in Leon's direction.

'It's OK,' Mr B said. 'My credit's good here. I've booked us in for the night. How many girls do you want? Two, three?'

'I'm a bit tired. I think I'll have an early night.'

Mr B stared at him, as though formulating another question, but was interrupted by the Madam who, with a clap of the hands, summoned three women to escort Mr B to his quarters. Leon's room was pointed out to him in an offhand manner and he slowly mounted the stairs, dragging one foot after the other. Halfway up, he collided with a tall, lean young man with softer, straighter hair than was usual among the Mutabese, wearing a slim fitting pink and white striped shirt. The man flashed Leon a brilliant orthodontist-crafted smile.

'Hello,' Leon said.

Another smile, even more inviting than the first, and a slight shimmy of hips in tight-fitting Armani jeans.

'My room.' Leon pointed at a door on the landing above. 'Number 7.' He made the shape of a seven with his hand. 'See you later?'

The young man gave no sign of having understood. They tried to sidestep each other but ended up still facing one another and laughed, and Leon noticed a faint scar running from the lower part of the man's right cheek to his jaw, the only flaw in an otherwise perfectly carved if delicate profile. Their eyes met, and they clapped each other on the shoulder, Leon thrilling to the solid, well-honed muscles underneath the man's soft cotton shirt. Within seconds the man had slipped away.

As he soaped himself in the dribble of water that passed for a shower, he couldn't stop thinking about the stranger, his perfect profile and his toned biceps.

★

Leon and Mr B ate dinner in the company of the Madam and six girls. The young man didn't join them, and Leon didn't ask after him. The enormity of the risk he'd taken was only just registering, and he hoped there would be no adverse repercussions. As the dinner table conversation was conducted in Mutabese, Leon, his resolution to become a vegetarian forgotten, devoted his entire energy to eating as much as possible of the tough, sinewy mutton stew on offer.

When they'd finished, Mr B selected three prostitutes, picked up two bottles of spirits and repaired to his room, leaving Leon with the Madam and the remaining women. Through graphic gestures the Madam offered each in turn, and then herself. Leon declined every offer politely with a shake of the head and a smile.

He was halfway up the stairs when he met the

young man sauntering down. 'We can't keep meeting like this,' he laughed, stepping aside.

'Yes, it's becoming something of a habit,' the man replied.

Leon breathed in to let him squeeze past. 'I thought you couldn't talk.'

The man looked at Leon over his shoulder. 'Whatever gave you that impression?'

Leon, disconcerted by the duration of their eye contact, struggled to collect his thoughts. 'Because last time you didn't say anything.'

'You should never judge a film by its trailer.'

With the man's teasing stare still fixed on him, Leon became even more flustered.

'No, er, of course not, I mean, er'...

The stranger extended his hand. 'Rolly.'

Leon took it in his own. It was warm and smooth.

'Nice name. I'm Leon.'

It was only when Rolly extricated his hand gently that Leon realised he was still holding on.

'What brings you to Mutabe, Leon?'

His voice was soft and gentle, like the breeze on a sunny English summer's day. So unlike Clive's grating nasal twang. And he was so much better looking than Clive, with a high forehead and a firm jaw, and a finely chiselled nose…

'Well?' Rolly said.

Leon started. What answer could he give? Floundering for a cover story, he came out with the first thing that sprang to mind. 'I'm looking for my sister, if she's still alive. Or, if she isn't, to find out what happened to her.'

'Interesting. Perhaps I could help. I know lots of people.'

Leon's heart missed a beat. 'Really? That would be fantastic.'

They were standing so close they were almost touching.

'It would be a pleasure.'

A seductively musky fragrance teased Leon's nostrils.

'When did you last see her?' Rolly asked.

Leon hesitated, knowing how ridiculous his answer would sound. 'I was a baby,' he mumbled.

'A baby? I see. What contact since then?'

Leon panicked. He was in danger of making an idiot of himself. 'Look, I don't know anything about her, not even her name. The only clue is that when I was found by my adoptive parents, I had this with me.' He unclasped his necklace and held it out. 'I'm hoping she has one too.'

Rolly moved in close, his warm, sweet breath bringing Leon out in goosebumps.

'Nice piece of work. Though I'm no expert, I'd say it's Bindese. Tell you what, a good friend of mine is a jeweller. If you're not busy, I could take you to her shop.'

'When?'

Rolly glanced at his Rolex. 'How about now? It's only eight. I'm free for a while and her shop stays open late.'

Leon looked down at his sweat-stained clothes. He couldn't go out like this. 'I don't have anything to wear,' he said, adding quickly to avoid arousing suspicion, 'my suitcase was stolen.'

Rolly smiled sympathetically. 'Happens all the time. Not to worry. I can lend you a t-shirt and some shorts.'

Leon's mind span. Who was this man who had turned up out of nowhere? Was he trustworthy? Was this a trap? Mr B had told him to trust no one and to remain hidden. He didn't want to endanger them both, yet he ached to spend more time with Rolly. Besides, going now might provide information on his sister. Adrenaline was coursing through his body; he was alert and ready for adventure. Sod the danger, he thought. I've been through so much, I no longer care. And sod Mr B. He's left me hanging about to go off with some tarts. Why shouldn't I do what I want?

'Why not?' Leon said. 'As soon as I've changed, I'll be ready.'

★

Rolly drove his bright red Mercedes coupé through the congested streets at high speed, continually honking the horn. Several times Leon closed his eyes, certain of a collision with another vehicle or a herd of cattle, but somehow Rolly managed to avoid them all. When Leon was finally delivered to a swanky shop on Disraeli Road in Victoria, Mutabe City's most fashionable area, he was shaking.

'The jeweller is called Mrs Daniels,' Rolly said. 'She's Mutabese but married an Englishman. She's a widow now. Dan Daniels drank himself to death.'

A memory stirred in Leon's brain, but he couldn't pin it down. 'The name sounds familiar.'

Rolly nodded. 'Not surprised. She's certainly well known in Mutabe City.'

They rang the bell and were greeted by a tall, svelte woman of about thirty-five. She wore a white silk blouse, a full-length black skirt and brandished a cigarette holder.

'Rolly, darling!' She exhaled a cloud of smoke. 'How divine to see you.' They embraced, hugging and kissing each other on the lips. Rolly slid his hands around her waist before stepping back to look at her.

'And who's your friend?' Mrs Daniels asked.

'This is Leon,' Rolly replied, 'a *very* good friend of mine.'

Mrs Daniels shot Leon a poisonous glance. He looked away, taking in his surroundings. The shop, with its discreet displays of precious gems, brooches and bracelets in gleaming ebony cabinets, would not have looked out of place in Bond Street.

Rolly and Mrs Daniels were now absorbed in a conversation in some dialect, with her hand resting proprietorially on his bottom. Leon, growing impatient, coughed politely.

With a muttered apology, Rolly took half a step back and broke into English, explaining the purpose of their visit.

'OK,' Mrs Daniels said briskly. 'Business first.' She took the necklace which Leon held out to her, and examined it through a thick magnifying glass, turning it first this way and then that. After several minutes she pronounced. 'Lovely piece of work. Made by one of the best silversmiths Mutabe ever produced.'

'Who's that?' Leon asked.

'Unfortunately, he died a few years back, but he invariably left his signature on his work.' She handed Leon the magnifying glass, indicating where to look. 'See that? He engraved a minuscule dragonfly, too small for the naked eye, on everything he did.'

Leon's gut tightened. Progress at last. 'What else can you tell me about him?'

'He only worked for the very rich, he charged a lot and his jewellery is much sought after. This is quite valuable. How did you come by it?'

Leon didn't want to go through the details, so he said his father had bought it somewhere before asking whether she thought the silversmith would have made others like it. She shook her head.

'Generally, he only made one-offs, but I suppose it

might depend who was asking. In Mutabe, there are some people it's wiser never to say no to.'

Mrs Daniels turned away. Leon touched her sleeve.

'What else can you tell me? Do you know who kept his books?'

Mrs Daniels looked down at her arm as though expecting to find a dirty handprint.

'Books?'

'Yes, business accounts, which might have listed his customers?'

She shrugged. 'If he kept any, they would probably have been incomplete, if not false.'

Leon was reluctant to give up on the only lead he had. 'Did he work with anyone else? Would anybody know about his customers?'

Mrs Daniels yawned. 'He worked on his own, as far as I know. That's all I can tell you.'

Leon pocketed the necklace, disappointed not to have discovered more.

Mrs Daniels directed her attention at Rolly. 'I'm giving a little soiree this evening. A few mutual friends. They'd love to see you again, as would I. I hope you'll be able to join us.'

'I've got something on,' he said sheepishly.

'Oh really, what?' Mrs Daniels asked.

'Nothing I can't cancel,' Rolly replied quickly, as though reprimanded.

'So, I'll see you at my place at eleven?' Mrs Daniels said.

'Sure. You won't mind if Leon joins us?' Rolly replied.

Mrs Daniels's eyelids flickered for a second. She glanced at Leon, who was struggling to hide his surprise and elation.

'No, I suppose not.' She kissed Rolly's mouth and squeezed his hand. 'See you later,' she breathed huskily. Then she nodded cursorily in Leon's direction.

They left with Leon's heart pounding with excitement.

*

Leon gazed at Rolly's profile as he drove them back to the brothel. He was so handsome — in a subtle, understated way — it was no wonder he was attractive to women. As this passed through his mind, he was speared by jealousy, an emotion he thought he'd put well behind him. He'd been dogged by it when he'd been with Clive - justifiably so, as it turned out. But he and Rolly were mere acquaintances with no obligations to each other. Even though intuition, or perhaps hope, suggested something more than friendship might be on offer, he may have misread the signs. It wouldn't be the first time. He sighed and turned his thoughts to Mrs Daniels. Who was she anyway? It was as though Rolly had read his mind.

'Interesting person, Morowa,' he said.

'Mrs Daniels?' Leon said, sure now he'd heard her discussed before.

'Yes. One of the richest women in Mutabe. Her late husband was West Africa's top diamond dealer. He was also a well-known British spy, though when legless, he boasted he worked for the Russians too. Died of cirrhosis ten years ago. She inherited the business and trebled it in size. It's said that she did a favourable deal with the Tribal Chiefs to trade all the diamonds from the Tribal Lands on their behalf.'

Leon knew now where he'd heard her name. It was at that meeting Mr B had taken him to shortly after he'd arrived. It didn't add up, though. 'If she's so rich, why does she work in the shop?'

'Bored. The shop is also a social centre for the Mutabe jet-set. They drop in for wine or coffee, and maybe see an expensive trinket and buy it.'

'Makes sense,' Leon said, angry at the thought of mega-rich socialites frittering money on baubles while others lived in poverty.

'In case you're wondering, she and I are old friends from university days,' Rolly continued. 'She knows everybody and everything.'

'I see.' Leon wasn't sure he needed to know more but ploughed on regardless. 'I thought you must be lovers.'

Rolly laughed. 'You're very direct for an English guy. Like everything in Mutabe, most relationships are pretty fluid. Personally, I've never believed in exclusivity.'

Is that right? Leon thought. If only he could have gone to that evening's soiree. But by then Mr B would be prowling around and, as Mr B was the only person with the power to facilitate his escape from Mutabe, he didn't want to antagonise him.

'I'm not sure I can join you this evening.'

Rolly glanced at him before refocusing his attention on the road. 'Whyever not? I thought you were keen?'

Leon improvised quickly. 'As I said earlier, nothing to wear.'

'No problem. Give me your measurements and I'll have some clothes delivered. You're in room 7, right?'

'Yes.' Leon said, resolving to sneak out after telling Mr B he was going to bed.

They pulled up outside the brothel at nine-thirty.

'See you later, bro.' Rolly patted Leon's backside as he slid out of the car. More than a friendly gesture, Leon thought, daring to let his hopes rise.

'I'll be back in an hour. Slip your measurements under my door, room 2,' Rolly added and roared off.

★

On entering the brothel, Leon encountered the Madam leaning against a wall, a lit cigarette hanging from her lower lip.

'Where's Mr B?' he asked.

'He sick,' she said, the cigarette bobbing up and down as she spoke.

'I'll go and see him. Which room?'

The Madam stared glassy-eyed. 'No want be disturbed.'

'Oh, you mean he's with some girls? You should have said.'

'No girls. Fever. He sick now and then. Come here for two, three days. Then better.'

Leon could have gathered her up in his arms and kissed her.

*

Nearly midnight and still no sign of Rolly. Leon resigned himself to being stood up again. It had happened frequently enough with Clive; extravagant promises broken and birthday treats, talked about for months in advance, forgotten. Leon tried to console himself with cold logic. It may be just as well. Being seen out in public would have exposed him and Mr B to unnecessary risks.

The bright red numerals on the electric clock now showed 00.05. Leon's eyelids were heavy, sleep would soon follow.

Rat-tat-tat. The brisk tattoo brought Leon straight onto his feet. Within seconds he'd opened the door. Rolly, giggling, fell in.

'Sorry, held up.'

'You're pissed.' Leon helped him to his feet and Rolly steadied himself with his hand against the wall.

'You ready?' he whispered loudly.

Leon looked down at his boxers, the only clothes he was wearing. 'Do I look ready?'

'Look ready to me,' Rolly said with a grin, swaying slightly. He made a concerted effort and stood up straight. 'Got clothes for you. Come on.'

He headed unsteadily down the corridor. Leon, grabbing a towel which he wrapped around himself, followed.

★

The clothes, a sensuous pale blue silk shirt, immaculate white chinos and soft leather deck shoes, all fitted well. Rolly looked Leon up and down.

'Wonderful. Ready now?'

Leon examined himself in the full-length mirror. The clothes were perfect, but Rolly certainly wasn't fit to drive. 'How can we go when you're drunk?'

Rolly grinned. 'Mutabe. None of your health and safety here. Survival of the fittest – only rule.'

'But we could injure or kill someone.' Leon had always been careful not to exceed the legal drink-drive limit. 'We could kill ourselves—'

Rolly put his fingers in his ears. 'No more! Too boring! I'm going. Coming?'

'Yes,' Leon heard himself say, and felt a wave of relief. Had he thought about it longer, he'd probably have declined the invitation.

★

After a mercifully uneventful journey through empty streets they arrived at imposing gates in a white wall fifteen feet high. Cameras continually swept the road while two guards in black uniforms patrolled outside. Rolly greeted them by name and returned their salutes. The gates swung open to reveal a wide drive leading up to a towering mansion with four faux turrets and a portcullis.

'Oh my God! This woman has seen too many Disney films,' Leon muttered.

Rolly laughed. 'And she's got too much money.' Driving had apparently sobered him up.

A Rolls Royce Phantom was exiting as they drove in. The passenger on the back seat looked familiar. He looked away when he saw Rolly.

'Well, if it isn't that wily old Mr E,' Rolly said. 'I wonder what he was doing here.'

A host of cars had been abandoned at haphazard angles around the drawbridge. Rolly, without removing the keys from the ignition, dumped his under a mango tree, and they sauntered across the moat and into the mock castle to the strains of a jazz band. In the hall, champagne and assorted canapes were offered to them by servants in crisp white dinner jackets. The noise increased tenfold as they entered an enormous ballroom, where the smell of marijuana hung heavily in the air. All around, couples of every permutation, men with women, women with women, men with men, were dancing, debating or canoodling. Small groups stood around the edges. In one corner, a muscular woman wearing only a golden thong, was in mid limbo under a pole held by two men in silver sling-backs and full-length white ball gowns, while a gaggle of female spectators whooped.

Rolly's eyes twinkled. 'Let's try and find Morowa.' He accosted a servant and spoke into his ear. The servant, shaking his head, pointed upwards. Rolly gave him a knowing grin.

'What was that all about?' Leon asked.

'Morowa's gone to bed with a headache.'

'Oh dear,' Leon replied, secretly delighted. 'Does she often get them?'

Rolly summoned the servant back and slipped him a rolled-up note. As he listened, Rolly's face creased into a broad smile. 'As I thought. She's with Sallay. Those two have been cosying up together a lot recently.'

'Sally. Isn't that a woman's name here?' Leon said, his hopes rising that Morowa wouldn't be competing with him for Rolly.

'It's Sallay, not Sally,' Rolly replied. 'But yes, it is.'

The noise in the room was becoming unbearable so they went through a door into the grounds. People were lounging everywhere. A floodlit swimming pool was full of merrymakers cavorting naked, while other, more serious folk, sat talking at tables illuminated by candles set in golden candelabra.

Rolly and Leon joined some women wearing long skirts and high heels, who were drinking cocktails at a nearby table surrounded by bushes of pale violet bougainvillea. The women were conversing softly in a dialect Rolly didn't understand. They acknowledged the men's presence and went back to their gossip. The air, scented seductively by myriad night flowers, smelled fresh and cool.

Leon told Rolly about his childhood, sharing his feelings of isolation and alienation. Rolly talked about his mother's death when he was six. His very rich and powerful father, who'd never shown any affection for him, had re-married and packed him off to boarding school in the UK. Although he was showered with money, apartments and cars on his return at the age of eighteen, his father refused to talk to him, and even tried to keep him out of the main family home. With the help of one of his step-mothers, who'd been sorry for him, he'd fought back and secured a small room there, though he rarely used it.

A servant brought foie gras, beluga caviar and fresh brandy alexanders. Leon felt himself mellowing as the alcohol worked through his system. What could be more idyllic than a beautiful, manicured garden, an even more beautiful – and sympathetic – man, exquisite food and sophisticated cocktails? A warm, naked foot alighted on the bare flesh exposed by his deck shoes. It could only be Rolly's. He slipped off his own shoe and a tingle ran along his spine as their toes met.

The group of women got up and drifted off, leaving Rolly and Leon alone.

Rolly placed his hand on Leon's arm. 'When did you know you were…?'

'I've always known, deep down, that I was different, though it took me years to find out why. And you?'

'Boarding school. The prefects passed the prettier young boys around and compared notes afterwards, awarding each of us a score. Traumatic at first, but it soon became normal. By the lower sixth, I was seducing the junior boys myself. But I bat for both teams, as you English say. You get more sex.'

Leon sipped his cocktail. 'You could live anywhere. Why do you live in Mutabe?'

'I spent eleven years abroad and was always an outsider. For all its faults, this is the only place I feel at home.'

Leon shifted in his chair and lowered his voice. 'Don't you worry about being prosecuted? They kill people for it here.'

Rolly ran his hand through his hair. 'Like all things in Mutabe, nothing is as it seems. A few unfortunates are executed, but generally because they've offended someone powerful and it's used as an excuse. Plenty of the upper echelons are gay, or at least bi. Take the

Lord Chief Justice, who passed sentence on the last batch. He keeps his male lover in a flat in Victoria, his mistress in Elizabeth, and his wife and children safely out of the way in a mansion in Alice.'

Leon laughed. 'Funny names for suburbs.'

'Shows how fond we are of old queens,' Rolly replied.

Leon popped a small, caviar-coated biscuit into his mouth thoughtfully. 'Doesn't that make you mad? Hanging people for what you're doing yourself.'

Rolly leaned back and narrowed his eyes. 'Yes, of course, but you have to be pragmatic. If they hadn't been executed for that, they would have been for some other crime, real or imagined. Their offence was to upset someone powerful.'

'You're so calm about it! What happened to justice?'

'We administer that ourselves.'

Leon was struck by the coldness of Rolly's voice. 'Are you speaking from personal experience?'

'I am.'

'Have you ever killed anyone?

'Yes, in self-defence.'

Leon took a deep breath. This conversation was moving in an alarming direction.

'But you're not planning to kill anyone else, are you?'

Rolly paused before replying. 'I am, but only because they deserve it. I'd never kill without a good reason.'

He sounded so calm and rational, it made Leon's head swim.

'What about the law courts and the police? What are they there for if people settle their own scores?'

'Window dressing, mainly. To persuade the rest of the world that we're a civilised country. In fact, the legal system is only accessible to the rich and powerful and bolsters their position. Don't look so shocked. It's not that different in the UK.'

'Perhaps not, but going back to what you said, who is it?'

Rolly put a finger to Leon's lips. 'You'll know when it happens, I promise you.'

Leon would have pressed for an answer, but was interrupted by the sight of Morowa, the skirt of her silver dress billowing out as she sashayed barefoot across the lush grass towards them, a champagne flute in one hand, her cigarette holder in the other. Rolly stood, arms outstretched in greeting.

'Morowa, darling, so glad your headache's better, and in such a short time. You must tell me your secret. Come and join us.' He pulled out a chair for her. 'You look gorgeous. How are you now?'

Morowa swept up her skirt and sat. 'Exhausted, but all the better for seeing you, Rolly darling.'

'Poor darling,' Rolly replied. 'You remember Leon, don't you?'

'Of course,' Morowa said, her eyes turning skyward at the distant sound of a helicopter. 'I had to send it to collect Kaday and Masseray. I don't know what's wrong with theirs. It's been out of action for weeks.' She stretched out, placed her hand on Rolly's arm and spoke to him in Mutabese. Rolly, nodding, turned to Leon.

'Morowa wants to show me something confidential. It'll take some time. When you get bored, her driver will give you a lift home. He'll be outside the main gate in the maroon Bentley Mulsanne. It's been great talking, it really has.'

Leon stood up, feeling like the child excluded from a gang. Rolly hugged him warmly.

'Another time,' he whispered in Leon's ear.

Leon watched them walk hand in hand back to the fairy tale castle. It was time to go. He gave them a few minutes, knocked back his drink and made his way, stepping over several bodies, some single, some coupled, sprawling on the grass, to the front door. Cursing his luck that an evening so full of promise had turned out so disappointingly, he found the chauffeur and told him his address. The chauffeur raised an eyebrow but said nothing.

*

The next morning, while washing himself in cold water in a plastic bowl in the corner of his room, he heard a soft knock. Suspecting a further attempt by one of the house girls to seduce him, with only his towel around his waist, he flung the door open. Rolly stood on the threshold, a look of surprise on his face. Leon ushered him inside.

'I didn't expect to see you. Thought you'd still be curled up with the lovely Morowa.'

Rolly's expression darkened. 'I warned you not to judge by appearances. Nothing is straightforward here.'

'Especially you,' Leon said, immediately regretting his words and expecting a sharp rebuke. Rolly's tone, however, was emollient.

'May I sit down?'

'Sure.'

'I want to help you understand Mutabe. We're not that different from the UK. You naively think your institutions, all grandly-named and housed in venerable buildings or towering office blocks, will enforce the rules and protect you, when it's self-interest that really drives them. That's why London, with its vast money laundering activities, is the crime capital of the world. Here we're more honestly dishonest. No one trusts anyone, especially the institutions, and we know if we're going to survive, let alone thrive, it'll be through alliances that we can make and maintain ourselves.'

Leon bit back the comment that corruption was part of everyday life in Mutabe in case it offended Rolly. 'Look, I never meant to run your country down.'

Rolly held up a hand. 'I'm sure you didn't but let me finish. In the jungle we have chimpanzees. Not many, because they've been hunted close to extinction. We can learn a lot from them, though. Chimps build alliances through grooming others. Even the alpha male does this, because otherwise the younger males might gang up and overthrow him. That's what we do in Mutabe too.'

'So, all you were doing was picking a few fleas off Morowa, was it?'

Leon watched Rolly's face intently. To his relief, it broke into a smile. 'In a manner of speaking, yes. Apart from being a delightful person and very sexy, she's very influential. Wealth counts here, and she's got mountains of it. It's best to be friends with her. She's a dangerous enemy.'

'I don't think she likes me much,' Leon said.

'She's jealous. She knows how attractive I find you.' Rolly reached out and took Leon's hand. 'I feel something for you I've never felt before.'

Leon's heart raced. 'I feel the same about you.'

Rolly stood up and they embraced, kissing deeply. Leon broke off.

'Wouldn't Morowa be upset if she knew we were doing this?' he asked.

'Oh, fuck Morowa,' Rolly said.

That's just what I'm going to stop you doing, Leon thought, pressing his lips hard against Rolly's.

★

Leon woke up with Rolly cradled in the crook of his arm. He kissed the top of Rolly's head and found himself on the verge of tears, so overwhelmed was he with happiness and a sense of fulfilment. Even though he'd only just met Rolly, it was as though he'd known him, and loved him, forever. Rolly, who was already awake, disentangled himself and sprang to his feet.

'Let's go out for lunch.'

'Gee! Can we go somewhere with local food and traditional dances?' Leon replied with an exaggerated American accent.

'You bet. I know just the place.'

Leon stood up. 'I hope their dishes are humongous. I could eat a horse.'

'Probably more likely to be a camel,' Rolly replied, slipping into his silk shirt. I'll see you in half an hour.'

★

After lunch, they visited the City National Park, where all Leon spotted were a couple of scrawny antelopes and a few brightly coloured birds.

'All the leopards were killed long ago for their pelts, and most other animals for their meat,' Rolly said. 'It sucks. We'll never attract tourists without anything for them to see.'

'Tourists?' Leon said. 'Why would they ever come here?'

'Precisely. It's one of my father's big ideas. He's developed an international advertising campaign featuring animals we don't have. No doubt he'll ship in a few substitutes or develop some other cunning wheeze to fool any visitors that arrive.'

Leon imagined an obese businessman with a fat cigar painting white horses with black stripes. 'Who is your father?'

'It's better you don't know.'

'I hate the way you keep things from me.' Leon was conscious that it sounded as though he was whining and hated himself for it. 'Why can't you tell me the truth?'

Rolly slung an arm round Leon's shoulder. 'Because I care about you. The truth in Mutabe can often prove fatal.'

For dinner, Rolly said he'd book a private room at the International Hotel. Leon's spirits sank. The name conjured up images of the Britannica, with its nearly inedible food, decrepit waiters, and rickety furniture.

'Couldn't we go somewhere a little more private?'

Rolly laughed. 'The International is *very* private.'

'But if it's anything like the Britannica—'

Rolly placed a hand on Leon's arm. 'It's nothing like the Britannica.'

They drove through the affluent Victoria area, past a lush park with elegant fountains and manicured lawns and into a broad boulevard where modern western cars – BMWs, Mercedes and Jaguars— drove unimpeded by bullock carts or mopeds loaded with baskets of chickens.

'I didn't know places like this existed here,' Leon said. 'It's all so calm.'

Rolly smiled. 'Because it's where the rich and privileged congregate.'

'Why doesn't Morowa live here, then?'

'Oh, she's got a place here, but she enjoys the more low-key lifestyle afforded by her castle.'

They pulled up outside the four-storey glass and concrete International Hotel, which glittered in the fading evening light. Two porters stepped forward to open their doors and escort them to the brightly lit lobby, while another took the keys to park the car. Beyond the lobby was an understated lounge, with elegant sofas and chairs dotted around in small clusters while waitresses in simple, smart black dresses ferried drinks from a gleaming metallic bar. The clientele was evenly divided between Africans and Caucasians, the men wearing suits and ties and the women cocktail dresses. Their conversations were quiet and intense, and Leon had the strong feeling that this is where the grooming of the real alphas took place. If only Clive could see me now, he mused.

Rolly acknowledged various guests with nods or handshakes as he steered Leon to a lift to take them to the third floor. There a young woman with a smile painted on her face greeted them, checked Rolly's booking and led them to a plush private dining room with a mahogany table, two matching carver chairs and a leather sofa. A well-stocked drinks cabinet stood in the corner. A waitress dressed in black entered, introduced herself and asked what they wanted to drink. Rolly ordered a bottle of Krug.

'This must be costing a fortune,' Leon whispered as soon as she had left.

Rolly shrugged. 'Money isn't a problem and I'm not expecting to live much longer.'

Leon's knees buckled and he reached for one of the carvers for support. Once he'd steadied himself, he looked anxiously into his new friend's face. 'Are you ill?'

Rolly laughed. 'I'm in the peak of health.'

'Is it because you are, you know...' Leon didn't like to say the word in case of eavesdroppers.

'No, it's not that. It's what I was referring to earlier when we spoke about administering justice. What I must do, you see, will prove terminal for both my target and myself.'

Leon's mouth hung open.

'You look like one of your famous codfish,' Rolly said.

Leon collected himself. 'Whatever you're thinking of doing, don't! Please.'

Rolly looked away. 'I must.'

Leon grabbed Rolly's shoulders with his hands. 'What is this plan? You've got to tell me.' The urge to shake him was almost overpowering.

Rolly turned his gaze on Leon. 'You won't change my mind. You can't.'

Leon couldn't hold back. He shook Rolly as hard as he could. 'Don't go through with it, please.' He stopped shaking and folded Rolly into an embrace. 'You're too precious.'

Rolly extricated himself with a deft flick of his shoulders and a twist of his body. 'Accept the inevitable. It's the only way.'

Tears started to well up in Leon's eyes. Rolly patted him on the cheek.

'Come on, cheer up! That's all in the future. Let's enjoy the present. I hope you don't mind. I ordered the banquet for us. It's eight courses and it's always delicious.'

The waitress returned with the bottle and poured them each a glass. Leon wiped his eyes with a handkerchief and blew his nose. He must compose himself.

'To us!' Rolly raised his champagne flute. Leon, his eyes still glinting, clinked his against it.

'To us!' He looked into his lover's eyes, noticing for the first time how light a shade of brown they were. He'd never forget that colour. He suppressed the wave of emotion still threatening to overwhelm him because he didn't want to spoil the mood. Now that his relationship with Rolly was fated to be so short-lived, he wished even more fervently that this evening would never end.

★

After an exquisite meal, at Leon's insistence they returned to the brothel. He hadn't been able to shake off the nagging thought that Mr B would recover sufficiently to notice his absence.

Before they went to sleep, Rolly announced he would leave early in the morning.

'Where are you going?' Leon asked. 'Can I come?'

'No,' Rolly replied. 'I told you I have things to do which I can't postpone. I promise you one thing though. I'll think of you till the day I die.'

Leon shuddered. 'Don't talk about dying, Rolly. Stay here with me. We could have so much fun. We could go anywhere, do anything.'

Rolly sighed. 'I have to go.'

Leon fought back his tears. 'I'll wait for you, however long it takes. I know we'll meet again.'

Rolly kissed him. 'Don't put yourself at risk. You must get out of Mutabe as soon as possible. It will become extremely dangerous for you when the authorities find out you know me.'

★

Leon was dimly aware of Rolly's planting a kiss on his forehead and creeping out of his room, but not sufficiently so to wake him from his slumbers.

A few hours later, shuffling around under the thin trickle of water in the shower, he noticed his silver elephant charm chain was missing. He turned everything in the room upside down without success. Perhaps it had slipped off him at the International, or perhaps — and his heart skipped a beat at the thought — Rolly had taken it as a keepsake.

★

Depressed at Rolly's departure and worried about his safety, Leon picked at his breakfast bowl of millet swimming in a thin grey gravy. The Madam sidled in to say that Mr B had recovered and would be with them soon.

Mr B announced his arrival with a loud refrain from a local song. Slapping the Madam on the bottom and tousling Leon's hair, he pulled a woman onto his knee and, with a lusty laugh, ran his hand up inside her blouse. She smiled politely, and Leon averted his eyes.

'Better now?' Leon asked coldly.

'Pretty much,' Mr B replied.

'Must have been a hell of a session to knock you out for two days,' Leon said, relishing the opportunity to get his own back.

Mr B glared at him. 'You obviously know nothing of the fevers that are endemic here.'

'I thought those women you went off with exhausted you.'

'Not so, but you can't beat sex for recuperation,' Mr B said, grabbing a handful of millet porridge and cramming it into his mouth. 'Not that you'd know much about that. I suppose you've been enjoying pitiably early nights.'

Leon smiled. 'I have spent quite a lot of time in bed.'

Mr B eased the woman's naked breast from her blouse, fondling its long, dark nipple with one hand while continuing to eat his breakfast with the other. 'We must plan our re-entry into Mutabe City.'

Leon stifled his growing anger at her treatment and softened his voice. His escape from Mutabe and his slim chances of a future rendezvous with Rolly depended on it.

'I'll pick up my things from the hotel, if you don't mind, and leave straight for the airport. I'm sure you can help me with the paperwork.'

Mr B stroked the nipple until it stood erect, then said, 'Leaving is out of the question. In any case, the airport will be under surveillance by any number of groups and is the least safe place. No, we must find the saboteurs and deal with them.'

Leon could see his chance of escaping from the country being extinguished. He wondered fleetingly what Peter and Marianne, if they really had been secret agents, would have done if they had been here, but he was on his own. He'd have to deal with it as best as he could.

'I'm no use to you anymore. I didn't make the rally, so people won't trust me. And pictures of me with the Fundamentalists will be all over the internet. I'm discredited. You might as well let me go.'

'Anything can be explained. You are still Chief Onagaku, heir to the Tribal Lands. Many revere that name.' Mr B tipped the woman off his lap. She tottered for a moment, her breast swinging. 'In any case, I don't have the power to authorise anything. Only once I re-establish myself will you be certain of leaving safely.'

'Surely they'll be delighted to see you again, Messrs C and D and all the rest of the alphabet? They'll roll out the red carpet and kill the fatted calf.'

To Leon's disgust, Mr B reached out for another of the prostitutes, pulled her towards him and slipped his hand up her skirt. Though she started gyrating rhythmically, the faraway look didn't leave her eyes.

'How little you understand,' Mr B said, kneading the woman's crotch while intermittently taking more millet with his other hand. 'My reputation will have been trashed by Donald's treachery, my place filled and my powers distributed. It will be a struggle to reinstate myself. When my survival becomes known, many people, including several of my erstwhile colleagues, will want me dead. That's where you come in. No one will link you with my disappearance. You must find out what you can and report back to me.'

'Enough!' Leon erupted. 'I've been kidnapped by Communists and Fundamentalists and been lucky to escape. If you think I'm going to stroll back as though nothing's happened and ask questions—'

'What choice do you have?' Mr B extracted his hand and pushed the woman aside. 'We can't remain here indefinitely. I'm your sole protector against those who see you as a threat. Only by you finding out who I have to deal with can I re-establish myself and secure your safety.'

'I might be murdered out there—'

'And we will both be killed if we stay here too long. Word gets about quickly in Mutabe. There's no time to lose. Now go!'

Chapter 14

Scrawny cattle, ill-tempered donkeys and people dressed in everything from dirty shorts to flowing robes pushed and shoved each other relentlessly in the teeming, traffic-congested streets. Leon, disoriented by the mooing, shouting and hooting and the miasma of sweat, fumes and excrement, bobbed helplessly in the torrent. Finally, abandoning restraint, he barged his way to a quieter spot. There he leant, panting, against the wall of a rusting corrugated iron kiosk as he tried to work out where he was.

A swarthy man with a small moustache, wearing a luminous green t-shirt and muddy white shorts, popped up in front of him, a broad grin on his round face. He looked vaguely familiar. 'Chief Onagaku!'

Leon, curbing the inclination to run, dropped his head and tried to edge away. Green t-shirt closed on him, smiling toothily. 'Chief Onagaku! Stop!'

A few passers-by stared.

Green t-shirt cupped his hands and cried out, 'Chief Onagaku has returned to liberate his people. Make way for the Chief!' A crowd formed around them.

'You've got the wrong person,' Leon said, looking around for a means of escape.

'No, I haven't,' Green t-shirt replied with unnerving confidence. Leon's heart was now racing. How could the stranger be so sure? Had he seen the FMF video? Was he FMF? If not, what was he? Leon glanced sideways at him. He looked friendly enough.

'Clear a path!' someone shouted.

The crowd parted and Leon, now clasped firmly by the stranger, was steered through the gap while his tribal name was chanted like an anthem. A drummer strode up, beating out a frenzied rhythm. He was joined by a woman with a shrill wooden pipe and another with a guitar. Some onlookers broke into a dance. The road in front of them cleared, the singing crowd squeezing to the sides. Leon tried to stop, break free, step aside, do anything to escape the terrifying public acclaim but was pinned by the unrelenting grip on his arm.

'You will end Oblanga's tyranny,' his companion rasped in his ear. 'We'll march to the Presidential Palace and demand his resignation.'

Leon recalled the outcome of the last rally called in his name. 'The guards might open fire. People might be killed.'

'Don't worry. The tribal legends tell that when the

Great Chief returns, he'll protect his followers and lead them to freedom and glory.'

Play along with them, Leon thought. I must be able to give this lot the slip. Keep them talking till I can. 'What makes you think I'm this Chief?'

The man laughed. 'Don't you remember me? Even if we hadn't met, I'd recognise you. Your picture is all over social media.'

Leon squinted at him in the bright sunlight. So much of what had taken place since his arrival was a blur. He shook his head. 'I can't place you. Who are you?'

At that moment they turned onto the wide tree-lined avenue leading up to a turreted white palace, which glistened in the hot sun. In front of them stood a company of soldiers dressed in dark green battle fatigues and armed with gleaming automatic weapons. The officer in charge barked an order and the soldiers fell into two ranks, the first kneeling, the second standing behind. At another command, they aimed their guns at the crowd.

'Halt!' Leon cried, terrified at the prospect of another massacre.

The crowd's momentum thrust him forward.

'Stop!' he shouted again.

This time others around him yelled and pushed back against the surging mass, which ground to a halt close enough for Leon to make out the intricate cross-hatched tribal gouges on the soldiers' skins.

'Talk to them,' Green t-shirt urged, hurling Leon forward so that he stood alone, two yards from the crowd and an uncomfortable ten from the forest of weapons.

Leon's instinct was to flee but there was no escape. Walls topped with spiked railings blocked him in on either side; behind him the crowd was solid. In front were the unblinking eyes of forty heavily armed soldiers. If he were going to die, he might as well do so bravely, he thought, recalling a similar predicament in the FMF camp.

After a few moments' strained silence during which his mind remained stubbornly blank, like water breaching a dam the words and gestures he'd spent three days learning, flooded back. He stretched out his arms and the crowd fell silent.

'I am Leon Onagaku, heir to the last great Chief. I come to claim his tribal rights and free my people from the yoke of oppression.' He parroted the rest of the speech, barely conscious of what he was saying, though he did recover his wits sufficiently to finish by adding, while staring at the soldiers, 'So, my friends, lay down your weapons and join us in this noble cause.'

Silence reigned for a full five seconds. Then, to Leon's surprise the soldiers, one by one, lowered their weapons and slung them on their backs while the crowd pressed forward to embrace them. Everyone cheered and hugged, and Leon was raised shoulder high in the middle of the shouting, dancing, singing mob. Eventually the soldiers, smiling and waving, strolled off, leaving the rest of them to snake their way towards the Palace gates.

Green t-shirt, who was one of those carrying him, bellowed in Mutabese and the crowd echoed his call. Those in the vanguard shook the gates and a few tried unsuccessfully to scale them. But everyone fell silent when a thunderous noise erupted, presaging the appearance of four camouflaged tanks. A company of soldiers in navy blue jackets and sky-blue trousers followed, their gold epaulets glinting in the sun. The soldiers positioned themselves behind the gates. Leon was lowered to the ground.

"The Imperial Guard!' Green t-shirt said. 'We won't get past them easily.' He pushed Leon forward. 'Go and negotiate.'

Leon, conscious of hundreds of smartphones filming him, once again found himself at the front. An orange and black helicopter with a machine-gun protruding from its open side door circled above them.

'I demand to speak with Oblanga,' Leon yelled, for want of anything better to say. The chant of 'Oblanga', was picked up by the throng, many of whom hammered out the beat on the railings with bits of metal or wood.

Another chant broke out, this time in local language, though in the flurry of words the names Oblanga and Onagaku were decipherable.

'They're placing an old tribal curse on him,' Green t-shirt told him. 'Oblanga's superstitious. If he's in there, it may get him out.'

Leon eyed him with a mixture of respect and suspicion. 'How do you know? And who the hell are you?'

'Jeff Gbeho. I'm a journalist for *The Record*, Mutabe's only truly independent newspaper. You probably don't remember, but I tried to interview you at the Britannica the day before the massacre. Today's events should make front page news, if I live to tell the story.'

Leon scrutinised Jeff's features closely. 'Yes, now I remember.'

The raucous noise trailed off as a balcony door opened and a woman in a blue business suit, carrying a clipboard and a microphone, appeared. She was followed by a soldier, a silver breastplate covering the chest of his scarlet regimental dress, the purple plumes on his gold helmet dancing in the wind and a cutlass gleaming in his hand. Behind him a short, stooped man in his seventies with close-cut curly white hair stumbled as he emerged, but quickly righted himself. Two burly guards in combat fatigues, wielding automatic weapons, brought up the rear. Loitering in the doorway's shadows, another figure in an off-white suit bore a close resemblance to Donald.

'It's Oblanga,' Jeff whispered.

An expectant hush settled on the crowd. Oblanga lifted an arm and the soldiers raised and aimed their weapons. 'It's going to be another massacre,' Leon said softly, cursing his helplessness. Those poor people all around him would soon be a pile of bloody corpses and it would be his fault.

Oblanga shouted in Mutabese and echoes from the sound system reverberated around the square. A few voices yelled back. Then, with his hands grasping the rail, he peered over the balcony. 'Who dares challenge me?'

Jeff nudged Leon. 'Answer him, my friend.'

A battered old megaphone was thrust into Leon's hands by someone behind him. Leon coughed to clear his throat and compose himself. Escape was out of the question. Despite his heart racing at what must have been 220 bpm or more, he had no option but to see this through. He took a deep breath and, struggling to keep his hands steady, held the megaphone in front of his mouth.

'I, Leon, heir to Chief Onagaku.' He paused, wondering what to add.

Jeff prodded him in the ribs. 'Order him to resign.'

Leon took another deep breath. He might as well keep going. 'You have committed serious crimes against the people, Mr Oblanga.' He paused for dramatic effect. 'In their name, I call upon you to stand down immediately.'

A few isolated cheers were followed by the buzz of several people translating what Leon had said, then a roar of approval arose from the crowd.

Oblanga's grimace was contemptuous. 'A foreigner, who does not even speak our language, tells me to resign? One I know to be a lackey of the British Secret Services, who are still bent on colonial dominion over Africa. If you leave Mutabe now you will not be harmed.'

If only I could, Leon thought, and wondered whether the opportunity might arise to negotiate his safe passage out of the country. What would it take? How would he go about it?

Jeff nudged him and whispered, 'He thinks you're the sort of coward who'd walk out on his people to save his own skin. Put him right, my friend.'

Leon emerged from his thoughts with a start and looked around at all the Mutabese who were relying on him to win back their freedom. He couldn't let them down, even if it meant… He couldn't quite bring himself to finish the thought. Jeff prodded him again and hissed, 'Go on!'

Leon took a deep breath. 'I may not speak Mutabese, but I was born here, and I represent no one, except the people. I will only go when they tell me to.'

After another brief delay for translation, the protesters started chanting 'Onagaku, Onagaku' and hurled themselves against the railings separating them from the military.

Oblanga held both hands aloft and the activity subsided, an expectant stillness settling on the demonstrators. 'I will meet this so-called descendant of Onagaku. Let him and two others through.'

'How do we know this isn't a trick?' Leon shouted.

'By Mungagette, I promise you safe passage.'

'That's our sacred ancestral spirit,' Jeff said. 'He daren't break his oath; he'll never enter the spirit world if he reneges.'

The crowd roared, and Leon could feel its sense of expectation. He suspected Oblanga's offer to be trap, but what were the alternatives? He surveyed the tanks and soldiers in front. Any direct attack would result in a massacre. On the other hand, failure on his part to pursue negotiations would probably lead to his being strung up by the disillusioned mob. He decided to risk going into the Palace on Oblanga's flimsy promise.

'All right. I accept your assurance.'

He turned to Jeff. 'You ready?'

Jeff took a step back. 'He wants to see you, not me.'

Leon fixed him with a cold stare. 'You got me into this mess. He said three people. You're one of them.' He noticed the worried frown on Jeff's face. 'Why, what's stopping you?'

Jeff wrung his hands and tried to take another step back but was blocked by the dense crowd. 'I know what goes on in there.'

'You said he wouldn't dare break his oath.'

Jeff nodded feebly. 'Yes, but I ... I'd rather not put it to the test.'

Leon put an arm around him. 'Well, that's just what we're going to do.'

Another man, small, grey-haired and with pock-marked skin forced his way through the mass of people and stood in front of Leon. 'I come with you.'

Leon looked him up and down, observing that with his open-necked blue checked shirt and red trousers, he was more smartly dressed than the other demonstrators.

'Who are you?'

'Desmond. I can help you. Know many people.'

'All right.' Leon turned to Jeff. 'He's up for it. How about you?'

Jeff stared back.

'Famous investigative journalist frightened?' Desmond laughed caustically. 'Wait till people hear.'

Jeff's shoulders slumped. He shot a poisonous look at Desmond. 'All right. I'll come.'

Oblanga gave an order and the gate swung open. Pushed roughly through by unseen hands, they found themselves in the Palace courtyard, a host of guns trained on them. The gates slammed shut behind them and, throughout a brief but highly intrusive frisking, Leon could feel the hard steel of a gun barrel pressing against the small of his back.

As soon as all three were declared weapon-free, a column formed around them. An officer and two soldiers strutted in front, while a dozen more marched behind. After passing through a few drab rooms and anonymous passageways, they came to a mahogany door bearing an intricate carving of a lion grappling with an elephant. The officer knocked and they were admitted by another posse of guards, who, after keeping them waiting for twenty minutes, carried out another thorough body search. Once cleared, they passed through gilded, chandelier-lit corridors which smelled musty despite the wheezing and groaning efforts of several rusty air-conditioning units. The last corridor, lined with peeling white and gold rococo chairs, opened out into an enormous rectangular chamber with a dark wooden floor traversed by a lush red carpet.

Leon gasped at the stateroom's opulence, wondering how many people had been exploited, and maybe even died, to make all this possible. Rich green wallpaper embossed with a silver oak leaf pattern adorned the walls and four golden chandeliers, each at least eight feet wide, hung from the high ceiling. At the far end of the room stood a dais bearing a diamond encrusted sky-blue throne, on which sat Oblanga, now wearing a small golden cap and a flowing white and gold gown, his swinging feet not touching the floor. He was flanked by a dozen men dressed in white robes and silver caps.

With Leon at their head, the three demonstrators were marched along the carpet to the throne.

'Kneel,' a voice boomed.

Oblanga winked at him three times in rapid succession. Leon was trying to make out why when a blow to the side of his head made the room spin and his knees buckle. Liquid trickled down his face. He put his tongue out and tasted blood. Jeff and Desmond were already kneeling. Sensing the rifle being swung back again, Leon followed suit, only realising then that what he had taken to be winks had been a facial tic.

Oblanga stood up unsteadily, his wrinkled face a petulant mask and his outstretched arms twitching. 'What brings you to my Palace? You couldn't think I'd resign. You,' Oblanga pointed waveringly at Leon, 'are a British agent, smuggled in to incite the people. Him,' he cocked a thumb at Jeff, 'he's working for the Chinese, and that little man there,' he nodded at Desmond, 'is a mystery which my interrogators will solve very quickly.'

'I am the heir to Chief Onagaku,' Leon said. 'I must be treated with respect.'

Oblanga winked several times. 'You are a liar and a fraud. Onagaku left no heirs. One way or another, you will soon confess everything.'

'You promised us safe passage,' Leon said before another sharp blow knocked him flat.

'Promises to dogs count for nothing,' Oblanga sneered. 'Take them away.'

Rough hands hauled the three to their feet and they were bundled back through rooms and along passageways until they arrived at a steep flight of stairs. The air, at first sour, became foetid as they were frogmarched down into a dark and gloomy basement, off which were several small doors. One was pulled open exposing them to a nauseating stench of faeces and stale urine. The three were thrown in and the door slammed shut. Inside was a rickety bunk bed, a torn grey blanket, a corroded bucket half full of slops, and a surveillance camera.

The three, covering their noses, perched on the lower bed.

'Wonder why they've put us in the same cell,' Leon said, pulling the blanket around his shoulders to stop himself from shivering in the cool, foul air.

'So we'll incriminate ourselves,' Jeff replied.

'Why only two beds?'

Jeff tugged at Leon's blanket. A small piece came away in his hand. He threw it onto the floor. 'To make us argue.'

Leon, realising he'd been selfish, offered the blanket to the others. Desmond declined. Jeff took it, ripped it into three pieces and handed Leon and Desmond one each.

As the hours passed, they became accustomed to the smell and took it in turns to lie on the bunk beds, the third person sitting at the foot of the lower one. No food or water arrived, and Leon tried to conjure up distracting memories of his favourite childhood holidays with Peter and Marianne. Frustratingly each led to thoughts of food, such as some sausages he'd enjoyed or an ice cream he'd eaten on a beach, which only made his hunger more acute. These recollections would then give way to more thoughts, inspired by films he'd seen, of the many ways in which his body might shortly be mutilated by his captors.

The sound of a key in the lock made them start. The door swung open, its hinges creaking. A bare-chested giant of a man with three deep black scars down each cheek waggled his index finger at Leon, who was slouching on the lower bunk.

'You! Come with me!'

Leon pulled himself up, remembering, as he approached the towering figure, all those times he'd been picked on by school bullies. But he wasn't Coconut now. He wasn't going let his fear show. When he reached the cell door, two guards seized his arms while a third snapped on a pair of handcuffs. He was dragged down a dank and airless corridor and pushed into a room with a table and a chair and made to sit in front of a bank of blindingly bright lights. A vicious slap stung his face, reopening his wound.

'You're going to talk,' said someone masked by the glare.

Leon trembled at the thought of more pain. 'I can tell you where Bankole is,' he said, hoping Mr B would be clever enough to avoid capture.

'We know where Bankole is, how long he's been there and who he's with.'

'I can describe the FMF camp to you.'

The voice laughed. 'The reason those amateurs still exist is because we tolerate them. Only a goat would want to live there anyway. Give us details of your British espionage network. Who controls it, what are the communication channels, how is it funded?'

'I don't know anything, honestly. If you don't believe me, give me one of those truth drugs.'

Another voice, deeper and more authoritative, cut in. 'An electric current passed through the scrotum is generally far more efficacious than sodium thiopental. So, let's start with the basics. You were recruited for British intelligence by Marianne Cartwright on the instructions of Charles Forrest, Head of MI6's West Africa Desk. Do you deny that?'

'Yes. Marianne's my mother and I only met Charles Forrest once. I didn't even know who he was. I thought he might be my mother's boyfriend.'

'It's common for step-parent agents to recruit their children. It's always more difficult to crack second generation cover stories. Let's not waste any more time. Who arranged for you to come here?'

'Mr Bankole. He— '

A stinging slap interrupted his flow.

'All right. So, we assume it was Marianne Cartwright. Who did she arrange for you to meet?'

'Mr Bankole— '

Another sharp slap brought tears to Leon's eyes. A steady trickle of blood oozed down his face and dripped onto his body.

'This is becoming tiresome, Mr Cartwright. We're going to have to employ more direct methods. We—'

The chirruping of a mobile phone cut the sentence short. A heated conversation in Mutabese ensued, during which the interrogator's tone rose from angry to near hysterical, while Leon trembled at the thought of all this rage being vented on him. The call ended, and Leon's captors conversed animatedly.

'We'll deal with you tomorrow,' the authoritative one said, and Leon heard footsteps and the door shutting. When they'd gone, the brilliant bank of lights was turned off and two guards hustled him back to his cell where, with his hands still handcuffed behind him, he was thrown to the floor.

'What happened to you?' Jeff enquired, helping Leon onto the lower bed, and mopping his wounds with a piece of blanket.

Leon shrugged the blanket aside; he could imagine the clumps of bacteria, like small ripe grapes, clinging to it, ready to infect his open wound. 'They think I'm a British agent.' He stared around the cell. 'Which I'm not! They were about to fry my testicles when one of them got a phone call and started shouting. Then I was brought back here.'

'Perhaps the revolution has started,' Jeff said, wrapping Leon's piece of blanket round himself despite its new blood stains. 'Because we've been here so long, the protesters will either have got bored and dispersed, which is what normally happens, or they'll have become irate, in which case they could have done anything: scaled the walls, kicked in the gate, who knows.'

'The Presidential Guard looked fearsome. If the crowd tried anything, there would have been a lot of bloodshed.'

'You never know,' Jeff replied. 'In Mutabe the concept of loyalty isn't strong. People can be bought cheaply and they'll only stay with you till they get a better offer.'

'But the Presidential Guard?'

'Well, unlike the regular troops, who will do anything for a few beers, they're paid quite well. And they all come from the Mosa tribe, so they've got a strong sense of loyalty. But if they thought something wasn't in their tribal interests, I could see them turning.' He stepped forward and examined Leon's still bleeding face. 'If I had anything to use, apart from this disgusting blanket, I'd clean your wound but, as you can see, they haven't even brought us any water.'

'I'm not looking forward to tomorrow.' Leon groaned and slumped onto the bed, his blood seeping into the pale grey mattress.

'In Mutabe we have a saying: "Tomorrow is another life",' Jeff said. 'So many of us fear we will die today, when tomorrow comes it's like being given a whole new life.'

'I like that,' Leon murmured. 'Sounds like the title of a book.'

Jeff smiled. 'It is, the one I'm currently writing. It's all—'

Their conversation was interrupted by the harsh grating sound of the small barred window in their cell door being eased back.

'Food,' Jeff said. But it wasn't a warder's face behind the bars in the observation hatch. Seconds later the door creaked open.

Without a word, Primrose entered.

Leon stared at her, his mouth gaping. 'What are you doing here?'

'Business. Go everywhere.' She unlocked Leon's handcuffs and then wiped his face with a handkerchief. 'You hurt, Mr Lion. You need to take better care of yourself.'

Leon shook his wrists vigorously to restore his circulation. 'I've never been so pleased to see anyone. How the hell did you know we were here?'

Primrose tapped her nose. 'Pillow talk.'

'Who are you, lady?' Desmond demanded.

Jeff ran his fingers through his thinning hair. 'I'm sure I've seen you somewhere before.'

Primrose turned her back on him and faced Leon. 'You need to get out now.'

Jeff shook his head. 'It'll come back to me.' He stepped out and surveyed the empty corridors. 'Where are the guards?'

'Riot outside Palace,' Primrose said. 'Everyone ordered to defend.' She thrust a small pistol into Leon's hands. 'Here, take this. Out, now, quickly-quickly. Go upstairs. Passage fifty metres on the left. Go to end. Through kitchen. Lorry waiting.'

'They rioted to save us.' Leon's voice cracked with emotion.

'No,' Primrose replied over her shoulder as she took the stairs two at a time. 'Crowd leaving when rumour price of rice double. Then riot.'

Leon and Jeff started to follow.

'Aren't you coming, Desmond?' Leon turned around and retraced his steps. Desmond, leaning against the bunk, shook his head.

'Catch us. Torture us.'

Jeff raced back to join them. 'We've got a good chance if we're quick.'

'Scared.' Desmond, a pleading expression on his face, stretched his hand out towards Leon's gun. Leon handed it to him.

'Have it. Didn't want it anyway.'

Desmond sat up, pointing it at him and then at Jeff. 'Sit,' he growled in a guttural voice, jumping to his feet and standing between them and the door. 'No one going nowhere.'

'What's got into you? We'll look after you, if that's what you're worried about,' Leon said.

Jeff's face was drawn. 'He's a police plant, sent to spy on us. That's it, isn't it, Desmond?'

Leon had edged, a millimetre at a time, away from Jeff so that they were a metre apart.

'Together,' Desmond shouted, pearls of perspiration glinting on his shiny black forehead as he backed towards the cell door.

'What will you do if we don't?' Leon said, avoiding looking at Primrose, who was sneaking up behind Desmond, a warder's truncheon in her hand. One swift blow bought Desmond to his knees, the second left him prostrate.

'I say leave,' Primrose hissed. 'Now go.'

Leon and Jeff bounded up the stairs, only to hear her voice boom out.

'Take this.' In her hand was the pistol she'd retrieved from the cell floor. Jeff rushed back to seize it.

'She your fairy godmother?' Jeff panted, trying to catch his breath when he rejoined Leon. 'If not, who's she working for? Your friends in MI6?'

'I'm nothing to do with MI6,' Leon yelled over his shoulder as he strode into the gloom of the passage, lit only by a distant dim bulb. His foot slid away from him on the wet floor and he crashed against the jagged wall, grazing his knuckles and face.

'Holy shit, that hurt!' He raised his fingers to his cheek. 'They won't have much difficulty tracking us. They can just follow the trail of blood.'

Jeff extended his hand and hauled Leon to his feet. 'You OK?'

Leon took a deep breath and tried to collect his thoughts. 'What were we saying? Oh yes, I remember. Why must she be working for anyone?'

'Because everyone is.'

'Are you?'

'In a way, yes.' Jeff helped Leon dust himself down. 'I play the major powers off against each other just as they do the Africans. I'm currently backing the Chinese; at other times it might be the Americans or the French. The way we've been exploited over the years has made prostitutes of us all. Our only option is to fight back using whatever weapons we can. You ready to move on?'

Leon rubbed his grazed hand. 'Suppose so.'

They inched their way towards the dangling bulb. Beyond that the tunnel continued into ever deepening darkness.

'Well, here goes.' Leon waved his hand like a windscreen wiper in front of his face to dislodge the thick cobweb tapestry as they felt their way along the rough walls, pausing occasionally to spit out strands of web. After several minutes, Leon crashed into a solid obstacle. He ran his hands over it. It was wood, with some metal spars. He groped a little further and located a handle, which, using all his strength, he turned. The door creaked open and a sliver of dazzling light broadened into a blinding glare. It took several seconds for his eyes to adjust. They were in a courtyard at the far side of which was another door, held open by an overflowing dustbin surrounded by a curtain of flies.

They filled their lungs with fresh air. From beyond the door came the bubbling, the whistling, and the tantalising aromas of food cooking. Occasionally someone, white-garbed and white-hatted, could be seen scurrying from one side of the kitchen to the other laden with yams and corn or carrying a steaming pot.

'We'll walk straight through,' Leon said, 'as though we have every right to be there. Hide that gun, Jeff, for God's sake.'

'I'll go first,' Jeff said, tucking the pistol into his belt.

Barely anyone glanced up as they strode through the sauna-thick steam, their empty stomachs groaning and their mouths salivating at the overwhelming smell of food. A lamb, turned slowly on a spit by a naked boy of seven or eight, was being basted by a youth in a loincloth, his black body glistening as though drenched in dew. Yams lay in big piles and, in a cauldron large enough to boil a buffalo, a sea of rice raged and spat.

A little further on, they came to a table on which rested a pitcher of water and several earthenware mugs. Affecting a casual air, they paused to drink, replaced the mugs and walked on.

Reaching the far end of the kitchen, they came upon another door, propped open by a stack of wooden crates. It led to a driveway where delivery lorries were unloading, overseen by a sentry absorbed in picking his nose.

'This must be it,' Leon said. They crept up into the

back of the first unloaded truck, squirming under a tarpaulin and peering through one of the many slits in its material.

The vehicle's engine burst into life, throbbing and belching black smoke. Soon they were crawling towards the main service gate, where a platoon of jeering and whooping soldiers in camouflage army fatigues were squatting and playing cards, some with piles of money in front of them, others with none. Sentries stood watching and smirking; too engrossed to pay any attention to an empty lorry exiting.

A bump in the road shifted the tarpaulin and cut off their view, so Leon and Jeff were reduced to listening to the hubbub of everyday life, punctuated by the loud cries of market traders and the braying of donkeys. Occasionally pungent odours of cinnamon, ginger and cloves would penetrate their refuge, teasing their noses and seducing the saliva from their cheeks.

Chapter 15

When the truck drew to a halt and the driver cut the engine, they waited for him to get out. Seconds ticked by and he was still there. Leon's pulse was racing and his mouth dry. He looked at Jeff, crouching in readiness beside him.

'Do you think he's waiting for someone?'

Jeff grimaced. 'Perhaps someone's going to put something on the back and we'll be discovered.'

Leon looked around as best he could. 'Think it's all clear. Let's go!'

They slipped out from under the cover and eased themselves over the side and down onto the road. But the driver must have seen them in his wing mirror, because he leaned, shouting, from his cabin.

Without looking back, they sprinted away, pushing past people and swerving to avoid their animals. When they turned the corner, they paused in a shop doorway to catch their breath. Leon glanced behind them.

'No sign, thankfully. What did he say?'

Jeff, still panting, took a deep breath. 'That he'll report us to the police. Hopefully he thinks we hitched a lift after he left the Palace.'

'Let's go down here, just in case.' Leon threw himself into the maze of alleyways running off the street. Jeff followed, clasping the pistol.

'These back streets are dangerous, my friend,' Jeff said, his head swivelling. 'Lots of people disappear in them.'

'The authorities won't find us easily then.'

'Not alive, no, though corpses, or what's left of them, are often spat back out onto the main roads.'

'Don't the police ever come here?'

'They sweep through occasionally, raping and pillaging, on the pretext of a clean-up. Afterwards the gangs come out of hiding and resume their rackets. It's like a tide washing in and out.'

Leon looked over both shoulders. 'Let's hope the tide's out now.' All around, habitations constructed of planks of wood, bits of plastic sheeting and rusting corrugated iron leant against each other, like playing cards. Cooking smells mingled with the stench of human and animal excrement, simultaneously teasing the taste buds and turning the stomach; clothes, often starched brilliant white, hung on makeshift lines between the shacks. Yet there was no one around and it was oddly quiet. Occasionally a small child would stray into their path and stand, blinking, in the bright sunshine before being summoned back into a shack's dark recesses by a female voice.

Leon tried to peer into some of the shanties, but the interiors were too dark to make anything out. 'Where is everybody?'

Jeff gazed all around, shielding his eyes with his hand. 'Watching us.'

Leon's stomach churned as they continued through the honeycomb of passageways. 'How will we get out?'

Jeff shrugged. 'If we stumble across another main road, we may be all right, but it'll be dark in a couple of hours and then we won't stand a chance.'

'Why don't we ask for help?'

'Then they'd know how vulnerable we are. Right now, all that's keeping us alive is uncertainty about what they'd be taking on.'

'Well, I'm prepared to give it a try. I'd rather die facing them than be picked off scurrying around like a rat in a maze. I'm going to talk to someone.'

Jeff laughed. 'Good luck with that. Most barely understand Mutabese, let alone English.'

Their debate terminated abruptly at the sight of a group of machete-wielding men dressed in sparkling white t-shirts and blue denim jeans, who were blocking their path. Behind stood another posse. Jeff pulled the pistol out of his trouser belt and pointed it at the largest man. At least six feet six tall, he had a bushy black beard, its furthest tendrils brushing the top of his gnarled brown leather belt. His face broke into a broad grin exposing a gap between his broken front teeth. He looked up. Following his gaze, they saw men with Kalashnikovs perched on the roofs above them. Their leader shouted, and the gunmen took aim.

'What did he say?' Leon whispered.

Jeff raised his hands. 'Who cares?'

Leon followed suit. 'We're friends. We're running from the police. Please help us.'

The smile on the leader's face faded to a frown.

Jeff repeated Leon's words in Mutabese. The frown deepened until one of his gang, small and wiry with close-cropped hair and a thin moustache, tugged his arm and whispered in his ear. The leader, nodding slowly, replied. Then the wiry man, in a faltering manner, uttered a few words.

'Thank God, he speaks some Mutabese,' Jeff said softly. 'He wants to know what we want.'

'Tell him we were prisoners in the Presidential Palace, but we escaped.'

Jeff spoke for a couple of minutes. The man finally nodded and then repeated something to the leader. Another few minutes' speech and translation brought back the message, 'How much money have you got?'

Leon turned out his pockets. 'Nothing. Go on, Jeff, do the same.'

Jeff grimaced. 'Oh, thanks.' Reluctantly he followed suit, producing a few crumpled notes, which were snatched immediately. Leon stepped forward, offering his hand. The men gripped their machetes tightly. The frozen tableau was broken seconds later when the bearded leader grasped Leon's hand and, laughing, clapped him on the back. He spoke to his interpreter, who translated for Jeff.

'He says we're brave but foolish. There are many dangers here, many ruthless gangs, but he'll see us safely out of shanty town.'

Leon put his hands together, bowing in what was intended as a universal message of humble gratitude.

'What are you doing?' Jeff yelled. 'If they think we're Muslims they'll kill us for sure.'

Leon dropped his arms to his sides and gave the locals his broadest smile. 'Not Muslim, just grateful.'

Suspicion was replaced by puzzlement in the men's expressions.

'What's his name?' Leon whispered to Jeff, who translated.

'Olatunde,' came the reply from the wiry man, and the leader bared his broken teeth in a friendly smile.

'I'm Leon, this is Jeff,' Leon said pointing with his thumb.

Olatunde spoke in a deep bass, jerking his head.

'He says he seen your face on wanted posters. Could kill you for reward, but if you against Oblanga, you our friends,' the translator said.

It took a few moments for Leon to grasp what had occurred. 'You speak English, why didn't you say?'

The man shrugged. 'Never show cards to other player.'

'What's your name?' Leon asked.

'Jojo.'

Olatunde barked what sounded like an order. Jojo translated.

'Olatunde say you leave now. We guide you but careful police not follow.'

Leon gave a thumbs up and Olatunde turned and led the way, while his gang brought up the rear. Now faces were appearing from every aperture in the ramshackle structures to view the procession. Turning left and right with bewildering frequency, they finally found themselves at the edge of the labyrinth. Jojo patted them on the back, Olatunde shook their hands and, in a second, their escort disappeared back into the maze. Leon mopped his forehead with his forearm.

'Phew! I wouldn't want to go through that again.'

'Probably safer there than here.' Jeff pulled Leon back into a doorway as a rusting police car coughed bumpily by, hooting continually to force a passage through the crowds.

Once it had gone, Leon and Jeff scanned the road. They were opposite an unusual mosque, its front portico defined by arcades with pointed arches. The paired square towers flanking the triangular pediment of its façade reminded Leon more of Christian than Islamic architecture. A donkey with baskets crammed with fruit and vegetables hanging from either side of its back passed by, led by a small fat man with a pale brown complexion and wearing a straw hat. A moped, like an irate wasp, wove its way between assorted animals, little boys groaning under the weight of panniers full of peanuts, and women balancing baskets on their heads with an easy grace.

'All looks pretty normal,' Leon remarked.

'No such thing in Mutabe,' Jeff replied.

A penetrating siren fractured Leon's composure. Another police car was struggling, despite its urgent wailing and its flashing lights, to thread its way through milling people. Leon and Jeff stepped back into the shadows of a merchant's hut while it crawled past. Mr Bankole was on the back seat next to a uniformed officer.

'It's Mr B! They've captured him!' Leon stepped forward, then stopped.

'Let him go,' Jeff said. 'He deserves to die.'

'Maybe, but he's my only ticket out of here.' Drawing a deep breath, Leon plucked the pistol from Jeff's belt and launched himself towards the vehicle, which was now hemmed in by a herd of cattle. Throwing open the front door, he pointed his shaking gun at the driver's temple. 'Stop! Turn off the engine!' He mimed a turning motion with his other hand. While the driver complied, his surprised colleague in the back was knocked senseless by a swift double-uppercut from the handcuffed Mr B.

Leon, now miming the removal of handcuffs, yelled, 'Give me the key.'

The driver stared at him blankly. Leon pointed at Mr B's wrists.

'The key!'

Mr B, his voice low and steady, said something and the driver slipped his hand into his pocket and held it out. Mr B took it and, fumbling with his handcuffs, released himself. Having deprived the policemen of their pistols, he forced the driver to get out and take his uniform off.

Leon looked around, anxious in case the teeming crowd around them intervened. No one met his eye, and only a few cast furtive glances at the disrobing policeman before averting their gazes.

The other officer was coming round. Mr B seized him by the shoulders and turfed him out onto the pavement, where he lay groaning. Having squeezed into the too small uniform, Mr B pushed the fully conscious policeman away and took over the driver's seat.

The policeman hauled his recovering colleague, who was now rubbing his chin gently and wincing, to his feet and they stood watching.

All around them a mass of people continued to swirl, seemingly oblivious to what was happening.

'It pays not to look when the police are involved,' Jeff said, reading Leon's thoughts.

'Get in,' Mr B screamed. Leon slid in beside him and Jeff took the back seat. Jeff waved a pistol through the car's window at the two forlorn policemen, one wearing only underpants and socks, and shouted something in Mutabese. They turned quickly and melted into the crowd.

'Won't they phone in and report us?' Leon asked.

Mr B navigated the police car into the slowly moving traffic. 'Not without the car radio. Anyway, an unarmed policeman has a life expectancy of about five minutes in these parts. If they don't want to find themselves hanging from a tree, the other will shed his uniform and they'll jog home.'

'Let's go back and drop them off somewhere safer.'

'No.' Mr B rolled his eyes as he overtook a bicycle in the thinning traffic and narrowly avoided several donkeys and an oncoming bullock cart. 'Now we've got a police car we can blag our way through security at the Interior Ministry. With these guns we can get some answers to who's been acting against us.'

'You mean shoot our way in?' Leon's voice quavered. Apart from once taking a few pot shots at the local fair to win Clive a fluffy pink hippo, he'd never used a gun.

'If necessary,' Mr B growled, frowning with concentration. He'd narrowly avoided a collision with a rusting milk lorry and a motorbike with a sidecar piled high with green mangoes.

'Couldn't we talk our way in?' Leon asked.

Swerving to avoid a one-legged beggar in a stained grey loincloth, Mr B laughed through gritted teeth. 'Our only advantage is surprise. They won't be expecting us, and certainly not in a police car.'

They'd been driving for several minutes when Leon remembered he hadn't introduced Jeff, who had been staring intently at the back of Mr B's neck.

'Oh, this is Jeff, by the way, Mr B. Jeff this is Mr Bankole.'

'We know each other.' Jeff's expression was grim. 'He had me sentenced to twelve months for an article in the *Record*. If my editor hadn't got me out after six, I wouldn't be here now.'

Mr B angled a glance in his rear-view mirror at Jeff. 'Yes, now I remember you and your invented stories about ministerial corruption.'

'Invented! I was punished for exposing the truth.'

'I hope it taught you a lesson.'

'It did. Not to trust you. By the way, there's a pistol at the back of your head. As soon as you stop this car, I'll blow your brains out.'

Mr B's hands gripped the wheel even more tightly, but his features remained composed and his voice level. 'You're alive, aren't you?'

'My wife and son aren't,' Jeff replied, his body taut with tension. 'While I was in prison, they lost their home, starved and died.'

Leon stifled a gasp; he had to overcome his revulsion and stop Jeff killing Mr B. He turned to face him.

'Jeff, that's terrible. I'm so sorry. You must tell me all about them. But listen. We've got to stick together, it's our only hope. Besides, he probably didn't know what was happening to your family and regrets the way it turned out. You do, don't you, Mr B?'

'Of course,' Mr B said with an exaggerated emphasis not even Leon could believe.

'Don't be so naïve, Leon,' Jeff said. 'His informers tell him everything.'

A sharp exchange in Mutabese followed, during which the car swerved, grazed the back of a bullock cart and nearly took out a row of men carrying beer crates on their heads. Silence reigned for a few minutes. Then another shouting match broke out before both participants fell quiet again. Mr B, swinging the steering wheel like a dodgem car driver, said something which sounded more conciliatory. Jeff paused for some seconds before replying.

'Have you resolved your differences?' Leon asked.

'I've agreed to kill him only after we've broken into the Interior Ministry,' Jeff said. 'There's too much in there I'd like to see and maybe destroy.'

'How do you know he won't kill you first?'

'He doesn't,' Mr B interposed.

Jeff grimaced. 'That's a risk I have to take. In the meantime, three of us stand a better chance than two, and he knows his way round. After all, he was Minister of the Interior not so long ago.' Jeff pushed his pistol into Mr B's thick neck muscle. 'What happened? Were you too corrupt even for them?'

'I was promoted,' Mr B said sullenly.

A thin spray of saliva accompanied Jeff's caustic

laugh. 'Promoted? Since when was Minister for Culture and the Arts senior to Minister of the Interior? Even then someone was out to get you. I hope no one kills you before I can.'

The car, now on a broad tree-lined avenue, slowed and swung right towards a towering set of wrought-iron gates painted a gleaming blue-black. On either side stood a couple of sentries. An armed personnel carrier was in the courtyard behind them. Six or seven soldiers squatted on their haunches in its shade.

'We're here,' Bankole said. 'You point your gun at Leon. Make sure they see it. I'll tell them we've got a prisoner for interrogation.'

'Won't they recognise you?' Leon asked.

'Unlikely. Mami Wata could drive in without being stopped.'

'Who's Mami Wata?' Leon whispered to Jeff.

'The water spirit. She has large and powerful snakes wrapped around her neck.'

As soon as Mr B rolled down his window and spoke, the gates swung open. They drove in, rounded the armoured personnel carrier and cut across the courtyard into a narrow road where they pulled up outside a wooden doorway reinforced with metal bars. The guard sitting beside it, a faded blue baseball cap pulled down over his eyes, his AK 47 resting between his knees, acknowledged their arrival with a limp wave.

'Traitor's Gate we call it,' Mr B said. 'We got the

idea from the British. Now get out. You.' He nodded at Jeff. 'Keep the prisoner covered. I'll go ahead.' He rapped on the door. The guard didn't look up. A couple of bright green, red-headed lovebirds in an adjacent tree squawked irritably. An aeroplane roared overhead laying a snowy vapour trail in the cerulean sky. The door remained closed. Mr B, yelling in Mutabese, banged harder. Still no response.

'Hey you!' Mr B kicked the thigh of the dozing sentry, who gripped his gun and pointed it unsteadily. Brushing it aside, Mr B seized him by the collar, dragged him to his feet and rammed him up against the wall. He held him so he dangled above the ground, his face no more than an inch away from Mr B's scowling features.

'Don't hurt him,' Leon said.

'You Yankees?' The sentry asked. 'What you want?'

Mr B tightened his grip and spoke slowly, this time in English.

'If you value your family's lives, not to mention your own, you'll let us in now.'

'No key, boss,' the man croaked.

'If you don't want those to be your last words, tell me where I can get one.' Mr B pressed on the soldier's throat so hard the terrified man's eyes bulged.

'Not know.'

'Why doesn't anyone answer the door?'

'Please no hurt, boss.'

Mr B let him drop and administered a sharp kick,

this time to the testicles. The sentry doubled over, his hands clasping his crotch, his forehead hitting the ground. Sensing that Mr B was aiming another, this time at the man's head, Leon pushed in front of him.

'Enough! This is getting us nowhere.' He reached down and shook the soldier's shoulder gently. 'Tell me my friend, why does no one come? Give us an honest answer and nothing will happen to you or your family.'

The soldier's mouth hung open, perhaps in surprise that a prisoner should be making such promises.

'We catch dealer. They sky-high now.' The soldier giggled. 'Me too, little spliff.'

'All of them?' Jeff asked. The sentry nodded.

Leon looked at his companions. 'Let's force our way in!'

Despite the door's formidable appearance, the lock was weak and gave way after a couple of hard kicks, swinging open to reveal a corridor and three supine bodies. As they tiptoed along, poking their heads into the many adjacent rooms, there were more somnolent figures, in a variety of poses: slumped at tables, sprawled on the floor, curled around toilet bowls. Save for the rise and fall of their chests, none stirred.

'This way.' Mr B led them to a staircase. He jerked his head upwards. 'The Director of Homeland Security's office is up here.' He bounded up the stairs, taking them three at a time, strode past a deserted workstation and burst through a door displaying a sign saying: *No admittance without prior appointment*. The office was empty. Before Leon and Jeff had time to catch their breath, Mr B was rifling through the filing cabinets and throwing selected contents onto the floor.

'What are we looking for?' Leon asked, already ankle deep in paper.

'I'll know when I see it,' Mr B said without slowing down.

Jeff glanced at the Apple gleaming in the middle of the desk. 'It'll probably be on his computer. Hold on. It's on sleep.' He leant over and tapped a couple of keys. 'Incredible! It's not even locked. And this is the Director of Homeland Security's office!' Within seconds he was scanning the computer's files.

Mr B held a beige manila file aloft. 'Got it!'

'What is it?' Leon said as he and Jeff crowded round.

'The so-called Watch List containing the names of the top threats to national security. Their removal is the Interior Department's priority.' He flicked through the list and, with what sounded more pride than hurt, said, 'And I'm number 1,' before scanning the dense paragraphs that followed his name. 'Lies,' he said when he'd finished. His eyes travelled down the page and onto several successive pages. He turned to Leon with a malicious grin. 'And you're right down at the bottom. In my day, you wouldn't even have made the list.'

Leon, on reading the scanty details against his name, was stung by the commentary: *'he is a threat only because of what he represents (the Onagaku legacy). A tiresome nuisance, he must be neutralised as a matter of good housekeeping rather than risk management.'*

'I'll give them tiresome nuisance,' he muttered under his breath. He tapped Mr B, who was engrossed in another file. 'What else have you found? Surely, we didn't break in here just to find out they want to kill us?'

'This file tells me Mr D, the treacherous bastard, is behind all of this, and the person he's using to front his operations is Donald. It also claims you are a low-level British agent, recruited to infiltrate my office and turn me, which you achieved through payment of twenty thousand dollars. As if I could be bought for such a trifling sum.'

'If I'm a British agent, how come you tracked me down and brought me to Mutabe?'

'This really is poor quality counter-espionage work. During my time, when we stitched someone up, we made a proper job of it. A waterproof story, photographic evidence, testimony from reliable sources. Why, I could do a much better job of making me look guilty than this amateurish drivel.' Mr B threw the file on the floor. 'Nothing but baseless assertions and unconfirmed rumours. When I'm back in charge I'll sack them all for incompetence.'

'What else is in there?' Leon asked, keen to deflect Mr B.

'Mr D is in cahoots with Mr C. They must have reneged on our arrangement. When they unseat Oblanga, they'll only share power two ways. That is, if one doesn't kill the other first.' He scrabbled together the papers which had spread around his feet, stuffed them back into the folder and tucked it under his arm. 'With this evidence, I can reveal their treachery to Oblanga. That'll leave me in pole position.'

Leon stared at him. 'You're like a bunch of kids. This is just a game to you. Meanwhile out there,' he nodded at the open window through which an assortment of disagreeable smells was wafting, 'people are living in squalor, barely able to subsist from one day to the next.'

Jeff clapped. 'Well said. You're all crooks.'

Mr B drew himself to his full height, dwarfing Leon. 'This is no game. And if you think British politicians are any better, you're deluded. They're as corrupt, only more subtle. Your Government is bankrolled by Russians. The Kremlin flooded social media with targeted disinformation to swing the last election. It planted a Russian agent as your Prime Minister's chief adviser and has managed to get several of his fellow agents appointed to strategic positions at Number 10. And those are just the egregious cases. They've wormed their way into the British establishment at every level and in every sphere: the media, business, sport.'

'I don't believe you,' Leon said. 'MI5 or someone would have vetted those government appointments.'

'It's a fact. Our intelligence services have verified it.'

Leon laughed. 'Those would be the same intelligence services that say I'm a British agent and turned you for only twenty grand, would it? Look, I accept that the the UK Government has many faults, but I don't believe it's been infiltrated, and I certainly don't accept that it's corrupt.'

Mr B raised his eyebrows. 'No? I could show you the deals they did when granting Mutabe independence, lining their own pockets for decades at our expense. And we were so grateful to be given our freedom, which was rightfully ours anyway, we accepted everything with an obsequious bow.'

'I don't know anything about that,' Leon replied, trying hard to dissociate himself from the guilt welling up in him because of his acquired Britishness, 'but, anyway, it's all in the past. You have to look forward.'

'The past?' Mr B exclaimed. 'They're still at it, with their favoured firms plundering our natural resources through bribery and extortion, and concealing the profits, worth several multiples of the Overseas Aid we receive, in tax shelters sponsored by the British Government.'

'I only have your word for that.'

'You live in fantasy land, Leon. Join the real world. Everyone is out to screw each other, but the British have made an art form of it. Worse still, they pretend to be respectable, with their all bankers, lawyers and accountants covering their tracks and laundering the proceeds.'

He barged past Leon, sending him reeling, and headed for the door, adding over his shoulder, 'Are you coming?'

Jeff appeared reluctant. 'I think we could do more damage by sending a few emails from here. This computer is linked to the secure state email system. Anything I send would come out under the signature of the Director of Homeland Security.'

Mr B stopped dead, turning slowly before re-tracing his steps. 'Though I hate to admit it, you're right.' He seated himself at the desktop. His typing, executed laboriously with two fingers, used local language, though Leon could tell from Jeff's chuckle that Mr B had composed something clever.

'Tell me,' he said.

'He's given orders for Donald's immediate arrest and interrogation, using all available means,' Jeff replied. 'The fellow's in for a bit of a shock.'

'Will they do it?' Leon asked. 'Isn't Donald too powerful?'

'The Director of Homeland Security has the President's full delegated authority on security matters,' Jeff explained.

'I've forbidden all contact between Donald and any other person,' Mr B said. 'If they take him unawares and sweep him off to solitary confinement, with luck none of his sponsors will find out for a couple of days. But they'll be unsettled by his disappearance, and when they do discover what's happened, they'll fear Oblanga is onto them.'

'What will happen then?' To Leon, it seemed a game in which only he didn't know the rules.

'I will already have alerted Oblanga to their treachery. Their choice will be to strike immediately, well before they're ready, or to flee and live off their Swiss bank accounts.'

'What will happen to Donald?'

Mr B laughed. 'He'll be in a bit of a mess. His confession should confirm Oblanga's worst fears.'

'And then?'

'What's left of him will be disposed of.'

Leon shuddered. Though he hadn't taken to Donald, the thought of his being tortured for several days and then killed made the hairs on the back of his neck stand up. 'Can't we do this without bloodshed?'

'Too late,' Mr B replied. 'I've sent the email. Now I've got to get to Oblanga. Come on.'

Chapter 16

Mr B waved and grinned as he drove them out past the guards. 'Security here is abysmal. I'll have this lot in the desert eating cockroach and scorpion kebabs for the rest of their lives.'

'Don't you want your best troops fighting the FMF?' Leon asked.

'Of course not. The last thing we want is to defeat them. Their supposed threat keeps the rest of the population compliant.'

'You're not serious?'

Mr B's lips twisted into a sneer. 'If we'd wanted to, we could have eliminated them years ago.'

'But they nearly killed you.'

Mr B, frowning, didn't reply.

Leon recalled the rumours he'd heard from Primrose soon after meeting her. 'The Government isn't sponsoring the FMF, is it?'

Mr B glowered. 'Where did you hear nonsense like that?'

'It's an old rumour,' Jeff said. 'That doesn't mean it's not true, of course.'

Mr B slammed his foot on the accelerator. 'Complete rubbish. Let's concentrate on the task in hand.'

'Where are we going?' Jeff asked.

'To the Presidential Palace, of course,' Mr B replied.

'But we've only just escaped from there,' Jeff said in a tremulous voice. 'They'll arrest us and shoot us.'

Mr B gave him a withering look. 'I don't intend to drive up to the front door.'

Leon sighed with relief. Mr B clearly had a plan. 'How will we get in then? And what will we do when we're inside?'

Mr B span the steering wheel sending the vehicle into a sharp skid on the sandy road to avoid a goatherd and a sizeable flock which had emerged without warning from a side track. 'You'll see when we get there.' The bleating and the goatherd's angry remonstrations faded as they sped away.

'This isn't the way to the Palace,' Jeff said.

Mr B's grip tightened on the steering wheel. 'You're getting on my nerves. I'd advise you to keep quiet.'

'You've forgotten,' Jeff replied, rubbing the barrel of his gun gently against the back of Mr B's head, 'that

I have a gun in my hand, and could blow your head off.'

Mr B snorted. 'You liberals are good at talking, not so good at acting. Go on. Blow my brains out and live with your conscience.'

Jeff's jaw tightened, and for a moment, Leon wondered whether he was going to. Instead he lowered his gun. 'Later.'

'Wimp.'

Jeff stroked his small moustache. 'We'll see.'

Threading their way through tight side streets and narrow alleyways, and then through a concertina of shanty town shacks, they finally came to open fields, and after a couple of miles, a sluggish brown river which stretched like a fat, slowly writhing earthworm towards the horizon. Mr B halted the car.

Leon looked around. With only a farm labourer's hovel a quarter of a mile away, they were in the middle of nowhere. 'Where the hell are we?'

Mr B cut the ignition. 'At the most convenient entrance to the Presidential Palace. It's something we learned from the Brits. Their old castles often had a secret water entrance.'

He jumped down the riverbank so that he was standing on a small beach of grey sand and started rooting about among the luxuriant plants. 'Got it!' he exclaimed, his hand around an anonymous metal box set into the rock. He pulled out an electronic pad and punched in some numbers. A door in the riverbank, entirely covered by dense vegetation, swung open to reveal a long, poorly lit tunnel heading back towards town.

Leon peered into the gloom. 'Will it take us all the way?'

Mr B stepped into the tunnel's mouth. 'Sure,' he said, his voice echoing. 'We plugged into a disused sewer system built by our colonial oppressors and refurbished it. Otherwise we could never have accomplished the task.'

Leon remembered how difficult it was to keep up with Mr B. 'It's a long way to the Palace from here.'

Mr B nodded. 'So, let's get walking.'

Jeff hesitated. 'How do you know it's not guarded?'

'I don't,' Mr B replied, 'though I do know that when I installed it, I didn't tell anyone.'

Jeff stared hard at Mr B. 'What about the workmen who refurbished it?'

Mr B met his stare without blinking. 'Oh, I took care of them.'

'You mean you eliminated them.'

Mr B looked away. 'Of course not. I made sure they got good jobs abroad.'

Jeff's face assumed an expression of exaggerated disbelief. 'And none of them ever wants to come home? How strange.'

★

Leon, conscious of fungal spores in the dank air, shielded his nose and mouth with his hand.

'The lighting runs off the city's electricity network,' Mr B said as he strode ahead. 'Even if there were a problem with the Palace's electrics and they checked all its circuits, they wouldn't discover the tunnel's existence.'

'What happens when everyone's power blacks out?' Leon asked. 'That's a daily occurrence here.'

Igmoring him, Mr B surged ahead along the slippery, moss-covered tiles, a heavy stack of manila folders under his arm.

Leon panted, waving to generate a draught in the otherwise airless conditions. 'How far is it?'

Mr B shifted the files from one arm to the other. 'Nearly two miles and we've done about two hundred yards. Save your breath, you'll need it.'

Their clothes were sodden and the sweat dripped off their faces as they scurried on in silence.

'Where do we come out?' Jeff asked at last, fingering his pistol.

'In a utility room in the Palace's basement housing the electricity circuits, aircon controls and telephone lines. It's immediately below Oblanga's private study, so we can climb up through a secret trap door.'

Jeff raised his eyebrows. 'What a coincidence!'

'I don't believe in coincidence, only in sound planning. When Oblanga's apartments were refurbished, I made sure it was constructed like that.'

Leon blew his nose, examined the contents of his handkerchief and shuddered. 'Won't his guards spot us?'

'They'll be outside his apartment. We'll be inside where only he and his family are allowed.'

Leon didn't bother to put his hand back over his nose. It was doubtful it had been reducing the number of spores he was inhaling, and it certainly hadn't done anything to reduce the smell of putrefying vegetation. 'His family?'

Mr B nodded. 'Four of his wives and his eldest son.'

'No other children?' Leon said.

'Plenty. Only he can't stand them, so they're all locked up in a nursery. He sees them every Friday at 5pm for fifteen minutes.'

'I didn't think he liked Mawusi either.' Jeff turned to Leon. 'That's his eldest son's name.'

Mr B grimaced. 'Can't stand him. A lazy, preening peacock who avoids responsibility. But he has some hold over his father. We'd all like to know what. I've had him tailed. He fritters away his time in sleazy bars and down-at-heel cafes with actors, writers and other degenerates. Unfortunately, we can't arrest him for that.'

Though Jeff bridled visibly, he said nothing.

Mr B looked at his watch. 'We're in luck. It's likely that the family will be out when we emerge. Mawusi's less predictable though he's rarely here.'

'What's the plan?' Leon asked, hoping his role in it would be minor.

'If Mawusi comes back first, we'll jump him. Then we'll wait. When Oblanga returns we'll confront him and explain C's and D's treachery. Once we've basked in his gratitude, I'll resume my duties and have them arrested for treason. There's enough in these files to condemn them without even having to fix the trial. I can't believe they were so sloppy. If you're going to carry out a coup, you must pay attention to detail.'

Chapter 17

They entered the President's private apartments. At the centre of Oblanga's study stood a mahogany desk. A blue Anglepoise lamp leant over a pile of papers like a crane over a building site. To one side were a leather sofa and two armchairs. The head of a snarling leopard was mounted on the closest wall, while on the one opposite hung two crossed elephant tusks above a photograph of ranks of young men wearing academic gowns entitled *Wadham College, 1962*. The third and fourth walls were covered with bookshelves.

Jeff scanned the shelves, pulled out a volume and leafed through it. 'Nice library.'

'He doesn't read much.' Mr B's sweep of the arm embraced both book-laden walls. 'All this is window dressing for press photos. Come with me. I'll show you around.'

Mr B led them first to the Presidential bedroom with its headboard crowned with ostrich feathers and its bed draped with a leopard-skin cover, then to the wives' bedrooms, all with the same green and gold fleurs-de-lis pattern wallpaper and curtains and finally, at the end of the suite, to another much smaller bedroom painted black, with a thick black pile carpet, matching curtains, a mirror on the ceiling and a six foot tall cardboard cut-out of a young bare-chested Cassius Clay in boxing shorts.

'The son's room.' Mr B spat the sentence and pulled the door to. 'Wonder where the wastrel is now. Let's go back to Oblanga's study. They should be back shortly. We can take up our positions and wait for him there.'

They were filing into the study when they heard women's chattering and laughing voices.

Mr B motioned for them to crouch behind the sofa. 'The wives. They'll shut up when he arrives.'

The cheerful hubbub lasted a quarter of an hour. Then an eerie silence fell. Leon, stretched out a stiff leg and emitted a low sigh. Mr B clamped his hand over Leon's mouth.

'Sssh!'

Although it seemed like an hour, it was less than ten minutes before the door was thrown open and Oblanga stalked in, his head hung low and his hands clasped in front of his chest as though in prayer. Mr B stood up.

'Mr President!'

Oblanga span round. 'How the hell…?' His expression changed from surprise to fear. 'You! What do you want?'

Mr B beckoned at Leon and Jeff to show themselves. Oblanga stepped back, his hand across his mouth.

'Those traitors too!'

'Don't be alarmed, sir, we're here to help you.' Mr B advanced on the President, who backed, winking uncontrollably, towards the window. Mr B held out the files.

'You're in great danger, sir.'

'From you,' Oblanga snapped. 'I thought you'd been dealt with.'

'The evidence is here. The same people who poisoned your mind against me are, at this moment, planning your death. If you'll permit me, I'll read a few extracts to corroborate my story.'

'And these two?' Oblanga's facial tic intensified as his gaze swept from Leon to Jeff and back again. 'That one's a British agent.'

Mr B spoke gently. 'All in good time, I will explain everything, Your Excellency. But first I need you to have C and D arrested before they launch their coup. They must be detained and interrogated immediately.'

With Mr B shadowing his every movement, Oblanga went to the desk and opened a drawer. He took out a large bottle half-full of bright red pills and crammed a handful into his mouth. When he'd succeeded in swallowing them, he slipped the bottle into his pocket.

'How do I know you're not the ones wanting to kill me?'

Mr B smiled reassuringly. 'Your Excellency, had we wished to kill you, you would be lying in a pool of blood and we would be on our way to the TV station to announce your death. It is therefore safe to infer that we mean you no harm. On the contrary, your well-being is our paramount concern. Now, I suggest I read a few of the more striking examples of heinous treachery to persuade you of the need for urgent action.'

Oblanga stepped to the window, opened it and looked out. A shrill cacophony of screeching filled the room as several green shapes wheeled and turned in the air outside.

'He's going to call the guards,' Jeff said quietly, his grip on his pistol tightening.

'Bloody lovebirds,' Oblanga muttered. 'Wake me up every morning.' He leant out of the window and shouted something at the guards below. A volley rang out, green feathers drifted past the widow and silence descended on the courtyard. He turned, winking rapidly.

'You don't have to read me anything. I know everyone is plotting against me. The only way I can survive is play you off against each other till each of you, in turn, makes a fatal mistake and can be eliminated. I appoint you Minister of the Interior. Now arrest C, D and Donald and interrogate them.

Once they crack, execute them.' He strolled up to Leon, stopping a couple of inches from his face. His yellowing eyes were criss-crossed with thin bloodworm veins, and his breath combined the stenches of sulphur and rotting fish. 'Now tell me about your accomplices. And make your explanation good, Bankole, or I'll have you arrested.'

Mr B brushed past him, plonked himself in the President's chair and planted his feet on the desk. 'I'm not sure you're in a position to have anyone here arrested,' he said, picking the dirt from behind his nails with an ivory letter opener. 'You see, unless C and D are taken into custody, there'll be a coup, and you'll be toppled. I'm the only one with sufficient authority to command the security forces to arrest them.'

'I'll do it myself,' Oblanga screamed, saliva dribbling down his chin, as he placed his hands on the desk to steady himself.

'You?' Mr B raised an eyebrow. 'Ten years ago, yes, definitely. Five years ago, maybe.' He sucked in his cheeks. 'Now? I'm not so sure. You haven't paid the armed forces on time, if at all, and they've had to scavenge to feed themselves. C and D, on the other hand, have worked hard to ingratiate themselves. They've bribed the generals with promises of top jobs in state corporations, they've been generous with handouts to the officers and turned a blind eye to the other ranks pillaging and raping during their excursions into our neighbours' territories. So, you see, if I were a betting man, I wouldn't risk money on them backing you. I, on the other hand, still command the forces' respect. They know I'm one of them by background, and that I've gone out of my way to look after them.'

Oblanga took the bottle of pills out of his pocket, poured several into his shaking hand and swallowed them.

Mr B rose slowly, pulled a tissue from a box on the desk, and brushed the chair where he'd been sitting.

'Excellency, please ...' He bowed graciously, sweeping his arm in the direction of the vacant seat.

Oblanga tottered forward and slumped down.

'Now let me explain my associates' true roles. Because of information fed to you by the deceitful C and D, you are under the impression they are spies. This is, of course, true. What is not true is that they are British agents. They are, in fact, mine. I recruited Onagaku here,' he indicated Leon with a slight wave of the hand, 'in Britain, brought him here and used him to penetrate both the PRF and the FMF. He wiped the Communist cell out, single-handedly, and, having been captured by the Muslims, managed, with my help to escape. He then infiltrated a rally organised by students, socialists and trade unionists, unseated its radical leaders to drain it of its power and supplanted them.'

Oblanga's body started shaking. 'But he told me I had to resign.'

'He was playing the part I asked him to play, Excellency. You know as well as I do that traitors are everywhere. Had he confided his true role to you, others would have heard, and he'd have been of no further use to me. He allowed himself to be thought guilty, secure in the knowledge I would extricate him.'

'Hmmmm.' Oblanga sat at the desk, his upper body now motionless, his feet beneath it pounding. 'It didn't look like an act to me.'

'You are merely complimenting him on his acting skill,' Mr B replied. 'Had he looked to you as though he was acting, others would doubtless have formed the same impression.'

'Why should I believe you?' Oblanga asked in a querulous voice, his arms and hands quivering.

Mr B's tone was emollient. 'Because, Excellency, you are a Mosa and I am a Binda. Our tribes are related. They come from villages only a few miles apart, whereas C and D are Ashangis and, as both our peoples know to their cost, Ashangis can never be trusted. Wasn't it, after all, the Ashangis who, all those centuries ago, grew fat by selling both of our tribes' forebears to the slave traders?'

Oblanga looked unconvinced.

Mr B pointed at the college photograph. 'Don't forget, Excellency, we're both Oxford men. C and D went to Cambridge.'

Oblanga's lips curled in distaste. 'You're right, we share a bond.'

'Then I'll give the order to arrest them.'

Mr B picked up a phone, punched in a number and, within seconds, was speaking rapidly in Mutabese. When he'd finished, he slammed the receiver back onto its cradle.

Oblanga looked at him sourly. 'Our peoples may be neighbours, but there's something about you I don't trust. I can see it in your eyes. You're like a hungry dog.'

Mr B's face radiated injured innocence. 'Excellency, you are very harsh. It's true I'm like a guard dog straining at the leash to hunt down malefactors on your behalf. Never though, have I been guilty of any act, nor even thought, injurious to your Government.'

'Hmmmm.' Oblanga wrung his hands.

'What more can I do to prove my loyalty?' Mr B asked. 'I've unearthed a plot, and at great personal risk, I've brought it to your attention.'

Oblanga reached into his desk drawer and produced a small bottle of blue pills. He took two out, placed them on the palm of his hand and then threw them into his mouth. He looked in turn at Leon and Jeff before his gaze came to rest on Mr B. 'You can go and investigate, but these two' – his bilious eyes scanned Leon and Jeff – 'must remain here as surety.'

Leon's mouth fell open. Jeff looked at him and sighed.

Mr B shrugged. 'Sure. No problem.'

'Be in no doubt,' Oblanga continued, 'if you act against me, they will suffer and then die.'

'You can't leave us here,' Leon cried. Memories of the cell they'd been in, of those terrifying torturers who were intent on changing the shape of his body, of the nauseating smells, flooded his mind. Mr B couldn't do it to him.

'You just watch him,' Jeff said.

'They must be treated well, though.' Mr B addressed Oblanga as though the other two were not present. 'They are not, after all, prisoners, but your guests.'

'So be it,' Oblanga said. 'I will accommodate them in the guests' wing, but they'll be under armed guard.'

'I'm sure they'll be comfortable enough.' Mr B turned to Leon and Jeff. 'Make the most of this unexpected holiday.' He saluted the President, walked backwards to the study door, saluted again, stepped through it and shut it behind him.

Oblanga picked up the phone, dialled and spoke into it. Then he sat motionless at his desk, apparently oblivious to his fidgeting visitors, until there was a knock. An officer in a crisp khaki uniform, his collars studded with gold stars, strolled in accompanied by two burly privates armed with machine-guns. Oblanga didn't look up.

The officer uttered something which sounded like a cross between an oath and a threat.

'We've got to go with him,' Jeff said. Leon inclined his head slightly, knowing he must allay Oblanga's fears to have any hope of surviving.

'We're at your service, Excellency, should you require us.' Leon bowed towards Oblanga, who continued to stare ahead as though scrutinising a patch on the opposite wall.

They left the room in single file, the officer leading, followed by Leon, Jeff and then the two guards. The route to their wing took many turns both to left and right along corridors which, near the Presidential apartments, were resplendent with fresh white wallpaper and gold leaf and, further away became increasingly musty and shabby. The overall upwards trajectory helped allay Leon's fears that they were heading back down to the dungeons. No one spoke, and Leon was pondering the circularity of life which had brought him back to the same place, albeit as a slightly higher category prisoner, when he caught a fleeting glimpse of a strangely familiar man flitting across the corridor ahead of them before disappearing. Leon blinked, unable to trust the evidence of his eyes. It couldn't have been, not here.

The procession continued for another five minutes until they arrived at a portico supported by two Corinthian style pillars. The officer halted, produced a key from his pocket and let them in. The door opened onto a spacious sitting room furnished with three leather sofas which had seen better days, a dining room with a dark mahogany table and eight chairs, three bedrooms, each fitted out with a king-sized double bed, and a bathroom with elaborate copper pipework feeding into taps that served a large circular tub. At the end of the corridor was a small kitchen reeking of fried fat.

'Maids bring food.' He pointed to his watch. 'Eight, one, seven.' He nodded towards the door. 'Guards'. He went to the window and looked down. 'Four floors. No jump.' He turned on his heel and, accompanied by the guards, left, shutting the door behind him. As the key clicked in the lock, Leon sank onto one of the sofas.

'Shit, what do we do now?'

Jeff put his finger to his lips, then cupped his ear with his hand. Leon stared around, expecting to see the tell-tale signs of listening devices, before remembering that, even in Mutabe, they would be undetectable without sophisticated anti-surveillance equipment. His mind went back to films where people went into the bathroom and ran the taps at full flow to mask their conversations. He motioned to Jeff, who accompanied him with a puzzled expression. Once inside, Leon shut the door and turned both taps on. A slow, brown trickle oozed out. When the bath had filled to about a quarter of an inch, amidst a loud clanking of the convoluted pipework, the flow dried up completely.

'I've always fancied trying one of those mud bath treatments you get in high class spas,' Leon said.

'You've probably used up today's water quota,' Jeff replied, leaving the room.

Chapter 18

They sat on the sofa. Above them was a stationary ceiling fan. Jeff eased himself up, went to the control switch on the wall and clicked it on. The fan made a faint whirring sound and, shedding some of its accumulated dust particles, started to rotate slowly, creating the faintest stir. Seconds later there was an acrid burning smell. By the time Jeff turned it off, a thin plume of black smoke was already collecting like a storm cloud.

'Perhaps if there's a fire...' Leon mumbled to himself, switching it on again. No more smoke emerged, no further smells were emitted and the fan stood resolutely still. Whatever it was that had caught fire had burnt out, leaving it useless.

They slumped back onto the sofa.

'Have you always lived in Mutabe?' Leon asked.

From the vigorous shaking of his hand, Leon gathered this was not a question Jeff wished to answer. He must think the place was bugged. He mopped his face and neck with a paper tissue from a box on the table and retreated to safer ground.

'Hot today,'

'Always is,' Jeff replied, his face glistening.

There was a knock on the door.

Jeff called out in Mutabese and the door opened to reveal two elderly maids, their white hair standing out against their ebony skins, each carrying a tray, which they deposited on the table. They lingered ostentatiously, presumably in the hope of a tip.

Leon smiled and said, 'Thank you,' in an exaggerated English accent. The maids looked hopefully from Leon to Jeff and back again, then, with their faces registering a mixture of contempt and disgust, left muttering to each other.

The removal of the stainless steel covers from the plates revealed thin, almost skeletal carcasses, roasted and then plastered with a glutinous yellow sauce, and piles of rice. Leon poked at the bony remains with his knife. 'Rabbit?'

Jeff laughed. 'We don't have them here. Rat more like. Fruit bat if we're lucky. Someone is making money charging the kitchen for quality produce and then substituting the worst kind of bushmeat.'

After a few moments' surgical dissection, Leon examined the small scraps of flesh it produced. He lifted a morsel to his lips, baulked and put it down again. Jeff, meanwhile, had devoured all his and nearly finished his rice. Leon tried again. The piece he forced between his reluctant lips didn't taste too bad, and the yellow sauce turned out to have an agreeable curry flavour in which cardamom predominated. He ate everything, lamenting only the absence of a toothpick.

When they finished, they pushed their trays away, put their feet on the table and drank some of the water from the flask left by the maids.

The rest of the afternoon dragged by. The dirty plates became magnets for a swarm of blue-bodied blowflies and were moved next to the door. Leon and Jeff stretched out on opposite sofas, waiting for supper to arrive.

'This is like being a lion in a zoo,' Leon said.

'Except most zoos don't threaten to shoot the wildlife.'

They lapsed into silence. This was broken by a rap on the door. Before they could respond, a tall man wearing a white tunic buttoned up to the neck, white trousers with a sharp crease, and a hat that looked like a white triangle with gold edging, entered carrying a silver tray on which were two tall cocktails, made up of striations of different colours. On the top level, which was purple, perched a small red and white umbrella, a glace cherry and a slice of lemon. Two straws protruded from each glass.

'Good evening, gentlemen,' the waiter said. 'His Excellency the President wishes you to enjoy some Mutabese hospitality. Your dinner will follow in approximately half an hour.'

They watched him withdraw, noting that he passed the fly-blown plates with barely a glance.

'They're trying to get us drunk so we incriminate ourselves,' Jeff whispered. 'I'm not touching mine.'

'Suits me to get pissed. What else is there to do?' Leon took a deep draught through his straw. He coughed and spluttered, his eyes watering. 'I think it's pure alcohol.'

'Exactly.'

'It's not so bad really.' Leon took another cautious sip. 'Once you get used to it. You ought to try it.'

'No thanks. You'll probably be blind by the morning.'

'Blind drunk, more like. I'd rather be drunk than sober and bored.'

By the time the two elderly maids arrived with supper, Leon was half-way through the second glass. The food was similar, the only difference being a browner sauce and a gingery flavour, though these subtleties were lost on Leon, whose vision was bleary and whose head had started to spin. Nevertheless, he tucked in, slurping noisily as brown streaks spread down his front.

'I'm going to bed now,' Jeff announced, 'and I'd suggest you do the same while you still can.'

Leon tilted the glass back and poured the rest of its contents down his throat. Then he slid slowly onto the floor where he sat propped up at an awkward angle against the sofa.

'I'm fine.' He articulated both words with great deliberation.

'We'll judge that tomorrow,' Jeff replied over his shoulder as he left the room.

The rest of the evening was a blur, though Leon had a dim and strangely pleasurable recollection of someone undressing him and helping him into bed.

★

The next morning, Leon found his mosquito net erected above his bed. He was in his boxers. When he moved his head to look around, the nausea that swept over him was so debilitating he didn't dare do it again. His mouth and throat were dry and cannons inside his skull pounded a twenty-one-gun salute on a continuous loop.

'Oh God, I wish I were dead,' he croaked.

The door opened, and Jeff strolled in carrying a tray. 'Thought you might like breakfast in bed.'

'Take it away.' Leon waved his arm feebly in Jeff's direction.

'It's good. This is a real western artery-clogger. Bacon and eggs, and lots of both.'

Leon put his hand over his mouth and shut his eyes, willing a renewed wave of nausea to pass.

'Mine was excellent. Of course, if you don't want yours…'

'Have it,' Leon groaned. 'Oh, by the way, thanks

for putting me to bed last night. I couldn't have made it on my own.'

Jeff frowned. 'I didn't. You must have imagined it.'

Leon's head span and he shut his eyes. 'I know I was drunk, but I have a clear recollection of someone helping me.'

Jeff shrugged. 'Strong stuff you were drinking. Rots the brain.'

The day passed slowly as Leon drifted in and out of sleep, occasionally forcing down a sip of water. It wasn't until the room started to darken with the onset of evening that he began to feel human again and in need of some light sustenance. Rising gingerly, he looked around for his clothes and was surprised to find them folded neatly on a chair near the bed. That was when he stepped back, eyes wide at the sight of his elephant charm necklace lying in a tight circle on the top.

'How the bloody hell did that get there?' An image of a slender but muscular body formed in his brain. Rolly! It can't have been. If it was, how did he get in? Primrose had access everywhere. He experienced a sharp pang. Rolly couldn't be a prostitute too, could he? Or someone in the Palace's lover? If only he'd spoken to Rolly, held him. With his head throbbing and overwhelmed by helpless self-pity, he was brought to the verge of tears.

★

Wiping his face with toilet paper, he wandered into the sitting room where he found Jeff perched, cross-legged, on a pile of cushions on the floor, eyelids closed and hands held out as though in silent supplication. He coughed, and Jeff opened his eyes.

'Sorry, didn't mean to interrupt your meditation.'

'No problem. Been meditating all day.'

'Has someone been in these rooms?'

Jeff looked surprised by the question. 'Only the waiters. Oh, and a cleaning woman came in and waved a duster around. Why?'

'Are you sure?'

'Positive. Why?'

There was a knock at the door and the elegant waiter, attired as before, entered, carrying two tall multi-coloured glasses, like those of the previous evening.

'Gentlemen, with the President's compliments. Enjoy.' He bowed as he placed the drinks carefully on the table and withdrew. As soon as he'd gone, Jeff took them to the bathroom, where he poured them into the toilet.

'That should see off a few germs,' he said on his return.

Dinner arrived exactly half an hour later. It looked similar to the previous night's, except the sauce had a reddish hue and was spicy. Leon ate in silence, his stomach convulsing at the first few mouthfuls and then slowly acquiescing.

Jeff took a couple of mouthfuls, threw down his cutlery and raced to the toilet. When he returned, his face was crumpled.

'What's the matter?' Leon asked.

'Lunch. It must have made me ill. I'm going to bed.'

Leon was thankful he'd missed it, though he was concerned about his companion. 'Anything I can do?'

Jeff, shaking his head, headed for his bedroom.

After ten minutes on his own, Leon was bored. He did a tour of the room, scrutinising every piece of furniture, fixture and fitting in detail. He didn't know what he was searching for but hoped he might stumble across something. Then he sat down and picked up the copy of the *Mutabe Times* that had been delivered earlier. The front page featured a picture of a delirious Bishop Mbutu rejoicing in the execution of seven army officers for homosexuality. The accompanying article spoke of the officers' refusal to undergo curative treatment for what was described as their abominable illness. Leon threw the paper aside in disgust.

There was another knock at the door and he got ready to hand their plates to the returning waitresses. Instead a large, well-endowed woman in a low-cut dress entered, smiling.

'Hello Mr Lion.'

'Primrose!' Leon shook his head. 'What are you doing here?'

'The President ask me to keep you company, Mr Lion. Very kind man.' She took Leon by the hand and stepped towards his bedroom. Once there, she whispered in Leon's ear, 'Take clothes off. Get in bed. I lie on top. We pretend.'

Leon followed instructions and soon Primrose was writhing and moaning on top of him as Leon simulated thrusting motions. Then she screamed ecstatically, and he puckered his face in blissful agony. It occurred to Leon while all this was going on, it was conceivable Primrose had somehow found and returned the necklace, and it hadn't been Rolly after all.

'Thank you for putting me to bed last night,' Leon whispered as they lay beside each other, panting.

'Not me honey. Must be other friend.'

'Are—'

Primrose placed a finger on his lips. 'Camera, microphones. I told to ask questions. Ready?'

Leon nodded.

'You like James Bond; all spies sexy like you?' she said loudly. 'You tell me. I keep secret.'

'I don't know, but I can tell you that I'm definitely the sexiest unemployed refrigeration engineer in this palace.'

Primrose guffawed. 'But you a spy, yes? Tell me. It very sexy.'

'Fraid not.'

'Who your friend, Jeff? He a spy?'

'He says he's a journalist. I only met him recently.'

'Come on, tell me. Then we do something special, something you never do before.'

'What's that?'

'Called Mutabese grip. Sound nice, eh? Tell me 'bout friends first. Anyone talk 'bout revolution?'

'Only this man called Donald. He wanted me to organise riots against the President. Of course, I refused.'

'And Mr Bankole?'

Leon stifled his surprise that he should be asked about Mr B. He'd always assumed Primrose to be in his pay. But as he had placed his trust in her to see him safely through this interrogation, he played along, shaking his head vigorously. 'No, he wants to protect the President. He thinks others are out to launch a coup and he's trying to stop them.'

'Honey, you earn grip.' Primrose disappeared under the sheet. Shortly after, Leon, thrashing about in apparent ecstasy, exclaimed, 'Yes, yes, yes!' and fell back in fake exhaustion and real sweat on the pillow. Primrose rose, leant over him and whispered, 'Flowerpot, sitting room.' She kissed him on the cheek and went into the bathroom. From there she left the apartment, the front door closing silently behind her.

Chapter 19

Leon waited an hour before pausing in front of the empty flowerpot as though lost in thought and running his hand inside it. His fingers bumped against a folded piece of paper, which he secreted in his palm and took to the toilet to read.

Be ready midnight. Gards sleep. Down 2 flite of stairs in front. Someone meet you. No bring Jeff.

Leon reread the unsigned note three times, tore it into small pieces and flushed it away, wishing his guilt at excluding Jeff was as easy to dispose of. Should he bring him anyway? After dithering for a while, he decided to follow orders. Disobeying might frighten off the person meeting him.

As soon as the grandfather clock chimed twelve, Leon, listening carefully for any sounds, emerged from his room, tiptoed to the apartment's main door and pushed it open. Two guards lay on their backs, their mouths open, snoring. He stepped quietly over them, although he suspected he could have stamped in hobnailed boots. The person who had arranged his escape had done a thorough job. The stairs were in complete darkness, so he had to feel his way until he'd descended two flights. Then he waited. And waited. Thoughts that he had been set up pressed on him. Was this an elaborate ruse to justify having him executed? He whistled softly. Perhaps someone else was there but had not heard him arrive. No response. He waited another ten minutes, terrified the guards would wake up and follow him. He was on the point of creeping back upstairs when he heard the soft click of a door and was dazzled by a shaft of light which disappeared as quickly as it had appeared. Then he heard the unmistakable sound of another human's breath in the absolute darkness.

'Primrose?' he whispered. A hand touched his side. He reached out and gripped it. It was firm and strong, though soft and smooth, unlike Primrose's gnarled palms.

'Who's there?'

'Sssssh!'

The hand pulled him down another flight of stairs and then held him back. He was handcuffed and a bag was slipped over his head and secured with a rope. Another click indicated the opening of a door. He stumbled and several pairs of hands steadied him. His repeated questions as to who his captors were and where they were taking him remained unanswered.

The convoluted journey seemed interminable in the stultifying blackness of the hood. He soon lost count of the number of steps, the direction in which they turned and the ascents and descents, and plodded obediently where directed by nudges and pushes. The streams of sweat trickling down his face and neck were like bloated slugs slithering across his skin, and his itching cheeks and chin constantly demanded scratching.

Another door opened, and he felt the cool relief of night air on his body. The hands on his back propelled him forward relentlessly until he was brought sharply to a stop. He heard the creaking hinges of a car door. Oh no, not this again, he thought. Who is it this time? PRF, FMF or some other disaffected initialism? His nagging suspicions about Primrose must have been correct.

Hands on his legs indicated he must step up. As he did so, he was guided into a sitting position next to someone. Another bulky person, smelling of cigarettes, got in and pressed against him. They drove for some time, the vehicle bumping up and down over numerous potholes.

Being blindfolded and bundled from one place to another is clearly a favoured mode of transport in this country, Leon thought, experiencing a sinking sense of deja-vu. He listened hard. All he could hear were the rumble of the tired diesel engine and a few noises from places or people they passed: the odd burst of shouting, the whine of a two-stroke motorcycle engine and, occasionally, the braying of a donkey.

Finally, they stopped. Leon was manhandled out of the vehicle and into a building, up some steps and, from the sound of a door opening and closing, into a room. From the freeze-drying sensation on his skin, he must be somewhere fiercely air-conditioned.

'Release him,' a familiar voice said.

'Oh, it's you,' Leon replied before they'd taken the hood off. Mr B, now resplendent in a general's khaki uniform, his epaulettes, collars and cuffs emblazoned with golden stars and crossed swords, was sitting in a high back rattan chair behind a marble topped wrought-iron table. A guard stood to attention at the door of the elegant cream coloured room. 'Why this ridiculous pantomime? You've obviously been reinstated. Why couldn't you just order my release?'

Mr B growled at the sentry, who saluted and left the room. He stood up slowly and walked towards Leon.

'In two hours, Mr C and Mr D will launch a coup. After some fierce fighting outside the Presidential Palace, it will fail. It will fail because I will intervene. The attempt will do three things; weaken the President, sign the death warrants of C and D, and demonstrate that Oblanga is dependent on me for his future. For obvious reasons, I didn't want to be seen in the environs before the putsch. You should thank me that you won't be in that particular bloodbath.'

'What about Jeff? He's still there.'

'He's a traitor.'

'He's a nationalist. He told me. He wants what's best for Mutabe.'

'Your naivety is boundless. He's in the pay of the Chinese. If the rebels take care of him, it will save us the trouble.' Mr B paused. 'How did Oblanga treat you? Not too badly, I hope.'

Leon, clinging to his belief in Jeff's integrity, only partly suppressed a pang of guilt. He should have woken him and given him the chance to escape.

'Well?' Mr B asked.

With considerable effort, Leon turned his mind to Mr B's question. 'The main problem was boredom. Even the meat was the same every day, only in a different coloured sauce.'

'But appetising?'

'You got used to it.'

Mr B laughed. 'I'm pleased you overcame your British squeamishness sufficiently to feast on roast kitten.'

'Kitten!' Leon put his hand to his mouth.

'Mawusi, the President's son, has a cat which gave birth to ten kittens. Oblanga decided you should benefit from her promiscuity.'

An urgent rap on the door presaged the entrance of a squat, barrel-chested soldier in camouflage fatigues and a beret set at a rakish angle. Having saluted, he rattled away in Mutabese, his voice rising in pitch as he progressed from animated hand gestures to hysterical arm windmilling.

It was obvious the news was not good. After a pause, like the lull before a storm, a howl of anger burst from Mr B's lips, forcing the soldier to bend forward as he braced his substantial frame against it.

'What's happened?' Leon asked, but Mr B was already on the phone, shouting orders.

More soldiers scurried in, saluted and were despatched with a few words. The phone rang again, Mr B answered it, listened for a second or two, screamed into it and slammed the receiver back on its cradle.

A willowy young man with a small moustache raced in.

'Akello!' Mr B said. 'Get the lorries loaded and tell the drivers to stand by to leave.'

Akello saluted and ran out of the room.

An explosion, loud enough to rattle the window frame but not close enough to shatter the glass, made Leon jump. It was followed by the pop-pop of automatic weapons, at first distant, then closer. Leon grasped Mr B's muscular shoulder.

'What the bloody hell's happening?'

Mr B stared at him blankly, as though surprised to find him still there. Then he collected himself. 'The coup started early. We didn't have time to alert the Presidential Guard and the rebels have seized the Palace. They may even have Oblanga.'

'You can still save him, can't you?'

'Not so easy. I was counting on the Presidential Guard for support. They won't do anything if Oblanga is being held. Without them we're seriously outnumbered. In addition, the rebels now hold the arsenal and the strategic defensive positions. If they lean on Oblanga, or do a deal, he may order the army to support them.'

Leon watched Mr B's face contort with hatred. 'I've been betrayed. Someone must have tipped them off.'

Akello entered at the double, stood to attention and saluted. 'Everything loaded and ready to go, sir.'

Mr B returned the salute, then lapsed into a silence broken only by a few subterranean mutterings. He was counting on the fingers of his hand.

'It's the Russians,' he announced after a while. 'Only they had something to gain from this. The Americans and the British would have preferred me, the Chinese would have remained neutral until they knew who was winning and the French were backing the status quo. I've long suspected that Messrs C and D were on Russia's payroll. Bastards.'

'What are you going to do?'

Mr B produced a pistol from a holster and started to examine it. 'We either advance, fight it out and possibly lose, or we retreat to fight another day.'

'Retreating and regrouping would be the more sensible, wouldn't it?' Leon's voice was barely audible above the sound of gunfire. 'When do we leave?'

Mr B stroked his chin. 'The odds are against us, but this may be the best chance we get. If we retreat, half my troops will change sides.'

Leon's bowels contracted. He would have argued for discretion, had he not been certain his counsel would be disregarded. 'Those guns sound awfully close. Haven't we left it too late?'

Mr B snatched the telephone, punched in a number and yelled into the receiver.

Akello ran into the room.

'Initiate Operation Sewer Rat!' Mr B shouted.

'Yes sir!' Akello saluted and left. The sound of gunfire intensified, then died away.

'Come on!' Mr B bounded into an adjacent room full of soldiers in battledress. He pushed his way through the seething mass of helmeted bodies with Leon in his wake until they reached the front door. It was only when they stepped onto the neat gravel path which bisected two rectangles of immaculately trimmed grass that Leon realised he was in the garden of a colonial-style half-timbered bungalow in an estate of similar buildings. Several soldiers lay on their bellies throughout the grounds, their weapons trained on the darkness.

'Where are we?'

Mr B's attention was devoted to scanning the neighbourhood. Shaking him by the sleeve, Leon repeated his question.

'St Lawrence. Expat sub-division, recently evacuated.'

Mr B's gaze swept across the surrounding area. 'We're going to march on the Palace. We may take them by surprise if we strike quickly.' He whistled, and Akello materialised by his side, a satellite phone in his hand. Mr B spoke into it. As though by magic, columns of troops fully equipped for battle appeared from each of the adjacent bungalows.

Mr B stuck out his chest as he took in the scene. 'I love this moment. The adrenaline flowing, the mind at its sharpest, the smell of greased guns.'

Leon shuddered. He hated it. His hands shaking, his legs trembling and his head swimming. 'Why can't you guys get together and negotiate? Fighting is barbaric.'

Mr B's lip curled. 'Only cowards and women negotiate. This is the manly way, the warrior's way.'

Leon restrained himself from shaking his finger in Mr B's face. 'No! What you show by negotiating is that you care about people's lives, about their safety, that you hate the misery war inflicts. We must learn to resolve our differences without bloodshed.'

A screaming sound ripped through the air. Leon was thrown to the ground by Mr B's powerful arms. An ear-bruising explosion followed, which hurled earth all over them. Mr B sat up and brushed the dirt off his uniform.

'Negotiate with that!'

Leon dislodged the soil from his hair. 'If I could talk to the person who fired it, I would.'

'You may well have your chance.' Mr B pointed. Flashes and bangs were getting closer and every so often they glimpsed figures darting from bungalow to bungalow. The prostrate soldiers nearby picked themselves up and surged towards these residences, periodically pausing to fire.

'Come on, let's get going,' Mr B shouted, bounding across the lawn and launching himself into a parked jeep. Leon followed, panting heavily.

'But how can we attack the rebels in the Presidential Palace if we're under siege here?'

Mr B gunned the jeep down the neat white line of the road. Well-clipped bushes stood on either side, broken every so often by fine-leafed trees whose bark shone silver in the headlights. 'War is 90% confusion. No one knows what the enemy, their own people, anyone, least of all themselves, are doing. He who seizes the initiative wins. My troops here will take care of that feeble assault. More are stationed at the crossroads. The two groups will converge at the Palace and rid Mutabe of these rebels.'

'And replace them with yourself?'

Mr B's look was one of concentrated contempt. 'As your Mr Darwin said, survival of the fittest. I'm the best person to govern so it's in the national interest I take control.'

'Says who?'

Before Mr B could answer there was a loud bang. The jeep careered off the road, through some bushes and plunged into a swimming pool, where it sank gently, a pool of oil, like blood, rising to the surface and coating the water. Mr B and Leon, dragged back by their clothes, laboured to swim to the side, where they clung to the rail, listening.

After a few minutes, Mr B nodded, and they hauled themselves, dripping, from the oily water. Their faces and their clothes were streaked with black liquid, which glistened in the glow from the ornamental lights dotted around.

'What do we do now?' Leon asked, removing first one shoe and then the other, and holding them up to drain.

'Walk,' Mr B snapped, squelching towards the road. Hearing the approach of a lorry they bobbed down behind thick bushes until Mr B identified it from its pennant as one of his. Then he jumped out, shouting and gesticulating. The lorry screeched to a halt. Mr B and Leon were pulled aboard into a cloud of rancid body odour and guided into the middle of the group by many helpful hands. Leon would have fallen to the vehicle's floor had the densely-packed, sweat-stained bodies not held him upright. All around were smiling faces, many scarred, though he didn't know whether from wounds or tribal markings. A large man with cracked front teeth and cesspit breath shouted something in his face, clapped him on the back and started intoning. The whole lorry swayed rhythmically as his chant, accompanied by his bouncing movements, caught on with the other soldiers. Then, with a graunch of the gears which made the whole vehicle shudder, the lorry lurched forward, spilling the half dozen or so who were nearest the back onto the road behind. A widespread cry went up and the driver stopped to collect those thrown off. Mr B despatched him on his way again with a blood curdling oath which Leon required no knowledge of local dialect to understand.

Within a few minutes, other lorries similarly packed with military personnel, fell in line with Leon's truck to form a lengthening convoy. As they neared the Presidential Palace, the soldiers in every vehicle started to chant and bob up and down again in what Leon assumed was a ritualistic war dance. Despite his best efforts to control himself, his adrenaline was flowing, drying his mouth and making his arms and legs twitch, and he was grateful for the support of the muscular, damp men all around him to keep him steady.

A round of gunfire brought the convoy to an abrupt halt. Its occupants leapt out, running in every direction while a few threw themselves down on the ground on their bellies, returning fire. Leon lay prostrate in the back of his now otherwise empty lorry, his hands over his ears and his eyes shut. Mr B, last seen hurling himself over the side with a deep-throated roar, had vanished into the black void, firing an assault rifle. The battle waged for a quarter of an hour, during which Leon counted five bullets passing close to him and leaving holes in the canvas cover.

A shrill whistle sounded, and Leon heard boots running away from him. He sat up and peeped out. Everyone had disappeared. He checked again. Apart from a few corpses littered around a lamppost, the area was clear.

He emerged quickly and, overriding his instinct for survival, headed for the sound of gunfire, hoping to find Mr B there. He had only gone fifty yards, scanning all around as he walked, when he was felled by a blow to the back of the head. He craned his neck painfully round, expecting to be confronted by the barrel of a gun. Instead, a tall man with a long bushy beard was staring down at him, a smile on his face. Olatunde! A couple of henchmen helped Leon to his feet.

'Sorry,' Jojo said. 'We thought you FMF. You lucky you alive.'

There was much shaking of hands and back slapping before the shanty town gang, saying they were on their way to attack the Palace, melted into the night. Still dizzy, Leon loped down the road away from the loudest gunfire. An explosion obliterated a car parked ahead and brought him to a dazed halt. Further on he could see soldiers sprinting, taking cover, and firing in what looked like an incomprehensible melee. He turned again and headed back towards the Presidential Palace.

When he arrived, the main gates were hanging open and the charred remains of a tank smouldered in the courtyard, wisps of smoke still rising from its turret. People were running everywhere, some in uniform, some in t-shirts and jeans. Most were carrying computers, printers, chairs, tables or anything else they could find.

Frantic screaming shredded the night air. In a dark, secluded corner of the courtyard, several soldiers were holding a naked girl up against a wall for one of their comrades to rape while others queued to take their turn. Her ripped clothes lay strewn around the ground, and her face, which Leon glimpsed through the sea of bodies, was contorted with pain. Horrified, Leon ran, yelling, at the rapists, only to be hit in the stomach and kicked in the genitals by some of the tangled knot of laughing and smoking spectators. As he doubled up on the ground, a soldier pressed a gun against his forehead and said, 'Go now or I kill you.' He dragged himself up and limped away, his hands clasped over his throbbing testicles. He slumped onto a nearby stone bench, tears rolling down his cheeks and sobs shaking his body.

Finally, the perpetrators set off into the bowels of the Palace through one of its basement level doors. The girl lay motionless on the ground, the soles of her feet a startling white in the gloom. Leon approached her cautiously, convinced she was dead, an impression reinforced by the rivulet of blood trickling from between her legs. He was backing off when a low moan drew him to her. The girl, she couldn't have been more than fifteen, tried to move, but all the life had drained from her. Leon stooped, saying a few kindly words, even though she wouldn't understand. He gathered her clothes, propped her up in a sitting position, and then slipped her torn and bedraggled blue dress over her head, gently guiding her passive hands and arms so it slipped into place. The girl stared blankly ahead. When he'd clothed her, he lifted her to her feet, anxious to get her away in case other rapists discovered her. But where would be safe?

'Pssst, Mr Lion!' An urgent whisper caught his attention. There in the shadows was Primrose, carrying an AK47 and dressed in camouflaged battle fatigues. She beckoned him over. Slowly, with the girl half walking, half being carried, they joined Primrose in the dark shadow afforded by a recessed doorway into the Palace.

'I didn't know prostitutes could use weapons like that.'

'You learn lot of things in my game. You Good Samaritan, Mr Lion.'

'Where can we put her that's safe? I can't hold her up much longer.'

Primrose produced a key and unlocked the door behind them. Then she helped Leon guide the stumbling girl into the dark room, locked the door, pulled down the thick blind and switched on the light. It was an office of some kind, with filing cabinets, two desks, both with grey desktop computers yellowing with age, a few chairs and, in the corner, an old chaise longue standing on three legs and a pile of books. They eased the girl down onto it. She lay motionless, staring at the ceiling, apparently oblivious to their questions. Leon held her hand, which remained limp and lifeless.

'She better soon.' Primrose was brisk to the point of brusqueness. 'Happen all time to poor people.'

'Who does these things?'

'Soldiers, politicians, landowners, employers. All do it. I gang raped two times as young girl.'

Leon's mind was reeling. 'Doesn't anyone do anything to stop it?'

Primrose gave vent to a sardonic laugh. 'Cat never walk away from cream.'

'Who is it? The Government, the rebels?'

'You not listen, Mr Lion. It all of them. All men who can, or,' she cast a glance at Leon, 'want to. Simple.'

Leon thought of his gentle, caring adoptive father. 'That's not true. Some men are kind.'

Primrose screwed up her face. 'A few, Mr Lion. Not many.'

'What about the police?'

Primrose, an expression of disbelief at his naivety on her face, shook her head. 'Worst. Arrest young girls, threaten then rape them.'

Leon clenched his fists. 'Bastards. I'm going to stop this. I don't know how, but I will. The police should be protecting people.' He inclined his head in the girl's direction. 'Especially the young and vulnerable.'

'You good man, Mr Lion, but no one sort out this mess.'

'We have to try, Primrose.'

Primrose put her hand under the girl's back and, lifting her, gave her water from a flask. When she took her arm away, the girl flopped like a limp rag doll. Leon hopped anxiously from one foot to the other.

'She needs medical attention. Where can we find a doctor?'

'All run away.' Primrose lifted the girl's dress and examined her. 'Bruises, cuts, that all,' she said. 'Hope not pregnant.'

'Who were they?'

Primrose smoothed the garment back into place. 'Maybe Oblanga's bodyguard, not sure. Soldiers change sides all time.'

'That does it. I'm going to confront Oblanga.'

'You crazy, Mr Lion. How you find him? Why he listen?' She stood up and pointed towards one of the chairs. 'Wait see winner, then decide what to do.'

Leon slid down into the chair only to take to his feet a few seconds later.

'No. I'm going.'

Primrose grabbed him by the shoulders and pushed him back. 'You get killed for nothing.'

Leon barged her aside. 'Maybe, but I can't just sit here.'

Primrose sighed. 'Good luck Mr Lion. We likely not meet again.'

'You've said that before.'

'You lucky that time. You usually a lucky man, Mr Lion?'

Primrose's jibe struck home. Would his luck run out? For a moment he wavered. Then he thought of the horrific scenes he'd witnessed. 'It doesn't have to be like this. I'm going in.'

Primrose pushed her gun into his hands. 'You take, Mr Lion.'

He hesitated for a moment, then waved it away. 'No thanks. I shall use peaceful means.'

Primrose shook her head. 'Crazy.'

Chapter 20

A door from the back of the office opened onto the rabbit warren of passageways running under the Palace. Leon unlocked it and stole tentatively into the gloom. From the far end came the unmistakeable sound of automatic weapons punctuated by occasional shouts and screams. Filled with a cold-steel determination, he made straight for it. After about a hundred yards the corridor turned sharply left. As he carefully rounded the corner, he narrowly avoided tripping over two awkwardly splayed bodies, their unseeing eyes staring at the ceiling, each of their heads surrounded by a pool of blood. He recognised them as two of the girl's rapists. To his astonishment, his squeamishness had vanished, and he stepped over them. A few yards further along another soldier in a similar uniform lay face downwards, his hands extended as though in surrender. Leon heaved him over. Half his face had been blown away. Forcing himself, Leon examined his remaining features. It was a third rapist.

'Justice,' he muttered.

The sound of racing footsteps made him look up. Three soldiers were running towards him, pointing weapons and yelling. Leon, his heart performing somersaults in his chest, raised his hands slowly in the air, expecting a hail of bullets to end his life.

The soldiers reached him, still shouting, and Leon recognised Akello, Mr B's lieutenant, at their head.

'Where have you been?' Akello said. 'Mr B's very worried 'bout you. Come with us.'

Akello led Leon along corridors and up and down stairs. Sometimes they passed through familiar sections. The rest of the time the Palace remained a bewildering honeycomb. Clusters of soldiers were standing at all major intersections, some smoking, some laughing, some sullen. Around one blood-soaked corner, dead bodies in different styles of uniforms were strewn. Some resembled peaceful sleepers, others twisted and broken mannequins.

They reached a door. Akello knocked, pushed it open and, saluting, stepped inside. Leon followed. President Oblanga and Mr B were seated side by side, hunched over a laptop's screen like schoolboys playing Minecraft.

'As you can see, we were in time to save the President,' Mr B announced. Oblanga's expression, however, was more one of resentment than gratitude and he avoided Leon's eye.

'You've triumphed, have you?' Leon asked.

Mr B's eyes narrowed. 'Happily, the President's authority has been restored.'

'What's happened to all those other alphabet letters? Messrs A to Z excluding B. Are they all dead?'

'Time will tell, but the important thing is they haven't seized control. Where were you while we were fighting?'

'Witnessing atrocities committed by his soldiers.' Leon pointed at Oblanga, who was now gazing into space.

'Enough! I suggest you bow to the President,' Mr B said. 'You must not forget the necessary marks of respect, especially in a war zone.'

Leon hesitated, then reluctantly inclined his head an inch. Raising it quickly, he said, 'I believe President Oblanga's soldiers have been guilty of serious crimes. No doubt he'll want to investigate and bring the culprits, or those of them who are still alive, to justice.'

'What crimes?' Mr B asked in an indifferent tone.

'Gang rape of minors, for one.'

Mr B waved his hand dismissively. 'Collateral damage. Now come here. I'm drafting a statement from the President to the people, and I want you, as heir to Chief Onagaku, to endorse it. It's essential we unite the country.'

'I'm not endorsing anything unless I know there'll be a full investigation and those responsible will be punished. If he agrees, and undertakes to see it through, fine. Otherwise, forget it.'

Mr B uttered a mirthless laugh. 'You're overestimating your importance. Your endorsement may help settle some of the tribal people who are somewhat restive now. That's all. If you don't...' He left the sentence unfinished and looked back at the computer screen.

Leon shuffled his feet. Their heads were now close together over the screen and they were conversing in local language. He coughed. Then did so again. He might as well be invisible. Humiliating seconds dragged by.

Mr B looked up, barked, 'Go away,' and resumed his conversation with Oblanga.

Filled with rage, Leon strode forward, swept the laptop up from the table in one deft movement and clasped it to his chest. 'I don't think we've finished our conversation. Appalling crimes have been committed, probably are still being committed, and neither of you is prepared to do anything.'

Mr B sat back, folded his arms and fixed Leon with an unblinking stare. 'Don't parade your naivety. People get killed. Premises get looted. Women get raped. That's what happens in war.'

'It doesn't have to be like that. If you had good officers, if you trained your soldiers, if you punished the miscreants, you could stamp that out.'

Mr B stood up and stretched his hand out. 'Computer. Now.'

Leon took a step back, holding the laptop aloft. 'They're probably paid next to nothing, if they're paid at all.'

Mr B signalled to Akello, who was lounging against the wall. He leapt forward and prodded Leon in the back with his pistol. Leon let the laptop crash onto the ground, its screen flying open and cracking into a myriad piece mosaic.

Mr B's nostrils flared. 'You don't know how close to death you are. Your spending a few days in solitary confinement will help us both cool off.'

He spoke in Mutabese to Akello, and Leon found himself being marched down until he was dumped into a cell that reeked of urine and faeces.

★

Hours later, a metallic bang and a shout announced the arrival, through a panel at the foot of the cell's door, of a battered enamel jug of water and a boiled yam on a tin plate. Despite the stench surrounding him, Leon fell on them, wondering as he finished whether he'd been too hasty in consuming everything. Dismissing this concern as theoretical, he manoeuvred the straw bedding into the least filthy part of the cell's floor and stretched out. He tried to ignore the rustling sounds around him with the inevitable consequence that images of ravenous rats muscled their way into his mind and refused to leave.

'What I need now,' he mumbled as he started to doze, 'is Primrose.'

Though the sound of the key turning in the cell door woke Leon, he remained in the foetal position, thinking it would be a guard. But the warm, passionate kiss on the nape of his neck caused him to spin round in irritation, convinced that some enterprising prostitute, having bribed his gaolers, was plying her trade.

'Rolly!'

Now dressed in a vivid yellow uniform with gold braid across his chest and stars on his epaulettes, Rolly put his finger to his lips with one hand and beckoned Leon to follow him through the gaping cell door with the other. Leon, still shaking his head to make sure he wasn't dreaming, complied and soon they were walking along another of those interminable corridors. Ducking into one of the many doors off it, they found themselves in a room full of military uniforms.

'Where did you spring from?' Leon asked as soon as the door closed.

'I'll explain in a minute,' Rolly said. 'I've missed you.'

Leon knew that he should be trying to make good his escape, that it was risky staying where they could be discovered at any time, but he didn't care. 'I've missed you too.'

They embraced and kissed, then undressed each other, their clothes lying in a tangled heap on the floor. Leon pulled Rolly gently to the ground, the perspiration running off them in rivulets and soaking into their discarded garments.

★

Leon turned over and lay on his back, a reservoir of sweat forming in his navel. 'Where have you been?'

Rolly, energised, stood up briskly and looked around. 'Holed up at Morowa's. I heard the secret police were after me, so I kept my head down and did some planning.'

Leon felt the sharp stab of jealousy. 'Morowa's? I'll bet planning isn't all you've been doing.'

'Chill, bro,' Rolly murmured, looking through the racks of uniforms. 'Nothing for you to worry about.' He stood back to get a better look at an outfit. 'I think this would suit you.' He held a purple jacket with gold epaulettes against Leon's recumbent figure. 'Perhaps a larger size?' Leon brushed it aside and stood up. That feeling of unreality was overwhelming him again. He'd found Rolly, or rather Rolly had found him, which had seemed like a miracle. Then Rolly confessed he'd spent the last few days with an obsessed nymphomaniac, yet nothing apparently had happened. Now they were trying on bizarre uniforms which wouldn't have been out of place in a Gilbert and Sullivan operetta. He banged his head with the palm of his hand.

Rolly pushed the jacket towards him again. 'Go on. Put it on.'

Leon slipped into it. 'Not too bad.'

'A perfect fit. Purple really is your colour. It goes with these.' Rolly picked out a pair of cream trousers with a thick gold stripe down each leg, and a white helmet topped with scarlet plumes.

Leon located his boxers in the pile of clothes and eased himself into them. He took the trousers and held them at arm's length. They looked about the right size.

'Try them,' Rolly urged as he rooted around among the rows of gleaming brown boots for a pair he thought would fit.

'Are we going to a fancy dress party, or does all this military stuff turn you on?' Leon said, stepping into the trousers.

Rolly laughed. 'I prefer latex. You'll need these clothes to accompany me. No one will stop you if you're wearing the dress regalia of the Imperial House Guard.'

'Accompany you where?'

'On my mission.'

'Not the mission you were talking about before? When you said you'd be killed?'

Rolly found a pair of brown boots and held them

out. 'That's the one. Seeing as I busted you out of jail, I thought you might want to help.'

'And risk my life?'

'Sure. We've all got to die sometime, and it's in a good cause.'

Leon couldn't believe it. He'd been rescued only to be invited to face near certain death in a quest he knew nothing about. He must keep his cool. 'I thought you warned me to steer clear, to go back to England.'

Rolly looked at himself in the mirror. 'But you didn't, did you? Which is why you ended up in a cell. As you're here, you might as well pitch in.'

'Well, what is this mission impossible then?'

Rolly stared Leon in the eye. 'To kill my father, of course.'

'Oh,' Leon gasped. This was even more incredible. He was being dressed in outlandish clothes to become an accomplice to the murder of someone he'd never met. 'Your father? Why? And what's he doing here anyway?' Leon had imagined Rolly's father to be a shifty entrepreneur.

Rolly grinned. 'He lives here; he's President Oblanga. I'm his despised son, Mawusi.'

'But...but...' Leon rocked back on his heels, struggling to assimilate the information. All he could think of saying was, 'But your name is Rolly.'

'That's the one I adopted. I hate Mawusi.'

This crazy place has just become even more baffling, Leon thought. How could Rolly have kept it from him that he was Oblanga's son? It had to be a wind-up. 'You're bullshitting me!'

Rolly shook his head.

Leon's mind was in turmoil. If Rolly had concealed this from him, what else did he have hidden? Could he ever trust him again? And what did it say about his own powers of observation? Shouldn't he have been able to guess from Rolly's high-handed manner and unwavering self-confidence?

'Don't tell me you didn't know,' Rolly continued. 'MI6 didn't give you much of a briefing, did they?'

Leon's shock and confusion gave way to irritation. 'Why does everyone think I work for British intelligence?'

Rolly gave him a wry half-smile. 'Because it's on your file.'

'My file?'

'Yes, after we met and I'd worked out who you were, I read the official reports.'

Leon shook his head. 'It isn't true. It's nonsense.'

'Perhaps you're working for the Russians then, like Marianne Cartwright.'

Leon's mouth hung open. 'Russians? What do you mean? Everyone else says she's a British spy.'

'Life's rarely that simple, especially here. I heard she was a double agent. Quite a coincidence that the Russians were implicated in your parents' murder and she was on hand to rescue you.'

'I don't believe it!' Leon's stridency masked his

doubts. Marianne had loved and nurtured him. That's all that mattered.

'Plenty of evidence on the files,' Rolly said. 'Though much of it is circumstantial.'

Leon put his hand to his forehead. Facts, opinions and perceptions all merged into one great blur; there was nothing firm to grasp hold of or rely on. If he'd learned one thing from his time in Mutabe, it was that anything anyone said would be contradicted shortly afterwards.

'Sorry if I shocked you,' Rolly said.

Leon wiped the perspiration from his brow with the back of his hand. Wearing this ceremonial jacket was making him melt. He'd thought Rolly was genuinely attracted to him. Now it appeared he had some ulterior purpose.

'You're secret service then? And you've been assigned to keep me under observation?'

Rolly guffawed. 'Far from it. Everyone in the Palace, just about, has access to the secret files. All it takes is a few simple passwords. My pet bushbaby could do it. Anyway, no time to chat. We've got things to do.'

Leon remembered his unanswered question. 'Why are you going to kill your father?'

'I was hoping I wouldn't have to. I've been feeding information to all these coup leaders in the hope they'd do the job for me. Only they're such bunglers. Now it's down to me.'

Leon thought of Peter. He couldn't imagine wanting to harm him. Yet Rolly was so cool about performing this unnatural act. 'You're his son. How can you justify killing him?'

Incredulity, anger and scorn vied for primacy in Rolly's face. Scorn won. 'Justify it! How about his persecuting and executing gays, especially my friends, even though he's gay himself?'

'What do you mean, he's gay himself?'

Rolly's voice softened and his hand touched Leon's arm in a confiding manner. 'My father masquerades as the big hetero. Deep down he'll fuck anything with an orifice. He knows I've got the evidence, and that I've arranged for it to be distributed worldwide should anything happen to me. If I hadn't had that insurance policy, I'd have been vulture food years ago.'

Rolly went to a cupboard, produced a key from his back pocket and opened it. The door swung slowly open to reveal a row of Kalashnikovs. He patted them. 'Loaded and ready to use.' He took one out and threw it to Leon. It could have been a cobra, such was the look of fear and disgust on Leon's face when he caught it. He held it at arms' length.

'Sorry Rolly. I could never kill anyone.' He laid the gun down on the desk. 'If you've got the goods on your old man, why don't you force him into exile? It'd be a more humane solution.'

'Because when he fucked my best friend and

then had him executed for homosexuality, I swore I'd revenge him.'

Leon grabbed a chair and sat down. 'Revenge feeds on itself. Someone has to be brave enough to call a halt.'

Rolly pulled out another rifle. 'If you're not prepared to help, I'll do it on my own.'

'I'll help you depose him; he may have committed crimes himself and he's certainly allowed others free rein to do terrible things, but I won't be party to his killing.'

Rolly shook his head. 'This isn't some cosy English suburb. Here it's kill or be killed, and I intend to do the killing.'

Chapter 21

Rolly swept out of the room. Leon froze, imagining him facing certain death at the hands of Oblanga's bodyguard. Then he jumped to his feet. He wouldn't be an accomplice to murder, but he could try to protect Rolly. Opening the door a crack, he squinted down the corridor. No one. He poked his head out and looked both ways, not sure which direction to take. He plumped for turning right and set off at speed. He was halfway down the corridor when he heard gunfire, followed by shouting. He pressed himself against the wall. Two men in identical costumes to his own swung round the corner, guns in hand, and yelled something as they sprinted past. Scared of being unmasked, Leon scurried away in the opposite direction. A little later he came upon another group. Four in different, highly coloured outfits with silver epaulettes stood shoulder to shoulder, apparently waiting for a photograph, while several more in drab brown clustered around on both sides of them, reminding Leon of the cover of the Sergeant Pepper album. Everyone was smiling. Some were giving the thumbs up sign. It appeared a festive scene until Leon noticed that the four each had one foot on the naked and mutilated body of a large man, whose face, turned towards him in a rictus of terminal agony, was unmistakably that of Mr D.

The soldiers spotted Leon. Yelling and beckoning vigorously, they summoned him over to join in. Leon looked around for a means of escape, only for his arms to be grabbed by the two soldiers he'd seen sprinting past, who had returned unnoticed. They guided him into the middle of the photo where he was made to place a foot on the stiffening corpse, his new friends standing on either side of him and jabbering while they were photographed. With peals of laughter, accompanied by much back slapping, they dispersed.

Leon continued along the corridor in a daze, the image of Mr D's grimace seared into his mind. He barely took any notice when he stumbled into Mr B emerging, pistol in hand, from an office.

'You! What are you doing here?'

'The President ordered my release,' Leon replied, pleased that for once his brain had not left him tongue-tied.

Mr B looked incredulous. 'Why are you dressed as a—'.

He was interrupted by a prolonged burst of

gunfire. 'We'll talk later,' he shouted, breaking into an undignified trot. He was overtaken by two soldiers in Imperial House Guard uniforms wielding silver sabres. Leon set off in pursuit, nearly catching up with the three of them by the time they rounded the next corner. A hail of bullets left the two soldiers lying in pools of blood on the floor. Mr B, now on one knee behind the corner, was reaching out periodically to exchange fire with the gunman.

'Shit!' Mr B threw the pistol on the ground. 'Damn thing's empty. Quick. He could be here in a couple of seconds.'

Leon peeped round the corner. The gunman, a vision in brilliant yellow, was marching steadily towards them. Leon stood up from his crouching position and stepped out to face him. For a second, he thought he was about to die as the gunman pointed his weapon in readiness to fire. Then Rolly recognised him.

Leon's fear turned to anger. 'What the– '

'I've done it, Leon.' A broad smile spread across Rolly's face. No child, confronted by a pile of sweets, could have looked more pleased.

'What?'

'I've killed him. The old bastard's dead.'

Mr B, listening from behind the corner, drew himself up to a standing position.

'This is Bankole,' he boomed, without revealing himself. 'Put your weapon down now.'

Rolly laughed. 'You really think you can boss me about when I've got a loaded gun and you haven't? Anyway, I've got nothing against you, Mr B. Of all the old bastard's henchmen, you were probably one of the least bad. I won't harm you.'

By now Rolly was only a couple of yards from the corner. Mr B, puffing out his chest, stepped out to face him.

'You killed the President?'

Rolly nodded. 'I have rid the country of that tyrant, yes.'

'And you want to take his place, I assume.'

Rolly's belly laugh shook his frame. 'That's the last thing I want. I'd like an apartment in King's Parade and a guaranteed income of a million dollars a year.'

Mr B's eyes popped. 'You're expecting the Government to pay you when you've just killed our president?'

Rolly lowered his gun and lolled against the wall. 'Come on Mr B. That old bastard was robbing this country of hundreds of millions a year. What's a million in commission for having delivered a saving like that?'

'You've committed a heinous crime. You should be executed, not rewarded.'

Rolly's eyes narrowed, he took a step forward and lifted his gun so that it was prodding Mr B's belly. 'If you're not careful, I could commit another, right now.' He jabbed at Mr B's solar plexus. 'All I've done is what you've been planning to do for months, if not years. You should thank me.'

It was a few moments before Mr B replied. 'Perhaps you should leave the country. It would make things easier. You could go to Paris. There's a large Mutabese presence there. Or London. Berlin even.'

'I don't want to go anywhere. This is my home. All my friends are here.'

Mr B's face remained impassive. 'I'll fix it,' he said. 'Before I do, we'll need to pin the blame for Oblanga's murder on someone. Someone expendable.' His gaze settled on Leon.

'No!' Leon grabbed Mr B by his lapels and stared up into his face. 'Blame Mr D.'

Mr B brushed Leon's hands off. 'Too many people saw Mr D die before the President was killed.'

'It might be easier to blame a foreign government,' Rolly said. 'The old bastard was stridently anti-communist, so we could point the finger at the Chinese.'

'Yes,' Mr B said. 'They're up to all sorts everywhere, so no one would think it too unlikely. Jeff Gbeho, if he's still alive, could be a suitable candidate. Meanwhile we'd better get you out of here. I'll get some of my boys to escort you.'

'I want to take him with me.' Rolly nodded at Leon and, in response to Mr B's surprised expression, added quickly, 'As a hostage.'

Mr B looked thoughtfully at Leon and then back at Rolly, and Leon wondered whether he'd rumbled their relationship. But when Mr B spoke, neither his face nor his voice betrayed any hint of suspicion. 'If you must. I'm not sure his life would be much of a guarantee.'

Rolly smiled. 'I'll take my chances.' He turned to Leon. 'Come on.'

Leon hesitated. He cared for Rolly in a way he never had for anyone before, not even Clive. Come to think of it, especially not Clive. Yet he was appalled by the murder. How could he ever forget that Rolly could kill in such a cold and premeditated way, and without any sign of compunction? On the other hand, if he didn't go with Rolly, where would he go? Mr B was ready to dispense with his services and he had no one else to protect him.

'OK,' he said wearily, casting a rueful glance at the tight bottom which had filled his thoughts so often.

Chapter 22

Rolly directed the armoured car to drop them in a remote corner of the Victoria suburb where flat-roofed, three and four storey houses encrusted with balconies, stood out white against the pre-dawn sky like so many abandoned wedding cakes.

He inserted a code and the black iron gates, each tipped with a golden spear point, swung open to reveal a pale pink gravel drive. It was fringed by rows of neatly clipped glossy bushes, three feet tall, crowned with floppy white flowers giving off the sweetest scent. Another code opened the front door. Before Leon realised what was happening, Rolly had lifted him, stumbled across the threshold with him in his arms, kissed him on the lips and put him down on a polished wood floor.

'Welcome to our new home,' Rolly said. 'We'll be very happy living here together.'

Leon straightened his jacket. 'Living here together? What are you talking about?'

'Well, you don't want to go on being Bankole's pawn, do you?'

Leon's hand smoothed his ruffled hair. 'I'm no one's pawn.'

'Now he's got what he wants, he doesn't need you. All this Chief Onagaku business was nonsense anyway. That ancestral bit might carry weight with the older tribal people, but for the younger generation, it means nothing.'

'So, you're suggesting I move in here? With you.'

Rolly shook his head. 'No, I'm suggesting you have moved in. If you need your things, I can arrange it. In a couple of days, when the fighting has died down, we can go into town, or what's left of it, and buy you some civilian clothes. The shops are used to coup attempts. They reopen quickly.'

It was as though Leon was watching a soap opera in which he'd missed some vital episodes. Until Rolly had shown himself to be a killer, he would have sacrificed anything to live with him. Now, with the memory of those two dead soldiers and Oblanga's murder he wasn't so sure. 'What makes you think I want to live with you?'

'Intuition. Let's go inside and sort ourselves out.'

Rolly started to turn away. Leon grasped his arm.

'I could ask your father for your hand in marriage. Oh, no I can't, because you shot him.'

Rolly laughed and punched Leon's shoulder. 'I love your sense of humour.'

With a proprietary air, Rolly sauntered off into one of the adjacent rooms while Leon lingered in the hall, transfixed by the image of the worried person staring out at him from the six-foot mirror with its gilt rococo frame.

'No one tells me what to do,' he said softly to his reflection. He heard Rolly's mobile phone ring and Rolly say, 'Oh, hi Morowa.'

'Enough,' he said. Seizing his opportunity while Rolly was distracted, he re-traced his steps down the drive. At his approach, the gates opened automatically. From the house he heard Rolly's voice, both pleading and panicking, calling out to him. He checked his step, uncertain whether to return and dithered in the open entrance. However much he loved him, he couldn't live with a murderer. He'd thought Rolly was the one. Before that, he'd thought Clive had been the one. Would he ever find a partner he could truly love who would love him in equal measure? He put his head down and pressed on. The gates closed behind him, and he could no longer hear his lover's desperate pleas.

The subdivision's road, with its flickering streetlights, was devoid of life, while the secluded white mansions' high walls acted like lampshades illuminating the sky. Behind some of the wrought-iron gates he encountered the bored stares of private security guards crouching or sitting on small stools. Each clutched a rifle or wore a revolver in a holster at his waist.

Leon had stopped to ask one of them for directions to Mutable City centre when he was thrown back by the sledgehammer noise of two low-flying jet fighters, no more than a hundred feet above the highest roof tops. He covered his ears as they circled three times, and then, in turn, unleashed their missiles.

Rolly's house exploded in a ball of fire, shards of debris hurtling several hundred feet into the air.

Leon clung to the wall for support, not sure whether his eardrums, or perhaps even his brain had burst. He looked around. The security men were lying flat on their stomachs, their hands clamped over their ears. Rolly's house blazed, black smoke billowing from it and curling down the street like a malevolent serpent.

'Rolly!' Leon screamed, overwhelmed by images of his friend being ripped apart in the blast. Sobbing and clasping his sleeve across his mouth and nose, he battled through the dense fumes until coughing overcame him and he fell to his knees. Distraught, he crawled away, propping himself up against a wall. No one could have survived that explosion. He hadn't even said goodbye.

Leon didn't know how long he'd been there. It could have been ten minutes or an hour. All he could think of was Rolly. He became aware of people peering out of their windows. Some emerged from houses, looking up at the sky and speaking in hushed tones. More joined them.

An old woman came over and offered him a glass of water, which he downed in a few gulps. A crowd formed as more neighbours arrived. Maids in simple cotton outfits and flip flops, live-in gardeners in t-shirts and shorts, and armed security guards mingled with the residents in their lustrous silk kimonos and wraps, each a blaze of primary colours. While the servants stared mournfully at the inferno, the plutocrats obviously derived amusement from it, their animated voices growing in volume.

A cultivated British accent stood out from the Mutabese hubbub. 'Yet another attempt on Oblanga's life.'

The speaker was tall and slim, with the dignified air of a senior politician, his wiry white hair capping his milk chocolate skin. Beside him, an Asian woman in a pale pink sharkskin suit was smoking a cigarette in a long holder.

'Wonder whether they got him this time.'

Leon waved his arm in the direction of the conflagration. 'The President's son,' he said, his voice hoarse. 'Inside.' Rolly's warm, embracing smile sprang into his mind. He wiped the tears from his eyes with the back of his hand.

'Mawusi!' The man whistled. 'Well, he's no loss.'

Had Leon not been so weak, the temptation to punch his smug face would have been overwhelming. 'You're talking of a person being incinerated,' he said, his voice quavering.

'A fag being despatched, you mean, and not before time,' the man replied. 'If I met the pilots who did it, I'd congratulate them. There are too many of his kind creeping around in the shadows, corrupting young people, destroying the fabric of our society. I'd burn them all.'

'They're disgusting,' his female companion chipped in. 'You know what they do to each other. Buggery—'

'Not now,' the man said with a shake of his hand. Attracted by the commotion, a crowd of wealthy residents was gathering.

The woman brandishing a cigarette holder flicked some ash onto the ground. 'They're sick, all of them. It would be a mercy to put them out of their misery.'

'You bastards,' Leon croaked. 'A human being has died in a horrific manner and you're revelling in it. What's wrong with you? Have you no humanity?'

The crowd shifted round to face him. His antagonists' eyes were hostile, their expressions aggressive.

'Who are you anyway?' one voice called out. 'Another pervert?'

'He can't be. He's an officer,' someone said.

An old man spat into the road. 'That's no guarantee.'

Leon detected the unmistakable smell of a crowd psyching itself up for violence. Memories of being surrounded by bullies in the school playground flooded his thoughts. He took a step back, planted his feet wide apart and stuck out his chest. He was Chief Onagaku now, not Coconut.

'Let's take him to Bishop Mbutu. He'll investigate him, officer or not,' a short fat woman in a silver dressing gown said. 'We'll get our guards to detain him.' She shouted and a couple of men in uniform shuffled forward. A hand grabbed his arm. He shook himself free, thinking that if ever he needed the help of his tribal forefathers, it was now.

'I am Chief Onagaku, leader of the Tribal Lands; anyone who trifles with me does so at his peril.'

His threat was enough to make his would-be persecutors hesitate. He seized the initiative. 'It's you that's sick, persecuting people for no good reason. Why are you so prejudiced?'

Discontent rumbled around the crowd, some of it in Mutabese, some in English. The threat of violence hung in the air like a putrid stench. Leon wondered why he wasn't scared, until he realised that with Rolly dead, he didn't care. He had nothing to live for. He'd face this rabble down or die in the attempt. Now was the time to employ all the acting techniques Mhlambo had taught him.

'The law will soon change. Mr Bankole will introduce a programme of reform which will drag Mutabe into the twenty-first century.'

'Bankole?' It was a tall man in a loose-fitting mauve shirt with a peacock picked out in startling green. 'He said that?'

'He did.'

'Oblanga will never agree!' a fat man with thick black-framed glasses shouted.

Leon raised his hands. 'Hear this everyone. Oblanga is dead. Mr Bankole is now in charge. I am his closest ally. One word from me and fighter planes will destroy this whole subdivision.'

The crowd fell into a stunned silence. Several people scanned the sky as though expecting the fighters to return immediately.

'Now, who will lend me his chauffeur to drive me to the Presidential Palace? I have important matters of state to attend to.'

No one moved.

'You!' Leon pointed at a fat man whose guts, loosely encased in a white silk shirt, spilled over his ivory chinos. 'I'm requisitioning your car and driver. Have them here in two minutes.'

The man nodded but stood motionless.

'Well get on with it!' Leon said. 'I'm in a hurry.'

The crowd parted as the man walked, as though in a dream, through them, returning a minute later with a boy of about sixteen, a growth of wispy hair on his upper lip.

'This is Frederick. He'll take you. The car's over there.' He nodded at a Bentley whose highly polished gunmetal grey bonnet was visible through the tall wrought-iron gates of a nearby mansion.

'Thanks.' Leon's curt response sounded

appropriate for someone in a position of authority. He was sure Rolly would have been impressed with his play acting. Rolly! He swallowed hard and blinked several times, trying to stave off the tears that were forcing their way into his eyes.

'I'll get my maid to bring you some breakfast to eat on the journey.' The man disappeared into the melee and Leon made his way to the car. The gates were opened, the vehicle's doors unlocked, and he settled into the plush leather upholstery in the back. His chauffeur, now in a peaked grey cap and a grey jacket with black piping, took the driver's seat. Shortly after, a corpulent maid waddled out of the house, a sizeable hamper on her arm.

'Thank you.' Leon's smile was expansive, as was his aristocratic wave. The car pulled majestically out of the drive as he lifted the hamper's lid: a chicken wing, a bowl of rice and several mangoes, guava and paw paws lay inside. His host had looked after him well. Unfortunately, he felt too sick to eat.

They sped through nearly deserted streets. Dawn was breaking, and a few early traders were opening the metal grills protecting their shop fronts or setting up stalls. There was little evidence of fighting. Occasionally they passed small knots of soldiers who paid them no attention. Throughout the journey, Leon spotted only a dozen corpses by the roadside, each shrouded by a cloud of blue-black flies. Not long before he would have been shocked and revolted at the sight. Now he was so emotionally calloused by violence, all he experienced was surprise that there weren't more.

The driver knew his way well, swinging the car through tight back streets to make short cuts between broad avenues. At last the Presidential Palace came into view. Outside it, six tanks, their barrels raised as though in readiness to obliterate a distant enemy, were stationed, along with a platoon of infantry.

Leon adopted an imperious manner. 'Drive through the main gates.'

No doubt impressed by the opulent quality of the car, the smartness of the driver's peaked cap and the relaxed way in which Leon, still attired in his military uniform, lounged on the back seat, the first two tiers of defenders let them through. At the main gates the car was surrounded by a dozen soldiers in dark green fatigues and black berets, several of whom pointed their weapons at the driver's window. Frederick lowered the glass and a babble ensued, brusque and assertive on the sentries' part, emollient and conciliatory on Frederick's.

Some soldiers came over to Leon's window. He lowered it.

'Chief Onagaku. Tell Mr Bankole I've arrived.' He raised his window in their surprised faces. Seconds later they were being waved through. He smiled to himself. This authority bullshit really worked.

Chapter 23

Even though the office into which Leon was ushered was large, it was dominated by the massive mahogany desk at its centre, behind which sat Mr B. He was resplendent in a crisp white general's uniform smeared with gold braid and adorned with gold epaulettes like those sported by doormen at the flashiest of fashionable hotels.

Mr B looked up from his computer screen. Leon found it difficult to interpret his expression. Surprise was evident. Annoyance was there in abundance. Perhaps there was even a hint of grudging admiration. What was absent was pleasure.

'You again!'

Mr B looked down as though this short sentence both commenced and concluded the conversation.

Leon stepped forward. 'Why did you kill him?'

Mr B's face betrayed no emotion. He didn't even bother to look up. But then Mr B was probably an accomplished liar. 'Who?'

Leon made a supreme effort to remain calm, counting silently as he inhaled. He held his breath, exhaling only when he was sure he could respond in a measured way. Yet all these steps failed to prevent a lump forming in his throat and tears pricking at his eyes.

'Rolly, of course.'

Mr B met Leon's stare. 'Who?'

Leon's voice was thick with emotion. 'The President's son.'

'Oh, Mawusi. Why would I do that? If it's true.'

Leon bridled, both at the response and Mr B's redirection of his attention back to his computer. 'Of course it's true! I was there when his house become a raging inferno.'

Mr B looked up again, his lip curling. 'While you somehow escaped.'

Resenting the implication, Leon pushed back his shoulders and took a deep breath.

'He was killed by fighter planes firing rockets. As you know, because you sent them.'

Mr B leant back in his chair and yawned. 'How do you draw that conclusion? There are dissident factions in the air force as much as in the army. That wasn't Mawusi's house anyway. Anyone attacking it would have been under the impression they were assassinating Oblanga.'

'It was a complete coincidence then that shortly after your men dropped us, giving us enough time to get inside, the house was obliterated?'

Mr B, eyes down again and apparently fully absorbed in his screen, didn't reply.

Had Mr B not been so formidably strong, Leon would have grabbed him by his be-starred lapels and yanked him out of his chair. Instead he contented himself by dropping his voice to a lower register and raising its volume.

'So, you're saying it must have been a coincidence—'

'I heard what you said.' Mr B sat back, placing his hands behind his head. 'Look, I had no reason to kill either of you. You may still be of some use to me in the Tribal Lands. As for Mawusi, he saved me the unpleasant job of despatching his father. The timing wasn't ideal, hence my keeping Oblanga's death a closely guarded secret. But if things were to turn ugly after my broadcast to the nation, he would have provided a murderer and a motive to serve up to the public. Unfortunately, those aeroplanes have deprived me of my insurance policy.'

Leon struggled to process this alternative version. He wanted someone to blame for the death of the man he loved. 'What do you mean, keep Oblanga's death secret?' he said at last.

Mr B eyed him suspiciously. 'Why, who have you told?'

The sinking sensation in his stomach reminded Leon of when he was seven. Marianne had organised a surprise birthday party for Peter, newly returned from an extended overseas tour of duty, and he'd let the secret slip.

'Some people in the subdivision, that's all.' He clenched his fists behind his back. Be assertive Leon, he urged himself. He must avoid appearing dispensable to Mr B, who was still the only person who could get him out of Mutabe. 'If you wanted it kept confidential you should have told me. I can't work with someone who can't communicate.'

Mr B's mouth dropped open, then clamped shut. 'What do you mean work together?'

Leon smiled inwardly. He had surprised himself. What he said had come out unconsciously. He mustn't lose the advantage. He thought quickly. 'You can count on my using the Onagaku reputation to deliver the Tribal Lands and help you re-establish order, subject to certain conditions.'

Mr B leaned forward, his hands flat on the desk in front of him. 'Which are?'

Leon seated himself in the chair opposite, crossing his legs and leaning back. Then he placed his hands behind his head, aping Mr B's earlier posture. 'Number one. An end to the army's lawlessness. No more murders, rapes, anything like that. From now on soldiers must be answerable for their crimes.'

Mr B's head shook with the lethargy of disbelief. 'What else?'

'Homosexuality must be legalised, and all gays pardoned and released from jail.'

'Impossible! Bishop Mbutu would never wear it. Neither would the Army.'

'Put it to the People. Let those in favour and those against campaign and let the People decide.'

Mr B spluttered, his eyes swivelling. 'The People! They're most against it.'

Leon sat forward, placing his hands, palm down, in front of him. He breathed deeply. 'That, Mr B,' he said, enunciating every word deliberately, 'is because they've been indoctrinated by their temporal and spiritual leaders. It's not like that in other, more advanced countries.'

'Like America? There are lots there who would gladly string faggots up from the nearest tree.'

Leon could tell from the jut of Mr B's jaw and the set of his shoulders that his mind was made up. Rather than dispiriting him, this filled him with enhanced determination.

'If you're going to use rednecks as your moral yardstick, don't forget that there are still plenty of those whose idea of a good night out is to put their bed linen over their heads and terrorise the black community.'

Mr B's eyes narrowed to slits. 'Why are you so interested in this cause?'

Leon hesitated. Declaring his own orientation could prove fatal. Should he be true to himself, or should he play a longer game, get whatever he could now and come back later for more? The latter seemed, at this moment, the more strategic.

''Well?' Mr B's voice was quietly menacing.

Leon dithered. Was he being cowardly by not confronting this bigot, and all the others in the country, and forcing them to admit their groundless prejudices?

Mr B's fingers were drumming a disquieting staccato on the table. Leon met his unblinking stare.

'I want to drag this country into the twenty-first century. Social reform is one part of that.'

Mr B shrugged. 'You don't realise how important the church is here. If I made any attempt to change that law, I'd alienate some of Mutabe's most powerful people. It's not worth it, for the sake of a few deviants.'

Leon, now quivering with pent-up anger, struggled to maintain a calm tone of voice. 'Homosexuality has always existed and always will. There's no point persecuting people for being themselves.'

Mr B waved his hand. 'A lifestyle choice, or perhaps a treatable illness. I'll tell you what. I'll introduce an amnesty. They can declare themselves without any risk of punishment if they undergo a programme designed by Mutabese doctors to cure them. Of course, if they slip back into their old ways—'

Leon decided to play his ace. 'You know Oblanga was bisexual, don't you?

Mr B's smile was condescending. 'Oblanga was a red-blooded Mutabese, as proved by his sixteen wives and fifty-three children.'

'He also had sexual relations with young men, including at least one he later executed for homosexuality.'

'Oh, not that old rumour.'

'It's true.'

The corners of Mr B's mouth turned down. ''Fraid not, my friend. If you're President, a lot of people will say things to damage you. Truth is always the first casualty of power.'

'Rolly, I mean Mawusi, told me,' Leon blurted out.

Mr B laughed. 'You believe the word of that murderer? He did whatever he could to hurt his father, including blowing his head off. Now, enough of this. I'm prepared to consider a modest suite of social changes to settle the populace down, but I'm not going to alienate Mbutu and all the other power brokers and subject Mutabe to the ridicule of our neighbours.'

There was a knock on the door and four burly men in white uniforms entered, bumped into each other, stood to attention and saluted. Mr B, now apparently oblivious to Leon's presence, swivelled in his chair and fixed them with an unwavering stare.

'Well?'

'Everything's in place as per your instructions, Excellency. Your car will leave for MBC tower in five minutes. They're primed to broadcast your announcement immediately. Troops are stationed at all the other TV companies. They'll close them down before you go on air to maximise your audience. Your statement is ready for delivery to all the newspapers.'

Mr B sat back in his chair and nodded. 'Excellent.'

The four functionaries took a step back, saluted again and prepared to turn.

'Before you go,' Mr B drawled, 'Perhaps you'd be good enough to update me on that other little task.'

Like well-rehearsed synchronised swimmers, the four froze, identical looks of consternation on their weather-beaten faces. The one who had spoken before cleared his throat, a guttural gurgle that echoed around the room.

'Nothing substantial to report, sir. A couple of unconfirmed sightings of Mr C, one of Mr A and a rumour Mr E was seen near Morowa Daniels' house in Victoria. We followed each up. Nothing.' He clasped his hands in front of his chest, though it wasn't clear whether this signalled anxiety, a plea for mercy or a desperate prayer. Mr B, his face impassive, let the four of them stand there in their growing discomfort. Leon wondered whether he was mulling over what he'd been told or was considering which one to kill first.

As the seconds dragged by, the silence weighed increasingly on each of the four's drooping shoulders.

Mr B picked up a document and scrutinised it. Then he put it down and repeated the action with another. The men in front of him remained rooted to the spot, searching his face for any clue as to his intentions. Having glanced at another two pieces of paper, he looked up again.

'You have forty-eight hours to locate and bring in all the targets. I don't have to tell you what will happen if you fail. Dismiss.'

'Yes sir,' the four men chorused and saluted, though to Leon their voices were less enthusiastic and their salutes more ragged. They turned and shuffled out.

Mr B looked at his watch. 'Time to go. You can come with me to confirm your undivided support.'

Without waiting for a response, Mr B sprang lightly to his feet and strode towards the door. Leon paused, then hurried after him.

Chapter 24

Leon's apotheosis as Chief Onagaku, leader of the Tribal Lands, was proclaimed and broadcast, and Mr B announced the death of Oblanga and his own temporary elevation to the Presidency, to 'restore calm and stability' to a war-torn country. Mr B even promised elections, much to Leon's surprise.

'I didn't say when, though, did I?' he retorted when Leon congratulated him on this pledge. 'In any case, getting elected is easy enough to fix, and while it doesn't count for much in Africa, it goes down well in the US.'

Following the broadcast, Leon was tasked with visiting the Tribal Lands, escorted by some of Mr B's personal guard, to win people over to Mr B's cause.

'I can't go empty-handed,' Leon said. 'I need to be able to talk to them about reforms.'

Mr B's head inclined to one side, then the other, as though weighing the merits of this argument. 'All right. Nothing too radical. Draw up your wish list and we'll discuss it.'

'Me?'

'Who else? You want them, you propose them.'

Leon couldn't believe his ears. 'Shouldn't the Civil Service do some research, formulate proposals with cost benefit analyses and all that?'

Mr B had half-turned away from him, evidently tiring of the conversation. 'Civil Service? What Civil Service?'

'There must be a Civil Service here. Every country has one.'

'We have plenty of people paid by the state to lounge around in air-conditioned offices. They're usually there through nepotism or bribery and are, without exception, both useless and untrustworthy. If you want it done, do it yourself.'

★

Leon had been given one of the less impressive suites in the Presidential Palace, though the decoration was in good order. The bright green paint looked fresh and the wallpaper, a delicate light green flecked with silver, bore none of the tears or blotches so prevalent in other parts of the building. What made the apartment less imposing was its size. It had a ceiling more befitting an English country cottage and its rooms were compact. This puzzled Leon as he reclined on his bed in his boxers, his newly acquired laptop balancing on his thighs.

The knock on the door, though not particularly loud, so startled him that the computer ended up by his ankles.

'God, I must be stressed,' he muttered.

There followed another knock, louder and more insistent.

'Coming!' Leon wrapped a sheet around himself and with it trailing like a bridal gown, stumbled towards the door, which he opened a crack. On the other side stood Primrose wearing a broad smile and a bright orange jump suit. He swung the door open.

'Hello Mr Lion. You join Ku Klux Klan?'

Leon laughed. It was difficult not to in Primrose's presence.

'Your usual sir?' Primrose continued, her voice echoing down the labyrinthine corridors.

Leon looked about. For whose benefit was this performance? No one was visible.

'Yes please, Primrose,' he responded equally loudly. 'Will my uncle be paying?'

'No sir. You pay this time.'

Leon stepped aside and, with a flourish of his hand, invited her to enter. Primrose sidled in, kicked off her silver stilettos and unzipped and stepped out of her jumpsuit to expose her muscular brown body with its well-toned sheen.

'Let's start with a bath,' she said, ripping the sheet away from him. Taking the startled Leon by the hand, she led him into the bathroom where she turned both bath taps and the shower on full. In England, the noise would have been deafening. In Mutabe, with its feeble mains pressure, it provided a background hum.

Primrose sat on the bathmat and motioned to Leon to sit opposite her. He complied gingerly, trying to avert his eyes from her forest of pubic hair, her fat lipped pudendum and her pendulous breasts with their blue-black nipples. It wasn't easy, they seemed to fill the room. Primrose leant across and nudged him on the shoulder.

'Come on Mr Lion. It nothing you not seen before.' Then she dropped her voice, so it merged with the sound of dribbling water. 'Important secret. People will kill uncle anytime now. Safer you go away, anywhere, maybe to Tribal Lands where your family come from.'

Leon forgot Primrose's nakedness. 'How do you know?'

'Everything spill out when men with me; first sperm, then secrets 'bout others, then secrets 'bout themselves.'

'Have you warned him?'

'Yes, but he think he superhero. No one can harm him.'

Leon could imagine Mr B swatting away death threats like troublesome gnats. 'Who's behind it?'

Primrose squeezed her left breast thoughtfully. 'Not sure... maybe Donald, maybe FMF.' She paused. 'I turn the taps off now; we get in bath. I give you rub down, you look happy.' She dropped her voice to an almost inaudible whisper. 'Cameras everywhere.'

With the taps off, Leon slid off his boxers and he and Primrose stepped hand in hand into the four inches of tepid brown sludge filling the bottom of the Victorian claw foot tub. Primrose set about her task, wielding a sponge and a loofa with practised ease. While Leon did not, indeed could not find her or what she was doing sexually arousing, it was pleasantly relaxing, so affecting a smile wasn't difficult. Being towelled down afterwards also brought back happy memories of childhood bath times with Marianne.

'You not forget,' she whispered, kissing two fingers and placing them on Leon's lips.

Leon nodded. 'I'm scheduled to visit the Tribal Lands soon anyway. If you're right, I can extend my stay.'

'I'm right, sweetie, believe me.'

Once the door had clicked shut behind her, Leon went back and sprawled on his bed. Mr B's assassination would certainly leave him vulnerable, but what should he do? He couldn't leave the country, and hiding, long term, somewhere in Mutable, even in the Tribal Lands, wasn't a feasible solution. And even if there were an attempt on Mr B's life, how likely would it be to succeed? The new President was more than capable of looking after himself and now also had an elite bodyguard. It almost certainly wouldn't happen. He pushed Primrose's information to the back of his mind and determined to get on with the task in hand. He picked up his laptop. The heading 'Social Reforms' remained unpopulated. How did one come up with a list of practicable and cost-effective measures? Should he suggest the introduction of a system like the National Health? He took his fingers away from the keypad. He somehow doubted Mutabe's economy, with its twin pillars of agricultural feudalism and sweatshop exploitation, would be ready. He needed something simpler which they might be able to afford. God it was hot! The air-conditioning must have stopped working. Like a slug on a skateboard, a bead of sweat slalomed down his face. It was far too hot to even think. He turned off his computer, laid out a sheet to pull over himself when the aircon came on again and turned off the light. He was hoping to have a nap to offset the night-time insomnia he'd suffered since witnessing Rolly's fate. Rolly! Hot tears pricked his eyes and he gulped. God, he missed him. He tried to think of something – anything – else. Childhood memories proved the best distraction, and soon he started to feel drowsy.

No sooner had he drifted off than he was awakened by a sharp knock. Before he could get out of bed the door banged open and the imposing figure of Mr B stood silhouetted against the harsh corridor lights.

Without being invited, Mr B, his body stooping to avoid the ceiling, strode in, turned on the lights and towered over Leon's bed. Leon pulled the sheet up to his chin like a 1950s B movie starlet.

'That trip to the Tribal Lands,' Mr B boomed.

'I leave the day after tomorrow. I want to nail these social reforms first.'

'Go now.' Mr B's voice had an urgency which made Leon's stomach perform a complicated series of somersaults.

'Why?' Leon asked, sensing how small and vulnerable he sounded.

'Trouble brewing. I want you to go to Port Villis.'

Primrose's information must be right, Leon thought, and Mr B was taking it seriously.

'Trouble? Are you in danger?'

Mr B harrumphed. 'You get going. A couple of my best people will accompany you.'

'Won't you need them here to protect you?'

'I'll be perfectly safe. Suitable clothes will be delivered right away.'

Leon gave up. He'd done his best. Perhaps the risks had been exaggerated anyway. 'What should I say to these tribal people?'

'Say anything. Offer them what you like. We must keep them onside. We can always backtrack later.'

'What's happened?' Leon asked, intrigued to see

how Mr B would allude to his own vulnerability without making himself appear weak. Mr B took a few moments to answer.

'The FMF have seized three hundred tribal schoolgirls in the North and they're threatening to make them marry their fighters.'

Leon winced at the thought. Then he remembered a previous conversation. 'You said the Government could crush the FMF at will.'

Mr B looked rattled. 'That was then. Now they've been supplemented by thousands of foreigners, many of them battle hardened in Syria and Iraq, who have brought sophisticated equipment with them. Of course, I'm preparing a force to take them on. Meanwhile, I need you to go out and assure the tribal leaders everything's in hand.'

'I'll leave in the morning,' Leon said, a sense of dread draining him of strength.

'Go now!' Mr B roared, ripping the sheet off and hurling it into the far corner. 'My men will be waiting outside in an hour to escort you.'

Chapter 25

Leon only had a few minutes to glance at what *Google* brought up on his screen about the Tribal Lands. *Wikipedia* defined them as the low-lying marshes between the Panmuir Highlands and the sea but gave little other information. A description of them in an article written by A J Forster, a renowned travel writer, didn't make them sound attractive. According to him, even during colonial times, the intense heat, high humidity and dense clouds of ravenous mosquitoes had combined to keep them a neglected backwater in which the malaria-ravaged locals subsisted on rice, chubby little frogs and snails the size of a man's fist. Forster went on to speculate that had it not been for Port Villis, the now-rusting conduit into Mutabe, the Tribal Lands would have had no strategic importance. Though trade through the port was only a fraction of what it had been in previous times, he observed, it still played an important part in the import of construction equipment and heavy goods, and the export of minerals and illegally logged timber. He went on to describe the city, saying that at its heart were dilapidated old colonial buildings stretching along roads still named after Hanoverian monarchs. These thoroughfares petered out into a maze of alleyways and a hotchpotch of shacks, often extending upwards in rickety second and third storeys that balanced precariously on the flimsy roofs of those below.

Leon snapped his computer shut. Hanoverian monarchs, he thought. Quite up to date for Mutabe.

★

Leon, smartly attired in an oatmeal linen suit, white shirt and green tie, approached the car he had been allocated to find Adwin, Mr B's chauffeur, and Akello, Mr B's trusted lieutenant, waiting for him. He shook hands with them. Adwin smiled, Akello barely looked at him. Adwin pointed to the front seat. He got in and made himself comfortable, and they set off.

'It's nice to have the chance to chat at last, Adwin,' Leon said. 'How long have you worked for Mr Bankole?'

'A couple of years.'

'What's he like?'

Adwin and Akello exchanged glances.

'He's fair. Better than the others,' Adwin replied. 'I wouldn't trust any of them though. The other day—'

Akello interrupted. 'Enough! Anyway, as regards your trip we've arranged for you to meet the tribal chiefs at the Queen Victoria.'

'It's not much good, but it's the best there is,' said Adwin.

'As good as the Britannica?' Leon asked, his voice dripping with sarcasm.

'Nowhere near,' Akello said, looking around him for a moment before resuming some game on his smartphone.

'You're always complaining. We could be meeting in a mud hut,' Adwin said.

Akello laughed. 'None of that lot would be seen dead in a mud hut.'

'Anyway, Leon,' Adwin continued, 'you'll be meeting the five most powerful tribal chiefs. I'll brief you. The thing to remember, though, is that you, as Chief Onagaku, have the highest status. They know it but will probably try it on, so you need to be firm.'

Leon pictured five bare-chested men, their faces and bodies gouged by tribal incisions and adorned with decorative designs, their powerful legs protruding from grass skirts. 'Will they be able to understand me?'

'Well, you've got a funny accent, but they'll probably make out most of what you say,' Akello replied.

Adwin gave him a reproving look. 'One went to Oxford, one to Bristol, one to Durham, one to Yale and the other was educated in Monash.'

'You're joking. Was everyone here educated abroad?' Leon asked.

'All the wealthy ones,' Akello replied.

'What about you?'

'Reading,' Adwin replied, smiling almost apologetically.

'How could you afford it?'

Adwin shrugged. 'My father was head of Customs and Immigration. Money wasn't a problem.'

Leon glanced at the shanties they were now passing. 'OK, but where did the tribal chiefs get the money to go to universities like that?' He thought of his own experience; the pile of debt that had mounted up even though he had studied at an unfashionable former Polytechnic and worked during term times in a café, and in the holidays in a sports shop.

'Diamonds,' Akello replied. 'Oblanga gave them a royalty on every diamond extracted in the Tribal Lands in return for their support.'

'It was, and still is a fortune,' Adwin added. 'And it's why they fell out with your granddaddy and his family and murdered them.'

'They did what?' Leon's jaw sagged. Yet again the facts he thought he'd established melted and re-formed as a different apparent truth, leaving him bewildered.

'No doubt about it.' Akello's tone was matter of fact. 'Rubbed them all out. Except you, of course.'

'I thought the British killed my family,' Leon said,

reluctant to let go of the previous version of events he'd been fed.

'The British? Why would they have done that? They were his biggest supporters.'

'Didn't he convert to Islam?'

Akello burst out laughing. 'Your granddaddy? Never! They killed him because he wanted to use the diamond money to build schools and hospitals instead of line the pockets of the tribal chiefs. He was an idealist.'

An idealist! Leon's chest swelled with pride. What a tragedy for Mutabe he'd been assassinated.

The car hit a pothole and Leon's head was slammed first against its roof and then against the side window. He rubbed the bruises, not sure whether this new information or the blow was contributing more to his dazed condition. Nagging away at him was the fear that this meeting with the tribal chiefs could lead to his being their next victim. So why was he really being sent? Was this a ruse by Mr B to get rid of him? He examined Akello's expression. If he were delivering Leon to his death, he was masking it well.

'They're not likely to welcome me, are they, if their forebears killed my grandfather?' Leon said, affecting a calm manner.

Akello stroked his cheek. 'You have to understand the Mutabese. Their predecessors might have killed him, but they would have respected him deeply too.'

Leon was left floundering by yet another Mutabese oxymoron. 'Respected him so much they killed him?'

'Death doesn't count for much here,' Adwin said, not taking his eyes off the pitted and scarred road ahead. 'We kill each other all the time. Sometimes it's because we don't like each other, sometimes it's because we bear grudges but usually it's because it suits our interests at that particular moment. Your granddaddy tried to block Oblanga's diamond deal, so he had to go. Nothing personal.'

'No, nothing personal at all,' Akello said. 'His family, your family I should say, was always deeply respected, even though five or six of them were assassinated by the lesser chiefs at one time or another. Don't forget your family provided the Overlord Tribal Chief for as long as anyone can remember, men who led them through wars, famines and epidemics. The people are grateful, even if occasionally they do away with one of them.'

'Tomorrow is another life,' Leon said, remembering Jeff's expression.

'That's it,' Adwin said. 'We live for today. If we survive till tomorrow everything resets: loyalties, alliances, grudges. Nothing stays the same for long.'

'I've noticed,' Leon said. 'Especially the truth. That resets every few hours.'

Adwin shook his head. 'You Europeans have a factual relationship with the truth. Ours is deeper and more emotional.'

They lapsed into silence as Leon tried to process what was, to him, such an alien worldview. After wrestling mentally with it for a while, he realised he couldn't. You must have to be brought up in that culture to understand it.

Adwin started his promised briefing on the five chiefs. Most of the detail failed to register with Leon as he gazed at the unending swamp with its teeming waterfowl and waders and little else. The five chiefs all appeared to have such similar backgrounds and lifestyles that they became a jumble. Aged between thirty-five and fifty-five, they all spent most of the year abroad in a mixture of Swiss chalets, New York penthouses and mansions in Belgravia or Knightsbridge. Their preferred mode of transport was private jet, using a small airstrip close to Port Villis, and while four out of the five had yachts, these were, without exception, moored in the Mediterranean.

Leon looked out of the window. They were still driving past swamps that stretched as far as he could see. Here and there a near naked figure was threading a path through the marshes, gathering snails. He collected his thoughts. 'Did you know my parents?'

Akello nodded. 'Yes, but not well.'

Leon's heart beat faster. 'What were they like?'

'Decent people. Both doctors working out in the Tribal Lands. I can't tell you much else. They valued their privacy and didn't mix much socially, especially after the Chief's death.'

'How many daughters did they have?'

Akello and Adwin looked at each other.

'One, I think,' Adwin said. Akello nodded.

'Yes, a little older than you.'

Leon's stomach sank. Further proof that Bankole had lied to him about his having another sister.

The car lurched again, throwing Leon across the front seat and hard against Adwin.

'Road's getting worse,' Adwin said.

'Should spend some diamond money on it,' Akello replied. They both burst out into loud laughter.

'Perhaps Morowa Daniels could contribute,' Adwin said. The laughter redoubled.

'What's so funny?' Leon asked.

'Nothing,' the other two chorused.

Chapter 26

As the car climbed towards Port Villis, the land became drier. Every few miles they passed a cluster of huts made from sun-baked mud mixed with cow dung. Goats lay tethered in the shade beside them, chickens scrabbled in the dirt and cows wandered listlessly in the fields nearby. Dotted around, medium-sized brown dogs broke occasionally from their dozing to scratch before slumping back into slumber.

Some of the fields had been turned over to crops, and men, women and children could be seen stooping or kneeling.

The car was already well into negotiating the sharp bends that heralded the tangled suburbs of Port Villis when the road changed from mud into pitted asphalt, sections of it marked by a white line which ran down its centre, faded, disappeared and then returned like a weak radio signal. There were people, animals and carts everywhere, and they had to reduce speed to little more than walking pace to thread their way through. Finally, they arrived at the old colonial centre.

The Queen Victoria was five storeys high. The stones from which it was constructed had a mottled appearance which, on closer examination, was caused by flaking paint. At each corner of the dark grey slate roof perched a giant gargoyle which Akello said had been positioned there to scare the locals. Perhaps even more frightening for them was the bronze statue which dominated the street and guarded the marble staircase that swept grandly up to the lacklustre and chipped wooden front door with its now dull bronze knocker and handle. The statue, which must have been twenty feet tall, was of a sour-faced Queen Victoria, riding side-saddle on a rearing charger. A shield with the royal coat of arms was attached to her left hand, which was holding the horse's reins. Her right hand closed around the handle of a fearsome sabre, pointing straight out in front of her. Her chest bore an armour breastplate while on her head perched a substantial ceremonial crown. Leon was wondering who had conceived this unlikely warrior queen image, when Akello read his thoughts.

'A gift from your great, great grandfather to the British as a peace offering from the tribes to their colonial masters. It was designed and cast by an émigré Russian sculptor in hiding from the Tsar's secret police. Shortly after completing it, he was found and killed.'

'Shame they didn't strike earlier,' Leon muttered.

Akello, still glued to his smartphone screen, took Leon by the elbow and led him to the staircase. Leon shook him off.

'You'd better watch where you're going. What so interesting, Akello?'

Akello grunted, not raising his eyes.

'Why have you still got all this Imperial stuff anyway?' Leon asked. 'Most countries dump all their colonial baggage – the street names, the grotesque statuary.'

'It was talked about often enough,' Adwin remarked, 'but no one could agree on what should replace them. The first government after independence was Chief Onagaku's and he was still pandering to the British. When Oblanga replaced him, he was pretending to be a Marxist and was backed by Moscow, but no one bought into Lenin Avenue or Marx Boulevard. Then, once he'd dumped the Russians and cosied up to the Americans, he wanted to name everything after himself, but he was a Mosa, so the other tribes objected. Things were rocky at the time and he needed their support, so he backed off and it all stayed the same.'

Leon was panting by the time he reached the top of the stairs. The lobby, clad in dark wood panelling and full of battered mahogany furniture with worn and faded velvet upholstery, reminded him of a dilapidated funeral parlour. The single bulb that still worked in the chandelier that bore a dozen, did little to penetrate the gloom, and Leon's eyes, still accustomed to the harsh glare outside, had difficulty adjusting.

Akello, still staring at the screen of his smartphone, thumped the bell press, and somewhere, deep in the bowels of the building, it sounded. As they waited, Leon started to make out his surroundings. What looked like a window from its ornately carved pelmet was, for some unknown reason, shrouded by floor length dark red curtains. High above it a small, circular window let in a thin strand of greyish light, which Leon found difficult to reconcile with the brilliant sunshine outside. In the corner was an escritoire, and beside it an elegant Louis XV style salon chair upholstered in gold floral damask with a gilt frame and one leg at a rakish angle. In the air a musty smell lingered, as of sweaty socks hung up to dry.

Akello leant on the bell-push with his elbow and kept it there. Meanwhile, Leon sank into a worn red sofa and a cloud of dust rose around him. He sneezed and got up again quickly. The lack of response clearly wasn't doing Akello's blood pressure much good. By now a vein was bulging on his forehead and his eyes gave every impression of being about to burst from their sockets. Meanwhile Adwin remained to one side, detached from proceedings.

To make matters worse, several flies had arrived and were hurling themselves, unharmed, through a curtain of desiccated cobwebs against the circular window's dusty panes.

When Akello gave up with the bell and stormed around the foyer shouting in Mutabese, Adwin called a number on his phone and spoke softly into it. A minute later, a wizened Chinese woman wearing a faded blue sarong, a white blouse with the sleeves rolled up and a bright red head scarf shuffled into the room in fluffy pink slippers. She looked from Akello, who had frozen in mid rant, to Adwin who was smiling. Akello resumed his diatribe, only to be hushed by Adwin.

'Easy, brother. Not her fault.'

The woman drew back the floor-length curtains and a brilliant shaft of sunlight speared the darkness.

'How do you know?' Akello's face was glistening with perspiration.

'I dialled the hotel's number and got this good lady, who was busy in the kitchen. I asked her to come to our assistance.'

'Why didn't it ring here?'

Adwin shrugged. 'Probably switched through to the kitchen.'

The woman, now wearing thin-rimmed round glasses, had slipped behind the counter, which dwarfed her, and was leafing through some papers. Had it not been for her papery skin, Leon thought, she could have been a child standing behind a church lectern.

Adwin scrutinised her lapel badge. 'Have you found our reservation, Mrs Chu?'

Mrs Chu coughed in a way that said quite plainly, don't interrupt. Akello stalked out of the hotel saying he needed air. Adwin adopted an expression of patient suffering like that of a martyred saint Leon had seen in a picture in Venice with Clive. Clive! What was that bastard doing while he sweltered in Mutabe? And Rolly. What would he be doing now, if he were still alive? Would he be here? How different life would be. He was on the verge of angry tears. What the hell was he doing here, witnessing atrocities like Rolly's incineration and that horrific rape? He forcibly dragged his thoughts back to the present, swatted a mosquito that was biting his forearm and eased himself nervously onto the Louis XV chair. Mrs Chu was still engrossed in her paperwork. This was going to take some time.

She coughed again; a self-satisfied, self-important cough. 'Everything in order,' she said in a wavering voice. 'Three suites, eight bedrooms booked. Breakfast seven, lunch one, dinner eight, all in Presidential Suite, first floor. Menu.' From a pile beside a typewriter, she handed a sheaf of limp pieces of yellowing paper bearing old fashioned typescript to Adwin.

Leon was intrigued. He extricated himself from his wobbling chair and peered over the counter.

Behind it sat a majestic Hermes 3000, a much sought-after collector's piece amongst those of Leon's UK friends whose disillusionment with modern life found expression in anything 'retro'.

'Where did you get that typewriter?'

Mrs Chu stared at Leon as one might a cockroach found feasting on that evening's meal, and Leon wondered whether she was deciding whether to squash or answer him. After a few long seconds, courtesy won. 'What you say?'

Leon repeated the question.

'Here when I arrive, forty years plus. Not new then.'

Clive had wanted a Hermes 3000, but Leon dissuaded him by pointing out the difficulty of maintaining it. 'Where do you get new ribbons?'

Mrs Chu grunted, 'Man near harbour.'

Adwin, who had been examining the menus, looked up. 'Shanty town people can get, copy or forge anything. And it's all cheap.'

Mrs Chu handed Adwin and Leon their keys, placing Akello's on the counter to await his return. She pointed up the dark wooden stairs.

'Two flights. Turn right.'

They picked up their bags and ascended the creaking staircase, stopping to inspect the Presidential Suite on the way. Leon was astounded. The room was light and airy, with a high ceiling from which two splendid chandeliers, each holding a hundred or so bulbs, hung over a highly polished table with ornately carved star legs radiating from three central posts beneath it. Places were already laid for eight, the silver cutlery glinting in the brilliance of the lights. Dominating each wall was a large portrait of Oblanga. In the first he was dressed in a Field Marshal's ceremonial uniform, in the second in an Admiral's, in the third in an Air Marshal's and in the fourth in a Roman Emperor's toga and laurel wreath. Most surprising of all, the room was clean and dust free. Leon sniffed the air. That musty smell, of decay, fungus and rotting timber, which haunted every old building he'd been in, was missing. He nudged Adwin.

'If the meal's half as fancy, should be a good dinner.'

On arriving at their adjacent quarters, Adwin said, 'We'll meet at seven to plan our strategy.'

Leon nodded, entered the darkness of his room and fumbled for a switch. The light revealed a large wooden bed, a lopsided wardrobe, and in the corner, a desk and chair. He went across to the sash window, flung it up and threw the external shutters wide open. The bright light that drenched him picked out myriad motes hovering in the air. Leon sat on the bed and a billowing dust cloud engulfed him. He stood up and opened the bathroom door to be confronted by a basin leaning at a slight angle, a cast iron bath with four bronze lions' feet and an elaborate towel rail, at least six feet tall and fashioned out of what looked like wrought copper. On it hung a towel.

After washing he set his alarm for quarter to seven, lay on the bed and fell into a troubled sleep studded with nightmares in which he and Rolly were stretched out side by side on racks in the Palace's dungeons while a nine foot gaoler wearing a leather mask severed their limbs one by one by, holding each bloody appendage up like a trophy.

Chapter 27

'Wake up! Wake up!' Adwin's feverish shaking finally sparked Leon back into consciousness.

'Is it quarter to seven already?'

'Akello's disappeared.'

Leon looked at his watch. Six-thirty. 'He'll be back. Probably exploring.'

'Not without this.' Adwin produced a smartphone. 'Found it on the floor. Never goes anywhere without it. His room's been ransacked. There was a struggle.'

'Why didn't we hear anything?'

'He's on the floor below.'

'Should we call the police?'

Adwin's contemptuous look killed the idea.

'What shall we do then?' Leon asked.

'Carry on,' Adwin replied. 'If they want a ransom, we'll hear from them.' His voice thickened and his eyes brimmed with tears. 'If they want information, then they'll probably kill him once he's cracked.'

'Who would do it?'

Adwin's nostrils flared. 'Almost anybody, but my money's on the tribal chiefs. They'll reckon that our feeling vulnerable will make us more inclined to cut them a favourable deal.'

Leon screwed up his face. 'Don't they know we haven't come to negotiate anything?'

Adwin gripped Leon's upper arm. 'We may have to, if we want to see Akello alive again.'

Leon shook himself free. 'We don't have the authority.' He'd been steeped in a work environment where no negotiation could take place without a clear management mandate as to what had to be achieved and what could be conceded.

Adwin's eyes narrowed. 'Bankole does. We'll find out what they want. Then it's up to you to persuade our new President it's in his interests to agree.'

Leon's heart missed a beat. 'Why me?'

'Bankole will believe what you say.'

'He won't trust you? You work for him.'

Adwin sniffled. 'I'd break down. Akello is my big brother.'

Their conversation was interrupted by the sound of cars arriving, doors slamming, and instructions being given in urgent tones. Leon squinted through the fine mesh that covered the open widow, noticing for the first time at its corner a gap big enough for an army of mosquitoes. Outside stood a cavalcade of gleaming Rolls Royces, Bentleys, and Mercedes. Rear doors were being held open by uniformed chauffeurs wearing buttoned-up collars and peaked caps despite the stultifying heat. Men in charcoal suits with dark glasses and bulging armpits were positioned at strategic points outside the hotel, next to the building opposite and along the street.

'We'd better get down there,' Adwin said, racing towards the door. Leon threw on his clothes and followed. By the time they got to the top of the stairs the lobby was full, the henchmen surrounding their tribal chiefs like worker bees protecting their queens.

One of them rang the bell repeatedly on the empty counter, the fingers of his other hand drumming an irritable tattoo.

Leo and Adwin reached the bottom of the stairs just as Madam Chu emerged through a small door in the corner of the room which had given every appearance of being nothing more than a wood panel. She wiped her hands on her apron.

'Yes,' she hissed and all eyes turned towards her. Leon and Adwin made their entrance unobserved and pushed their way through the heavily muscled torsos which surrounded the five tribal leaders, who were conspicuous by the smart cut of their suits and their ostentatious jewellery. Leon prodded the first he came to. The man, who was tall and slender with a neat moustache, turned to him. Leon seized his hand and pumped it up and down, the man's heavy gold bracelet – a string of sovereigns interspersed with clusters of diamonds – clinking as he did so.

'Onagaku,' he exclaimed. 'Pleased to make your acquaintance, brother. Welcome.'

The man's look of astonishment gave way to a sly smile and a surreptitious wink at one of his fellow chiefs. 'Chikelu,' he said.

Adwin whispered in Leon's ear. 'You're not meant to do that. They must kneel before you and await your touch on each of their heads before getting up.'

'You should have told me earlier,' Leon whispered. He gestured for the other four chiefs to approach and, beaming with fixed intensity, shook their hands.

'Follow me brothers,' he said, setting off in the direction of the Presidential Suite. The waiters sprang to attention as they entered. Leon dismissed them with a wave.

'Gentlemen, sit down, please.' Now was the time for some more play-acting. With his blood pounding in his ears, he took a deep breath, lowered his voice and launched in.

'I was hoping for constructive discussions. Unfortunately, that is not to be.'

His listeners looked at each other.

'One of my party, Akello by name, has disappeared. If he's not returned unharmed by tomorrow morning at six, there will be consequences.'

A hubbub of local languages broke out amongst the tribal chiefs. Kabokeme cleared his throat.

'What do mean "consequences"?'

Leon hadn't thought this far but was saved from embarrassment by the sound of an airliner passing overhead. The whole building reverberated. Adwin, latching onto the noisy clue, came to his aid.

'You heard how the President's private house was destroyed by the Air Force?'

The chiefs nodded uncertainly.

'Need I say more?'

Leon struck what he hoped was a Churchillian pose and lowered his voice to enhance its gravitas. 'The meeting is cancelled. We'll adjourn until, let's say, seven tomorrow morning. If Akello has been returned in good shape, we'll recommence over breakfast in the Presidential Suite. If he hasn't, let me bid you farewell. Good day, gentlemen.'

The tribal chiefs, babbling raucously, sounded angry and confused. Then Kabokeme spoke out.

'We know nothing of this man's disappearance. You have no grounds to threaten us.'

Leon was enjoying play-acting. Perhaps he'd missed his vocation. He sat up straight, his gaze sweeping over each of them in turn. 'I don't intend to debate the matter. You have until tomorrow morning. If you don't deliver ......'

The five chiefs fell silent. Then Omiata – short, fat, pockmarked and in a silvery suit which glinted under the chandeliers—said, 'What if he's been killed?'

Imitating Mr B's favourite expression, Leon curled his lip. He hoped he wasn't hamming too obviously.

'Our forces are primed. Dead, maimed, no show. All the same. Good day.'

The tribal chiefs shuffled out of the room muttering, their voices becoming more animated as they passed into the corridor.

'What do we do now?' Adwin asked.

Cooking smells were wafting on the still, humid air. Leon surveyed the table.

'I suggest we eat. We've got a lot of food to get through.' He summoned the waiters, who were loitering outside, and soon the first steaming dish of millet with a slight tang of kidney – or perhaps urine – was placed in front of them.

'Just the thing for a hot African evening.' Leon wiped a drop of sweat from his forehead with his cuff. 'What is it?'

'Green monkey porridge. It's a delicacy here. It takes the kidneys from five adults to make one portion.'

Leon's stomach churned, and he wished he hadn't asked. However, this was no time to show weakness. 'What happens to the rest of the animal?'

Adwin shrugged. 'Probably sold as bush meat. Some say AIDS started with people eating infected green monkeys.' Pushing his plate aside, he picked up a piece of okra and nibbled it.

Leon grasped his spoon and fork. 'I thought HIV came from chimpanzees.'

Adwin frowned. 'Whatever.' He threw an uneaten

piece of okra onto his plate. 'What if they don't bring Akello back? We can't carry out our threat, so they'll know we're powerless.'

Leon blew on a spoonful of porridge, partly to cool it, partly to postpone the moment when he'd have to put it in his mouth. 'Tomorrow is another life, my friend. Enjoy your food.' He paused, his spoon hovering in the air. 'Speaking of which, I'll make sure I have a full English tomorrow morning, if they can manage that.' He forced himself to take a mouthful. It didn't taste too bad.

He stole a glance at Adwin, wondering whether he'd been taken in by this show of nonchalance. The truth was Leon was still sleeping badly, often waking from nightmares in the early hours in a pool of sweat. He felt sick every morning, only recovering his appetite gradually as he suppressed the dark, corrosive memories haunting him and concentrated on the present.

Adwin placed his crumpled napkin on the table. 'Excuse me,' he said in a leaden voice. 'I'm not hungry. I'm going to bed. Early start tomorrow.'

Leon's eyes followed him as he left the room. Once alone, the need to act evaporated and he put his knife and fork down. In truth, he too had no appetite, though the prospect of bed offered few attractions either.

Chapter 28

After a largely sleepless night interspersed with ragged dreams in which mutilated and bloodied bodies stalked him and a helpless, naked girl repeatedly cried out for help, Leon awoke early with a throbbing head and a deep sense of personal worthlessness. He would have turned over and tried to get back to sleep had thoughts of Akello not jolted him, with the power of an electric shock, into an upright position. He peered tentatively through his curtains. No one was stirring in the still dark street outside. He showered, shaved – nicking his face twice and applying pads of cotton wool to staunch the flow of blood – and dressed quickly before slipping quietly down the stairs in his socks to the unlit foyer. A figure loomed out of the shadows and an involuntary gasp escaped Leon.

'Ssssh!' Adwin placed his hand over Leon's mouth. 'Nothing yet.'

Leon looked at his watch. Five o'clock. He unbolted the front door and stepped onto the top of the flight of stairs. A cloud was drifting slowly across a sky dotted with bright stars and pierced by a thin, curved moon. What looked like a shooting star turned out to be an aeroplane, winking at him. Port Villis was gradually coming to life. Dim lights punctuated the city's darkness. Adwin joined him, offering him a cigarette.

Drawing deeply, they contemplated the tranquillity of the scene. A man leading a donkey laden with baskets jammed to the brim with vegetables hove into view. A small boy in rags ran behind, stooping to pick up whatever fell out. Apart from them the street was deserted.

Leon looked at his watch again. They weren't going to deliver. Perhaps they weren't holding Akello, or he was so horribly maimed they couldn't return him, or he was dead. The man and little boy passed by, their donkey leaving a steaming pile of ordure at the foot of the hotel's steps. Someone's bound to tread in that, Leon mused. His thoughts were ruptured by the roar of a black saloon travelling at speed, followed by the squeal of tyres as it slowed outside the hotel, the dull thud as it ejected a large sack, and its throaty acceleration away.

Throwing his cigarette on the ground, Leon, with Adwin close behind, galloped down the steps towards the dark shape lying on the pavement. They tore at the sacking until Akello's face emerged, his eyes covered with tape. They uncovered the rest of him. He was bound hand and foot but appeared unharmed.

'Drugged,' Adwin said, releasing him and peeling off the tape. 'Help me carry him upstairs.'

Leon hadn't realised how unwieldy an inert body could be. Struggling up the stairs carrying Akello's feet, while the sweat-drenched Adwin laboured under his shoulders, Leon feared the muscles in his own back would rip apart. With his lungs screaming for oxygen, he clattered Akello's knees against the banister on a bend in the staircase. His arms were aching to breaking point but Adwin's determination kept him going until they were in Akello's room and able to deposit him on the bed.

'Are you going to call a doctor?' Leon asked. Adwin shook his head. He lifted Akello's wrist, held his fingers on his pulse and stared at his watch.

'He'll live,' he said. 'We'll let him sleep it off.'

'I'd like to know who's been holding him before we talk to our friends again.'

Adwin sighed. 'I doubt we'll get much sense out of him for several hours, and we're due to have breakfast with them in less than thirty minutes.'

'We'll have to wing it,' Leon said. 'Let's go down to the private dining room and grab the best seats. This is one meeting we can't afford to stuff up.'

Chapter 29

'Gentlemen, to business!' Six expectant faces turned towards him, their forks suspended in mid-air.

'Phones off. I don't want any interruptions.'

Once the grumbling chiefs had complied, Leon continued. 'Mr B is in full control of the country. The armed forces have sworn their allegiance. The Americans, the Chinese and the British are backing him, and the French remain neutral.'

'What about the Russians?' Omiata asked, his mouth still full of food.

Averting his eyes, Leon said, 'Who cares about the Russians? We've got everyone who matters. The point is Mr D is dead and Mr Bankole is now unassailable.'

'So unassailable he can't even rescue those schoolgirls from the Muslims,' Chikelu sneered.

'Part of the purpose of my being here is to reassure you that that matter is in hand and the schoolgirls' release will be effected imminently,' Leon replied.

'If Bankole is so strong, why are you here? He obviously needs our help.' Kabokeme looked at Leon like a smug schoolboy gloating over a teacher's mistake. Leon met his stare.

'Of course, Mr Bankole would like your full support and cooperation. These are uncertain times and unity is essential if we are to come through them stronger and more stable.'

'Stronger and more stable?' Chikelu asked. 'What nonsense is that? This country is deeply divided, not only by tribe but also by religion and political affiliation.'

Leon's neck prickled with the heat under his chafing collar. 'That's precisely why he wants your support.'

Five pairs of eyes focused intently on him. Omiata spoke first.

'What's he prepared to offer us? Our diamond concession isn't enough. We need to be granted rights over all minerals in the Tribal Lands.'

'Without our support, life could get very difficult for Bankole,' Chikelu said. 'Personally, I'm fond of the fellow. He was my fag at Harrow, but business is business.'

Leon steadied his nerves. 'I'm here to give you six months' notice of the termination of your concessions unless you swear your allegiance to Mr Bankole.'

Leon's intention had been to shock and he achieved it. An intake of breath and a brief silence was followed by an outburst of shouting.

Kabokeme leapt up, shaking his thin fist. 'How dare you come here and threaten us?'

Leon sat perfectly still, like a neutral observer at a prize fight, and concentrated on his breathing: count to seven, hold, exhale.

Chikelu thumped the table. 'No one tells us what to do.'

'You can rant and rave as much as you like,' Leon said calmly. 'The armed forces will strike at any who are disloyal to the new regime. All you have to do is pledge full support publicly and these ugly scenes will be forgotten.'

'Why should we?' Chikelu roared.

Leon folded his arms. 'Because, as I said earlier, Mr B is unassailable.'

At that moment, the door was flung open and Akello, dressed only in his briefs, staggered into the room, his eyes staring wildly, his body shaking.

'Dead!' he shouted and collapsed on the floor in front of Leon.

Leon's initial surprise was followed rapidly by irritation at having his performance interrupted. 'Probably delirious,' he said.

Adwin sank to his knees and shook Akello. 'Who's dead?'

Akello opened his bloodshot eyes. 'Bankole...

shot … ,' he croaked before passing out.

The room exploded in uproar and Leon swayed unsteadily in his chair. Dead! He can't be. It must be a mistake. But if it isn't… Then Chikelu was screaming at him and shaking his fist, as though holding Leon personally responsible. While he couldn't understand the words, their meaning was clear. He'd threatened these people and they wanted revenge. He eyed the door, but the path to it was blocked by the tribal chiefs.

'Quiet!' Kabokeme slammed the table with both fists and the clamour gradually abated. 'We must find out who's taken over.'

The five chiefs busied themselves with their phones while Leon, in shock, mused on Mr B's demise. He cursed Mr B for inveigling him into this mess, but he couldn't blame him, because it had been his own decision to come. Images of Mr B lifting and carrying him on his shoulders in the desert, scavenging for birds' eggs and digging water out of the sand replayed in his mind. He'd been a manipulative bastard, but he'd saved Leon's life. Though Mr B had undoubtedly had many faults, the person who succeeded might be worse.

'Perhaps no one has,' Leon ventured, speculating that a power vacuum might be more helpful to his cause.

Chikelu looked at him scornfully. 'In Mutabe, someone always takes over, and quickly.'

There was a knock on the door and Mrs Chu entered. 'Announcement, national TV, five minutes.'

'Where's the TV?' Omiata asked.

'Lounge,' Mrs Chu said, backing towards the door. She got away just before the stampede out of the room.

★

The ancient TV took several minutes to warm up. When a picture did emerge from the screen's multi-coloured confetti storm, a groan ran round the room.

It was Donald, waving his fist at an enthusiastic crowd outside the Palace and declaiming in Mutabese.

'What's he saying?' Chikelu demanded.

'Don't you understand? Leon asked.

'Of course not. I speak my people's language, Malusi, French and English.'

Kabokeme translated. 'He says the culprit has been caught and executed.'

A close-up of a bloodied corpse filled the screen. Leon's jaw dropped.

'Jeff!'

Chikelu swivelled round. 'You know him?'

Leon nodded.

Kabokeme continued translating. 'Now he says Mutabe needs strong and stable government, which only he can provide. He's declaring martial law, with movement prohibited between towns and an overnight curfew from six till six.' He held his head in his hands. 'It couldn't be worse. Donald hates the Tribal Lands, and he's backed by the Russians.'

Chikelu shuddered. 'From what I've heard, he's been funding the FMF for years. We're an obvious target for them too.'

'We'd better get back to Mutabe City,' Adwin whispered to Leon. 'He'll know we're here and he'll send his agents after us.'

'Aren't we safer well away from him?' Leon asked.

Adwin shook his head. 'The needle is safest in the haystack. Let's lift Akello into the car and get going before they set up roadblocks.' He turned to leave the room. Leon, about to follow, was held back by Chikelu.

'Where are you going?'

'Mutabe City,' Leon replied.

'To do what? Hide?' Chikelu's eyes narrowed and his nostrils flared. He gripped Leon by his shirt. 'This is a crisis. Tribal lore foretells that at the time of greatest danger, a saviour chieftain will arrive from afar. You can't let your people down.'

Leon wriggled, but to no avail. 'I can't save anyone. It's best I go home.'

'Home!' Chikelu bellowed, tightening his grip. 'This is your home. It's where your father, and his father, and his father before him were born. It's where you were born.'

Leon pushed Chikelu away. 'And it's where I would

343

have lived if your relatives hadn't killed them all!'

Chikelu flicked his wrist. 'An accident of history. It doesn't absolve you from your tribal duty.'

'What do you expect me to do? I'm not a soldier, I can't fight.'

'Maybe not, but Donald would love to use you as a puppet to keep our people quiet until he exterminates them.'

'In fact, he'd rather that than have you killed,' Kabokeme said.

'Until he has no more use for you,' Omiata added.

'So, this is what you must do,' Chikelu said. 'Seek an audience with Donald, offer him your assistance and when you've gained his confidence, kill him.'

Leon swallowed hard. 'Kill him? How?'

'Up to you,' Kabokeme said. 'Once he's dead, we'll declare our support, the Tribal Lands will rise up and you'll be saved from punishment.'

Leon gulped. 'What if it's too late? I might have been tortured to death by then.'

Kabokeme's broad smile exposed a set of gleaming white teeth. 'Then we'll give you the most lavish funeral ever. Even bigger and better than the British gave that cruel imperialist, Winston Churchill.'

Leon felt sick. He didn't have it in him to kill anyone, however justifiably. Yet he couldn't be the cause of the tribes being slaughtered either. 'What if I won't do it?'

Chikelu stared at him. 'Then you are a traitor to

your people, and we'll kill you now.' He slipped his right hand into his jacket. Leon looked desperately at the other tribal chiefs' impassive faces. Chikelu's hand emerged clasping a small black revolver. Leon glanced at Adwin, whose forehead was beaded with sweat. He ran the back of his hand along his own and it came back wet. Better to agree than die now, he thought. At least it would buy time.

'I'll do it,' he croaked.

'Splendid!' Kabokeme clapped him on the back. 'I knew you wouldn't let us down.'

'But just to make sure you go through with it, we'll keep your friends with us.' Chikelu gestured with his chin first at Adwin and then at the supine Akello.

'But I need them to drive and navigate,' Leon spluttered. 'Otherwise how will I find my way?'

'Easy,' said Kabokeme. 'It's due east. Navigate by the sun.'

'I can't drive,' Leon lied.

Chikelu laughed. 'By the time you're halfway there, you'll have learned.'

Chapter 30

All attempts to re-assert himself by striking a power pose before getting into the car proved ineffective. Leon could feel himself becoming Coconut again. He moved the seat back. Meanwhile images of what Donald might do to him burned into his brain. He adjusted the rear-view mirror. Some of the chiefs' bodyguards were lounging against the hotel wall, looking in his direction and laughing. He was about to move off when a head poked through his open window. It was Chikelu, and he was pointing a gun. Leon recoiled. Chikelu, laughing, spun the revolver on his index finger and dropped it into his lap.

'You might need this.'

Leon picked it up and handed it back through the window. 'No thanks. Not my style.'

The smile disappeared from Chikelu's face. 'As you wish. Don't forget though, you must kill him.'

Leon nodded, though it was much more likely that Donald would kill him.

'If you don't,' Chikelu added, 'your two friends will exit this Earth in a most unpleasant manner.'

Without waiting for Chikelu to step back, Leon let out the clutch and pressed down on the accelerator, relishing the mirror view of his tormentor tottering back as the car sped off.

The journey to Mutabe City proved uneventful. Roadblocks hadn't appeared, and the traffic was light. With his elbow resting on the car window, Leon considered his options. Of course, he could forget Adwin and Akello – what were they to him anyway – and try to cross the border. But the more he thought about it, the less comfortable he was about ditching them. Yet he couldn't become an assassin either. He didn't have Rolly's courage. He needed time to think. He was wracking his brain for somewhere to hide when the image of a luxuriant beard, a high forehead and bushy eyebrows formed in his mind. Then, like the Cheshire Cat's, the rest of the face took shape. Olatunde! He'd find him and his shanty town warriors and throw himself on their mercy. He experienced a flicker of optimism. With a sufficiently healthy incentive it was even possible they might do the deed for him.

As he neared Mutabe City, dark clouds piled up and the air became sultry. The first few heavy drops plopped onto the windscreen. Then there was a drum roll of water on the car, and a curtain of rain obscured all but ten feet of vision. He cursed. He'd intended to cruise around until he saw the mosque which looked like a church and seek out Olatunde. Now he could see virtually nothing. His irritation was tempered by relief a few minutes later when he passed open roadblocks, abandoned by drenched soldiers huddling in the dilapidated porches of nearby houses.

Within ten minutes the rain ceased. The air smelled clean and fresh. The sun broke through retreating clouds and people emerged from every direction. Leon put his hand on the horn and his foot on the accelerator; he was getting the hang of driving Mutabe-style.

It took an hour to locate the distinctive mosque. He nosed the car in between carts and old lorries, finding a space outside a corrugated steel kiosk. Turning the ignition off and pocketing the key, he leaped out, nimbly sidestepping a shouting vendor, and ran down the alleyway into shanty town. When he reached a junction of several routes he called, 'Olatunde! Jojo!' A few nervous faces peeped out from their ramshackle dwellings then disappeared. The place seemed deserted until two men with AK47s appeared and stared at him. One had a golden earring in his left ear, the other had two scars, the first running the length of his forehead, the second describing a near perfect circle round his chin.

Leon held out his arms. 'At last! Please take me to Olatunde.'

The men continued to stare.

'Ola-tun-de,' Leon repeated, emphasising every syllable.

No reaction.

'Jojo?' Leon said, more tentatively.

The scarred man's expression was hard to read. 'You friend Olatunde?'

Leon nodded.

'Then you enemy,' the other said, spitting a globule of saliva into the dirt at Leon's feet and slipping his finger over his gun's trigger.

The scarred man pushed him so roughly against a wall, Leon lost his balance. As he righted himself, the other shouted something in alarm, they both looked over their shoulders and, without a further word, sprinted away. A group led by a tall man with a bushy beard was approaching fast.

Olatunde, flanked by heavily armed gunmen, towered over Leon. Jojo, small and wiry, pushed between them.

'You again! You bring bad people.'

'They were going to kill me.' Leon wrung his hands. 'I must hide. Can you help?'

Jojo conferred with the others, their voices rising and their arms gesticulating. Olatunde clapped his hands twice and they fell silent. He said something in a low voice to Jojo.

'Olatunde ask who you hide from? Those people who run away? If so, no need. They dead tomorrow.'

'No, not them. It's Donald,' Leon replied. Jojo translated and the gang members muttered what sounded like expletives.

'Why?' Jojo asked.

Leon wondered how to explain in simple language. 'I'm Chief Onagaku from the Tribal Lands,' he enunciated slowly. 'He wants to kill me, and I want to kill him.'

Jojo translated and a rapid conversation with Olatunde ensued.

'You no speak language,' Jojo said. 'How you be chief?'

'I'm the chieftain foretold in tribal lore. I've returned from afar to save my people, but I need your help.'

The gangsters huddled around Olatunde, speaking rapidly and softly. Eventually, Jojo broke free.

'You expected. We are the Mandese. Oblanga stole our land to give to big bosses. You promise to get it back, we help you.'

Leon extended his hand. 'It's a deal.'

Olatunde gripped it so firmly Leon winced. Then, still holding it, he said something.

Leon looked at Jojo enquiringly.

'He say you kill Donald now.'

Chapter 31

Leon lay on a thin, bedraggled mattress on the floor of his hut. A single lightbulb, fed by a cable inserted into a public power main, dangled from the ceiling. His only other privilege was a television fed from the same illegal electricity supply. He spent his time watching US sitcoms and nature programmes dubbed into Mutabese. Sometimes these would be interrupted by a newsflash when a young man in a suit or a woman in flowing robes would rattle off an update of the day's events, often accompanied by newsreels featuring Donald, who was evidently now President.

The television went off between midnight and six, leaving Leon to wallow in his own thoughts. Usually these were about Rolly and were tear-filled, with grief over his lover's tragic death now centre stage and revulsion at his murderous acts banished to the wings. The way that they had ended their relationship would haunt him forever.

At other times, when Leon's thoughts strayed to Mr B's demise, he experienced a different sense of loss, like that of the death of an unreliable uncle. Mr B had misled him and used him, but he'd also saved his life.

Sometimes Adwin and Akello's plight came to mind, and he feared his procrastination might be imperilling their safety.

And yet, he was no Rolly. He couldn't imagine killing anyone, not even Donald. Even the practicalities baffled him. The President would be surrounded by armed guards and any concealed weapons would be discovered and removed. His mind went endlessly through the options, always arriving at the same conclusion; he was powerless.

'When you do something?' Jojo asked one morning as he handed him jackfruit slices on a metal plate. 'You expensive. Eat more than family.'

'Planning, Jojo, planning. To fail to plan is to plan to fail.'

Jojo looked at him coldly. 'Do nothing is fail,' he said and left.

Leon finished the fruit and turned on his side as the newscaster appeared on the screen to give one of his periodic reports. As a result of his total immersion in Mutabese TV, Leon had picked up a few words, but not enough to make out what was being said.

First Donald was shown shaking various people's hands, then Bishop Mbutu baptising some babies.

Leon's eyelids were starting to close when he was startled into the upright position. The screen was filled with Rolly's face. Then the camera backed off to show Rolly being bundled, handcuffed, into a police van by a couple of bruisers.

Leon couldn't believe it. Rolly had survived the airstrike. But how? The building had been destroyed. Leon rubbed his eyes and shook his head. Perhaps he'd imagined it. It wouldn't have been the first time he'd fallen asleep and had dreams he thought real.

Jojo entered again. Before he could open his mouth, Leon sprang up and grasped his shoulders.

'Rolly, er, I mean Mawusi in prison?'

Jojo looked bewildered.

'Oblanga's son.'

Jojo's face lit up. 'Hang tomorrow.'

Leon recoiled. Then adrenaline surged through his body. He must act immediately. 'Tomorrow? We've got to rescue him. Where is he?'

Jojo shook himself free of Leon's hands. 'Shamat. Fortress. No one get in, no one get out.'

'I'll get in and I'll get him out,' Leon said.

'Mawusi not important. When kill Donald? Olatunde want action now.'

'He'll get it,' Leon said, breezily masking his doubts. But how would he get into Shamat? Walk up to the front door and knock? With no money, he couldn't even use bribery. He slumped onto the bed, head in hands. Think, Leon, think, he urged himself. The only people with access would be those providing supplies or services, like food or laundry. All would be strictly controlled. The only activities not likely to be monitored closely would be those of a very personal nature. The larger than life image of a beaming Primrose sashayed into his mind. It was as though, for her, doors didn't exist.

★

Leon picked up his keys and strode out into the alleyways, miraculously finding his car where he'd left it. The driver's window had been smashed and the car was now home to a family sprawling over its seats. He leant in and politely requested them to leave. They paid him no attention. He wrenched the driver's door open and bellowed at them to get out, making up in volume and body language what he lacked in comprehensibility. With barely a murmur they complied, and he slid in. He remembered where Primrose often plied her trade and how to get there. Amidst a cloud of blue smoke, like a rusting missile aimed at a city centre, the car started to home wheezily in on its target.

Chapter 32

'Hello sweetie. Want some company?' The woman's enormous frame, encased in flowing green and pink striped robes, blocked Leon's view of the Hotel Britannica's Hippo bar.

'I'm looking for Primrose,' he said, trying unsuccessfully to sidestep her.

'Primrose busy. I sexier, got more tricks. You come with me.' She seized Leon's hand, dragging him towards a flight of stairs.

'I'll wait for her,' Leon said, yanking his arm free.

'She so special? She only got pussy and mouth like me. No different 'cept I younger, got bigger titties.'

'She knows what I like.' Leon edged past her and squeezed behind a table near the door. The prostitute looked him up and down.

'An' what so special 'bout you? You pretty ordinary guy.'

More confident now he was protected by the table, Leon affected an air of boredom.

'I pay, I choose.'

The woman gave him the sort of look people normally reserve for dung beetles and sauntered off, swinging her substantial hips.

Leon looked around. The bar hadn't changed much: seedy businessmen, girls with a glint of desperation in their eyes. On the far wall the head of a hippopotamus, its skin papery with age, its mouth baring its mottled yellow teeth, roared in silent disapproval.

An ageing waiter hobbled over. Leon ordered a beer and settled down to wait. No matter how long it took, he would remain there until Primrose appeared. He was so engrossed in his thoughts he barely noticed the slim young man with a shaven head slide onto the seat next to his and, in a soft voice say, 'You come; someone big want you.'

Leon started at the unexpected interruption, his heart racing, his mouth suddenly dry. He glanced down at his glass. 'Haven't finished my beer yet.'

The man edged closer. 'No joke, mister. You in trouble. We know about you.'

Despite the heat, a shiver ran through Leon's body. Was this about his relationship with Rolly, or the politics he'd been drawn into? 'Know what?'

The man looked Leon in the eye. 'Everything. We got evidence. Photographs. You do what we say, or police arrest you. You not so pretty after they ask questions. Then you hang.'

Masking the fear engulfing him, Leon sighed and stood up. Out of the corner of his eye, he saw Primrose enter through a far door. Too late, he thought.

'I need to pee,' he declared. He'd used the lavatory excuse in the desert. Would it work a second time?

'Later, no time now.'

'Later too late. I piss pants if I don't go now.'

Grudgingly the man acquiesced and followed him. Leon, staring down at the urinal in front of him, took his time while the man stood against the marble-clad wall, picking his nails. A sharp crack was followed by a louder thump. Leon looked round. The man lay prone on the floor, with Primrose standing over him, rubbing the edge of her right palm.

'Primrose!' Leon zipped his trousers quickly. 'Did you just knock him out?'

'Out of practice, Mr Lion. Hurt me more than him.'

'How did you do it?'

'Knock out many men in my business.'

Leon briefly pondered the statement. Primrose appeared remarkably, perhaps unbelievably adept at taking care of herself. Then he remembered why he wanted to see her, and all other thoughts went out of his head. 'I'm so pleased to see you.'

'Friends say you ask for me. We go out and you tell me why.'

She led him along a narrow passageway which opened onto a courtyard where some waiters sat smoking and playing cards. They saluted as Primrose walked past. She acknowledged them with a casual wave and proceeded through a door on the other side which led into a storeroom with small, high windows.

'Now you tell me.'

Leon hesitated, suddenly unsure whether to trust her.

'Less you want me to go, start talking, Mr Lion. No got all day.'

He took a deep breath and told her all that had befallen him since their last meeting, culminating in his resolve to rescue Rolly.

'Shamat!' The word exploded out of Primrose's mouth. 'I got no access there, Mr Lion. No girl has. Maybe all funny like you, prefer boys.'

'What can I do, Primrose? He's going to be hanged tomorrow unless I can get him out.'

'Nothing Mr Lion, 'cept say bye bye to your frien'.'

A thought struck Leon. 'But you could still sneak me into the Presidential Palace?'

Primrose nodded uncertainly.

'And into Donald's suite of offices?'

'Too risky, Mr Lion. If I caught there with you, that it for me.'

'Well, if you get me into the Palace, I'll find a computer and send a message to the Governor ordering him to release Rolly.'

Primrose's eyes widened. 'He no believe that, Mr Lion. He check.'

Of course, Leon thought, she was right. He'd have to send instructions that Rolly was to be brought to the Palace and rescue him from there.

'What's the Governor's name? I can probably look him up in the email directory.'

'Dimka. Nasty man.'

'OK, you get me in. I'll do the rest. When do we start?'

'Right now, Mr Lion. I got clients here strain their pants to see me. They not wait forever.'

Chapter 33

The Palace security's porosity was a matter of constant amazement to Leon, who wondered how Oblanga had avoided assassination for so long and voiced this thought.

'He no good, but he no good for everyone,' Primrose replied. 'With him gone, army, air force, Americans, British, French, Russians, Chinese fight who be President. Big mess, people hurt. Safer keep Oblanga, make him do what they want.'

To Leon it seemed a curious logic. 'Isn't Donald in full control now?'

'He no strong enough. Country still divided.'

'How will it end?'

'More die till another strongman, another Oblanga come.'

Leon's heart sank at this depressing forecast. He redirected his thoughts to Rolly's rescue, regretting not having paid more attention when Mr B had got

Jeff and him into the Palace. 'How are we going to get in? Through the underground tunnel out past shanty town?'

Primrose shook her head. 'I know way much closer.'

★

Primrose navigated while Leon drove. Heading away from the Palace and into the suburbs, they came to a small concrete building disguised as an electricity sub-station inside a barbed wire compound. It was plastered with signs in three languages, the English one saying, *High voltage keep out!* Primrose, after a thorough surveillance of the street, took out a set of keys and opened the compound gate. Once inside, she punched a series of numbers into the keypad on the wall and a heavy steel door swung open, revealing a well-lit passageway painted white.

'This how Oblanga's boyfriends got in. This passage go straight to Presidential wing.'

'And his girlfriends?'

'We go in front door. More girlfriends you have, more men respect you.'

'And his wives?'

'They used to it. They not like him. Prefer he use prostitutes.'

In an alcove near the entrance stood an electric golf cart plugged into a charging point. Primrose jumped in and seized the steering wheel. Leon climbed in behind her. Soon they were whirring along. Every so often they passed a camera; Leon hid his face and Primrose waved.

'Probably no one watching,' she said. 'Not bother with this tunnel.'

The passageway ended at a lift shaft where three other carts had been left. Primrose pressed the lift button and, seconds later, when it arrived, inserted what looked like a credit card and hit the top light with her thumb. They rose quietly; the lift was one of the few things, outside the International Hotel, Leon had seen work efficiently. When they reached their destination, after looking all around, they stepped out. The place was empty. Leon recognised Oblanga's old office. It was unoccupied, though a television screen on the wall was relaying a meeting taking place somewhere else in the building. Donald, along with two companions, was sitting opposite Zaynabou, who was speaking, and one other.

'You take out Mbutu, we declare sharia law, together we move into the Tribal Lands— your army, my fighters. Once we get rid of the infidels, you give us mineral concessions.'

Donald shook his head. 'No, your people provoke the Tribal Chiefs, then escalate the fighting. I send the army in to restore order, declare martial law and arrest the chiefs. Then I reallocate the concessions and you declare sharia law there and only there. I won't oppose it.'

Zaynabou frowned. 'I lose many men fighting tribes. Militia strong. Need army to help. Tanks, aeroplanes.'

'We've been paying you for years. It's time you delivered.'

'Money's not enough. We need full military support.'

Donald thumped the table. 'Impossible. Though the Americans will know I am behind the attack on the tribes, I mustn't give them any evidence. That way they can reassure their masters in Washington to continue to support me.'

'No army help, no fight,' Zaynabou said, standing up. 'It won't play so well for you if it become public you've been funding us.'

His colleague followed suit and they walked stiffly from the room, leaving Donald staring at their backs. When they had gone, he said something to the man on his right, who spoke into a mobile phone.

'He say to kill them,' Primrose translated, 'An' the other man arrange it. Bomb under car.'

'He doesn't mess about,' Leon said. He tapped the keyboard of the open laptop on the desk and found, to his relief, it wasn't password protected. It took a few seconds to search the email directory for Dimka's address and send a terse message ordering him to deliver Mawusi covertly to the Presidential Palace. Now all he had to do was hide while waiting to see whether Dimka fell for it.

Chapter 34

Primrose steered Leon to a windowless room not much larger than a broom cupboard, its shelves overflowing with battered manila folders. 'You stay here, Mr Lion. I gotta go. Client 'bout to 'splode. Be back soon.'

Leon settled down to wait. He pulled out a bundle of files and leafed through one. It chronicled every detail of the life of a public figure, identified only by a code, right down to the number of meals he'd eaten and what they'd consisted of. It finished with a sheet bearing the word 'neutralised' and the date, along with a signed receipt for a cash payment. After his recent experience in the Hippo bar, he suspected a similar dossier might exist for him, and the person Primrose had laid out had been his hitman. He put it aside; it would be less upsetting to do nothing. He glanced at his watch. Awaiting Primrose's return didn't make sense. He could still be cooped up here while Rolly was brought, presented to an uncomprehending Donald and taken away again. He must leave the relative safety of this room and find somewhere to observe the Palace's comings and goings.

After checking carefully, he stepped into a familiar corridor and soon found himself outside a door he remembered. He poked his head in and entered cautiously. It was still full of dress uniforms. This time he selected a general's khaki tunic – replete with insignias and several rows of medal ribbons – which fitted perfectly, and trousers which he could squeeze into. Thus attired, he re-entered the corridor determined to bluff his way past anyone he met. His first challenge came quickly. Rounding a corner, he was confronted by two guards, who pointed their weapons at him. Brushing the barrels away with a sweep of the arm, he stared the soldiers up and down, affecting a look of contempt. The first sentry's belt buckle was tarnished, so he pointed to it and uttered the Mutabese for 'disgusting', one of the few words he'd picked up. The man mumbled apologetically. Turning to the other, he scrutinised his scuffed boots, shook his head and then shouted 'shun'. To his delight the men stood to attention, allowing Leon to walk between them and through a door. On the other side was a small lobby which reeked of hash, and three snoring sentries. He sneaked past them into an area he'd never seen before. In front of him stretched a large operations room, its walls covered with maps. At its centre stood a wooden table, some twenty feet long surrounded by rows of empty desks, each bearing a laptop. At the far end a bank of about fifty screens was mounted across the entire wall. These showed aspects of the Palace: all approaches to it, its environs and many, perhaps all, of its rooms. A prominent red button sat on a white pad in the middle of the table. While he was wondering what purpose it served, his eye was caught by an unmistakable figure on one of the screens. He would recognise that lithe body and tight bottom anywhere. Rolly had arrived! Though he was being shoved roughly by the two thuggish prison officers escorting him across the front courtyard from a black van, he maintained his air of insouciance.

By shifting his gaze from one screen to another, Leon could follow his progress. Within five minutes, Rolly and his two guards were nearing Donald's private suite. Leon reached across and pressed the red button.

Alarms blared as he made his way through the shouting, scurrying soldiers, orderlies and civilians now thronging every corridor, eventually reaching Rolly, who was pushed up against a wall with a guard's gun at his throat. Rolly's eyes widened at his approach, but he didn't move a muscle or make a sound.

Leon would have to risk using English. His grasp of Mutabese did not extend to ordering the guards to hand Rolly over. 'The prisoner is now in my care.'

This statement was met by a blank stare.

'Now!' he shouted.

The guards looked at each other. All around them swirled a mass of people running in different directions. Whatever the alarm signified, the effect had been dramatic. Leon drew himself up to his full height.

'Dismiss!'

The guards saluted and melted into the human maelstrom. Leon gripped Rolly by the scruff of his neck, that neck he'd so often dreamed of, and frogmarched him down the corridor towards the uniform room. As soon as the door was closed and the key turned, they locked in a passionate embrace. Leon emerged first for air.

'How the hell did you survive?'

Rolly smiled. 'Morowa tipped me off that the aeroplanes were coming and I hid in my father's bombproof shelter. I tried to find you. Then I saw you on the security monitor, leaving through the front gate. You should have stayed with me. It was very cosy. We could have had a great time.'

Leon hugged him. 'Let's make up for it now.' He started to unbutton Rolly's shirt, but Rolly pushed him away.

'Later. We have things to do.'

Leon grasped Rolly's arm. 'What things?'

Rolly shook Leon's hand off. 'You'll soon see.' He surveyed the room. 'Now for my disguise.' He slipped into a naval admiral's uniform and examined the cutlass, before lifting it and bringing it down hard on a ceremonial hat adorned with ostrich plumes. It cleaved the hat cleanly in two. 'Sharp enough,' he said. 'Quick! Come with me.'

'Where are we going?' Leon said to Rolly's departing back.

They were in the crowded corridor again. The alarm was still sounding, and people were scurrying in every direction, many carrying briefcases and boxes of documents.

'What alarm did I set off?' Leon asked.

'The big one. It means Palace under serious attack, evacuate immediately.'

They made their way to Donald's suite of offices, battling against the hordes, and arrived there just as a voice boomed through the loudspeaker system three times, the last in English, 'Intruders have penetrated the building. Shoot to kill.'

Outside Donald's office a guard stood, machine-gun at the ready. Rolly, drawing himself up to his full height, barked an order, pointed behind him and the guard turned and scuttled off.

'Military training here is a joke,' Rolly said, pushing open the door to reveal Donald screaming into a red phone, the veins standing out like runner beans on his forehead. He was so absorbed he didn't look up until Rolly, his sword drawn, was nearly beside him. Donald's eyes widened before he reached for the holster under his armpit. As he drew his pistol, Rolly's arm swept back, almost lazily, and swung the cutlass down in a swishing arc, neatly removing Donald's head from his neck. Blood pumped out of the open arteries for a few moments before the torso crashed heavily to the ground. Donald's decapitated head rolled slowly across the floor, coming to rest at Leon's foot, its wide-open blue eyes staring vacantly into his face.

Leon nudged the head away with his toe. His guts lurched but settled back into place; he must be getting used to atrocities. Rolly seated himself calmly in the recently vacated and still warm presidential seat, stretched his hand out towards a bank of buttons and levers, and grasped and turned a small, anonymous grey handle. The alarm fell silent.

'How could you kill him like that?' Leon stepped aside to avoid the blood that was spreading across the floor towards his shoes.

'I did it for all the gays he's tortured and killed. Now let's get on, we have an announcement to make.'

'Announcement?' Leon said feebly.

'Yes. This room is linked to the national television service. We can interrupt scheduled programmes at any time to make broadcasts to the nation. The picture quality isn't that great, but it will do.'

'What are you going to say?'

'That Donald is dead and introduce the next president.'

Leon's heart sank. So this was just another power grab, yet one more blood-stained coup. Rolly was about to declare himself as the new leader.

Rolly fiddled with some buttons, hissed, 'Sit down,' and motioned for Leon to bring up a chair beside him.

Intensely bright lights illuminated the room and the small TV camera on the desk started to whirr. A red light on top of it lit up and Rolly, drawing a deep breath, broke into Mutabese, speaking in grave and measured tones. After two minutes he lifted the camera and directed it first at Donald's head and then his decapitated body. Just as Leon feared that he was going to be sick after all, Rolly placed it back on the desk pointing at him. Rolly, now out of picture, kept talking and Leon understood nothing until Rolly said, 'President Onagaku,' and started clapping.

'Over to you Mr President. Say a few words, please.'

Leon was too stunned to speak.

'Go on,' Rolly whispered. 'Speak to your people.'

Leon had had similar dreams before, for that's what it must be. Now was the time to say what he really thought; it couldn't have any consequences as he'd wake up soon.

'My people,' he intoned in a stentorian voice, 'I did not choose to become President, but now I have, what I promise you is a fair society. That means equality between men and women, between tribes, between religions and between heterosexuals, homosexuals and transsexuals. I will introduce workers' rights and curb exploitative bosses. I will introduce healthcare funded by general taxation, and compulsory free education for all children.' His promise to Olatunde came back to him. 'I will also return the land that Oblanga took away from the people, like the Mandese, and gave to unscrupulous landlords, and return it to its rightful owners.

Oh, and of course, I do not intend to be President by proclamation. I will organise free and fair elections, with everyone over the age of sixteen having a vote. I look forward to sharing my detailed plans with you in future. Meanwhile, remain calm and go about your normal business peaceably. Goodbye for now.'

Rolly threw a couple of switches, the camera turned off and the lights dimmed. Leon wiped his hand across his brow, glowing with pride at his own oratorical skills.

'How did I do?'

'Congratulations,' Rolly said in an even voice. 'That speech will have united the country.'

'Thank you,' Leon said humbly. His oratory must have been more powerful than he'd suspected.

'Against you,' Rolly continued. 'All that sexual equality stuff will have angered Mutabese men and quite a few traditional women too. You'll have the church for an enemy for recognising all religions, not to mention the gay content. The powerful landlords will want to kill you to avoid losing their estates. People who work the land will hate you because you want to force their children to go to school instead of providing free labour. Those who run businesses or have servants will detest you because of workers' rights. And everyone who has an income will loathe you because you want to increase taxes. Worse still, the army and police won't like it because they want to keep people ignorant, so they can control them better.'

'Is that what you think too?' Leon asked huskily.

Rolly laughed. 'I thought it was magnificent, but I fear you may have signed your own death warrant, and probably mine too. We'd better get out of here before the crowds gather. Then we can smuggle you out of the country and back to the UK.'

'I'm not going anywhere. I believed everything I said, and I'm going to see it through.'

Rolly sighed. 'I believe it too, but that's not the way to make it happen. First you must sell your vision to people. Then you build alliances by cutting deals with the power brokers. Finally, you buy off potential trouble-makers who have lost out.'

Leon grunted. Rolly's words sounded a bit too much like traditional politics. Leon had said what he believed, and he wanted to make it happen now, not in the distant future. 'Well, yes, but every time you make an alliance, every time you soften the blow for the losers, don't you compromise your vision?'

Rolly leant forward. 'Of course. But isn't it better to achieve 50% than antagonise everyone and emerge with nothing?'

Leon nodded. 'I suppose so.' He paused. 'Do you really think there'll be an uprising against me? I could set a record for being in office the shortest time.'

Rolly turned on the radio and listened intently to the announcer, who was talking fast in Mutabese. His expression became grim. He switched channels several times. Each time he grimaced.

Despite the Palace's air conditioning, the sweat trickled down Leon's face.

'Bad news?'

'I'll try one more, it's probably the most influential.'

Even though Leon couldn't understand the words, from the announcer's near hysterical gabbling and the frequent references to Onagaku, they were obviously in trouble.

Rolly looked up. His voice was calm and factual. 'The army runs this radio station. He's talking in Bindese about an undemocratic uprising by an imposter pretending to be Onagaku's grandson and urging people to make their way here. According to him, a tank division has already been despatched. You'd really better go home.'

'Will you come with me?'

'No, I don't think so. I was at school there. The UK's too cold and grey for my liking.'

'We could go somewhere else. America, France, anywhere.'

Rolly raised his hand. 'Enough! We've got to get out, but there's something I must do first. Wait here.'

He leaped up and raced off, leaving the door open behind him. Leon started to follow, then thought better of it. He turned the television on to be greeted by the sight of angry crowds gathering in one of the main squares. The seconds turned into minutes and Leon started to worry that Rolly had been waylaid. What the hell could be so important? He set off into the empty corridor and followed it up to a junction with another. The Palace appeared deserted. He was wondering which way to turn when he saw Rolly running towards him with a package in his hand.

'Got it!'

'What is it?'

Rolly tucked it into his inside pocket. 'Tell you later. Come on, let's go!'

Leon felt a surge of irritation. 'You're the one who held us up by buggering off.'

Rolly waved away Leon's protest. 'Quick, back into Donald's office.'

They ran into the room, stepping over Donald's body. There was an explosion outside. Rolly went to the window. People, shouting and wielding sticks, machetes and axes, were flooding through the unguarded Palace gates, which were swinging open in the stiff breeze.

'Too late! Now we can't get to the tunnels. We're trapped.'

The increasing clamour bore testament to the crowd's rapid progress through the Palace. Shots rang out, often followed by screams. Leon stepped beside Rolly and put his arm round his shoulders.

'Well, if we're going to be shot, I'd rather I was in your arms when it happened.'

Rolly pushed him away. 'You idiot. They won't shoot us. They'll chop us into little pieces with their machetes, starting with our genitals which they'll cut off and stuff into our mouths.' He picked up Donald's blood-stained pistol, which had fallen onto the floor, wiped it with a tissue and held it against his forehead. 'If you're wise, you'll follow my example and allow yourself the luxury of a clean death.'

From the increasing volume of noise, the crowd was now close.

'You can't do that,' Leon exclaimed, trying to pull Rolly's arm away from his head.

'You watch me.'

'At least we should say our farewells first.'

Rolly lowered the gun and they embraced.

'I love you, Rolly,' Leon said.

'I love you, too,' Rolly replied, before again pointing the gun at his forehead.

The door opened, the crowd's shouting became even louder, and a familiar face appeared. It was Primrose, dressed in a camouflaged jump suit. She was carrying an AK47, and was accompanied by Akello and Adwin, similarly attired and armed.

'Primrose!' Leon exclaimed. 'What are you doing here? And Adwin, Akello, you got away.'

'Thanks to Primrose,' Akello said.

'We fight, you escape,' Primrose said to Leon. She nodded towards the left-hand side of the stairs. 'Akello, you go, Adwin other side. I go middle.' She turned to Leon. 'Go, go, go!'

Akello and Adwin scuttled out to take up their positions. Almost immediately there was gunfire outside the room.

Leon gawped. Primrose seemed to be in her element.

'Why are you doing this? Why are Akello and Adwin with you? They used to work for Bankole.'

'No time explain. Mawusi and you run, now.'

'But you'll all be killed.'

Primrose's expression was grim. 'Maybe, maybe not.'

'I'll stay here,' Leon said, 'and face these people down. This country needs change, and if no else is prepared to lead it, I will.'

'No good idea,' Primrose said. 'Bishop Mbutu. Photographs, you and Mawusi, on social media. If not kill you for speech, will for gay boy sex.'

Rolly took out his mobile and scrolled through some screens. His hand leapt to his mouth. 'Shit! She's right.' Then his face lit up and he made a brief call in Mutabese.

'Who were you talking to?' Leon asked.

Rolly dismissed the question with a flick of his hand. 'Later. Follow me to the roof.' He opened a panel in the wall and depressed a lever. A bookshelf slid to one side revealing a flight of stairs.

'Goodbye, Primrose, whoever you are, and whoever you're working for.' Leon kissed her on both cheeks. 'Say farewell and thank you to Adwin and Akello for me.'

'Good luck, Mr Lion. Hope meet again.'

Primrose left to take up her position on the landing while Leon and Rolly bounded up to the roof. From time to time they heard more gunshots.

'What will they do?' Leon asked, when they arrived at the top. 'They'll be all right while their ammunition lasts, but then?'

Rolly peered over the parapet. 'Look here,' he said. 'That's odd.'

Leon joined him. Below he could see a big man with a bushy beard leading a score of raggedly dressed armed men. 'Olatunde!'

'You know him?'

'Yes. I think he's come to rescue me. Perhaps he can save Primrose and the boys.'

The sound of a helicopter approaching distracted them. When it touched down and its door swung open, Leon recognised the pilot.

'Morowa! What's she doing here?'

'I asked her to rescue us,' Rolly replied.

'I'd rather wait for Olatunde,' Leon said angrily.

Rolly grabbed him by the collar and dragged him to the parapet. 'Don't be stupid. What do you see? How is your brave but ill-equipped friend going to combat those?'

Leon looked down to see a dozen tanks trundling into the Palace courtyard, followed by hundreds of infantrymen. Rolly gave a thumbs up to Morowa, who was gesturing wildly.

'We have to get out now.'

The sound of gunfire increased. Leon peeped over the parapet. Out of a side door he saw Primrose, Akello and Adwin running in one direction. From another door, Olatunde and some of his followers had emerged and were fleeing the opposite way. That meant that as soon as they discovered the way up to the roof, the mob and the soldiers would be with them.

Leon and Rolly reached the helicopter just as the door swung open and men waving knives, sticks and machetes spilled onto the roof.

'Welcome on board, darling,' Morowa said, as the helicopter took off, leaving the swirling masses behind. She extended her cheek for Rolly to kiss. Soon their pursuers were specks in the distance, no bigger than ants. Leon took a deep breath. He and Rolly had survived.

'Tomorrow is another life,' he murmured.

Chapter 34

'You look as though you need this.' Morowa handed Rolly a bottle of Armagnac. He opened it, took a deep draught and passed it to Leon.

'Glad they got out,' Leon spluttered, clutching the bottle to his chest. 'Who the hell was Primrose anyway?'

Rolly prised the bottle out of Leon's grasp. 'Who knows? This is Mutabe. Perhaps she's working for Mr C, or for the British, or for several people and countries at the same time.' He lifted the Armagnac to his lips.

'Where would you like me to drop Leon off, Rolly?' Morowa asked.

Leon's head span. They were going to dump him! After everything Rolly had said, everything they'd been through together. He started to shake.

Rolly's eyes met his. 'He's coming with us.'

'With us!' Morowa exploded. 'I don't think so.'

'Where are you going?' Leon said.

'To Port Villis,' Rolly replied. 'My father kept an ocean-going yacht there just in case. Then onto Switzerland.'

Morowa's eyes narrowed. 'You're going to have to choose, Rolly. It's him or me. You have nothing now. I can offer you a life of pleasure and luxury; apartments in London, Paris and New York, and all the spending money you want. What can he offer you?'

Leon thought of Marianne's cramped flat. He had nothing but himself. 'We'd rent somewhere. I can find another job, given time. It might be a bit of a problem getting you into the UK, but I'm sure you could claim political asylum. The important thing is we'd be together.'

'Together!' Morowa exclaimed. 'Only if he arranges for you to be smuggled in on some small boat or hidden in a lorry, to live as an illegal immigrant.'

Rolly, humming softly to himself, sat staring at his hands.

'Say something, Rolly, for God's sake,' Morowa screamed as the helicopter dropped several feet.

'I have no intention of leaving Mutabe for good,' Rolly replied, gazing at the countryside below them. 'I may have to stay in Switzerland for a short while, but I intend to return. I have unfinished business.'

'Then I have the resources and the contacts to facilitate that. Leon can't offer you anything,' Morowa said. 'He's useless.'

I'm not Coconut and I'm not useless, Leon thought, determined to make his own pitch, however thin it might sound against Morowa's offer. 'I offer you unconditional love, companionship while you're in exile and support on your return.'

'Pah! Pathetic,' Morowa spat as the aircraft's nose dipped momentarily, throwing them all off balance.

'The bids are in then,' Rolly said with a twinkle in his eye. 'I assume those are both your final offers. If so, I'll have to consider them carefully.'

'Let me add one thing,' Morowa said. 'I have it on good authority Mr E will shortly strike a decisive blow against Mr C and his followers and will seize the Presidency. I have, how can I put it, some influence with Mr E. With him in power, you would receive a full pardon and could return to Mutabe in the next few weeks.'

Rolly looked at her coldly. 'I never had much time for Mr E. As for his becoming President, his chances are, at best, slim. The armed forces are bound to back Mr C.'

'Maybe, but Mr E's been cultivating the PRF. They'll support him.'

Rolly raised his eyebrows. 'And you think having the Communists on his side will endear him to the people?'

Morowa's brows furrowed, and her voice became hard. 'That aside, it's still a straightforward enough decision. You've been spoilt all your life. You'd never survive penury.'

Leon watched Rolly's face as he spoke. There was something mischievous in his expression.

'Fortunately, that won't be a problem. I can still live a life of luxury, with all the apartments and cars I want.' He produced the package he'd had in his hand earlier. 'I have here the key to my father's billions.'

The air went out of Leon and he struggled to breath. So that was what Rolly had risked their lives to go and find. Morowa gasped but quickly collected herself.

'All right, you're a wealthy man now, so choose. Him or me.'

Leon's initial shock was replaced by a flash of anger. 'That's Mutabe's money, not yours, Rolly. If you choose me, you won't fritter it all on having a good time. You'll spend it improving people's lives, on building schools and hospitals, on giving back the land stolen from the smallholders.'

A look of disgust crossed Morowa's face. 'With me, you can spend the money on whatever you like. What's Mutabe done for you? They hate our kind here. They'd kill us and stick our heads on spikes if they could.'

'Then we have to educate them,' Leon exclaimed.

'Impossible!' Morowa retorted. 'They're barely better than animals.'

'I'll tell you both one thing,' Rolly said. 'I'll decide how I spend the money. No one else.'

Rolly looked first at Morowa, then at him, and

then back at her, and Leon wondered whether he was playing eenie, meanie, miney, mo.

'Choose!' Morowa shouted as the helicopter swung first to one side and then the other.

'I have,' Rolly said, laughing. 'I decided long ago.'

'Well, who is it?' Morowa screeched.

Rolly glanced at Morowa and then looked at Leon, his stare lingering for some seconds. 'I'll tell you when we get to the yacht.'

Acknowledgements:

Cover design concept and artwork: Hilary Thripp

Cover design implementation: Roger Kohn

I'd like to thank the following for their advice and encouragement:

Patricia Alcock, Ross Baglin, Tony Baker, Jonathan Clark-Wood-Sowa, Martin Cummins, Michael Fleming, Pat Goodwin, Joanne Higginson, Kevin Kelly, Roger Kohn, John Linnell, Emma McQuillen, Graham Minett, Mike Ray, Lynda Strudwick, Jane Wallace.

And of course the 'home team' – Hilary, James, Tamzin, Meli and Kristian – for their unwavering support.

 Matador